A DREAM COME TRUE

Duke Tremaine, the most sought-after bachelor in Washington, D.C., frowned as the last passengers descended the airplane steps. Why wasn't Faith Jarvis among them? Then, suddenly, he felt a warm hand on his, and beautiful long eyelashes blinked up at him.

"Don't you remember me, Duke? I'm Faith. Ben's sister."

"Faith! How dumb of me. I was looking for a little girl. Why didn't Ben warn me that you've grown into the loveliest woman in the world."

Faith smiled, dazzling him with her warmth. At that moment Duke Tremaine stopped looking for the woman of his dreams. He realized he had known her all along.

Books by Emilie Loring

- FOR ALL YOUR LIFE
- WHAT THEN IS LOVE
- I TAKE THIS MAN
- MY DEAREST LOVE
- LOOK TO THE STARS
- BEHIND THE CLOUD
- THE SHADOW OF SUSPICION
- WITH THIS RING
- BEYOND THE SOUND OF GUNS
- HOW CAN THE HEART FORGET
- TO LOVE AND TO HONOR
- LOVE CAME LAUGHING BY
- I HEAR ADVENTURE CALLING
- THROW WIDE THE DOOR
- BECKONING TRAILS
- BRIGHT SKIES
- THERE IS ALWAYS LOVE
- STARS IN YOUR EYES
- KEEPERS OF THE FAITH
- WHERE BEAUTY DWELLS
- FOLLOW YOUR HEART
- RAINBOW AT DUSK
- WHEN HEARTS ARE LIGHT AGAIN

Published by Bantam Books, Inc.

EMILIE LORING

ACROSS
THE YEARS

BANTAM BOOKS · TORONTO · NEW YORK · LONDON

The names of all characters in this novel, all episodes, are fictitious. Use of a name which is the same as that of any living person is accidental.

This low-priced Bantam Book
has been completely reset in a type face
designed for easy reading, and was printed
from new plates. It contains the complete
text of the original hard-cover edition.
NOT ONE WORD HAS BEEN OMITTED.

✦

ACROSS THE YEARS
A Bantam Book / published by arrangement with
Little, Brown and Company, Inc.

PRINTING HISTORY
Little, Brown edition published September 1939
2nd printing . . . November 1939
3rd printing . . . September 1940
Grosset & Dunlap edition published June 1947

Bantam edition published January 1967
2nd printing
3rd printing
4th printing
5th printing
6th printing

Published simultaneously in the United States and Canada

Bantam Books are published by Bantam Books, Inc., a subsidiary
of Grosset & Dunlap, Inc. Its trade-mark, consisting of the words
"Bantam Books" and the portrayal of a bantam, is registered in the
United States Patent Office and in other countries. Marca Registrada.
Bantam Books, Inc., 271 Madison Avenue, New York, N.Y. 10016.

PRINTED IN THE UNITED STATES OF AMERICA

PROLOGUE

SUNLIGHT turned the silver wings of the departing plane to opalescent gauze. It floated against the hard blue sky like a weightless spirit. A faint sigh drifted back before it vanished beyond the rim of mountains that seemed little more than violet mists enclosing miles and miles of shimmering desert, accented here and there with sparse vegetation. Billions of alkali dust particles hung in the dry, choking air. A lizard wriggled to the tip of a low rock ridge and stretched in the sun.

The two men holding the bridles of their horses followed the dim shape with their eyes till it melted into nothing.

"Well, Duke, we've rung up the curtain on the opening act," remarked the elder of the two. He squared thick shoulders in their tweeds, his pugnacious jaw set in determination, excitement deepened the blue of his eyes. "And if I'm not mistaken we've got something breath-taking in its importance." He mopped his forehead beaded with sweat.

The younger man's eyes swept across the desert to the horizon. A mere hint of white in the black hair at his temples accentuated the bronze of his face. A vital face. Strength of purpose in each line of it. Tenderness and humor in the mouth. Keenness and knowledge in the gray eyes.

"You're right, Senator," he agreed, "but unless you've changed your mind about keeping the discovery of the invention, the fact that you've agreed to finance the testing of it, a profound secret between us three, you, I, and the man in the plane, it will be heard round the world if you don't furl that white handkerchief that's big enough for a flag of truce. A desert as apparently lifeless as this may have eyes peering over the top of one of those ridges or ears parked behind that pile of bones which instinct tells me was once a steer. You're a marked man these days, remember. They're watching you."

Senator Joe Teele swung easily into the saddle of the piebald mare.

"Marked because I have a mind of my own and intend to stand by my convictions as to the needs of this country whether my constituents return me to Congress or not. 'Set

1

our own house in order *first*,' I'll hammer at that till it's done
—or I am. I'm out to preserve human life and American
liberty in a time when it faces more great problems than ever
before in its history, by strengthening ourselves, before
strengthening our friends. One answer to that is, air superiori-
ty. We'd better get going."

"Right," Duke Tremaine agreed and mounted the rangy
bay horse.

"We'll separate when we reach the crossroads, Duke. Better for us not to be seen together," Senator Teele said as they
rode on. "If this invention we've nailed today stands the test
it will save thousands of lives and planes. When we're sure of
it I'll take it before the aeronautics commission. If before that
a hint of what we've put through today should get on the air
high-class spies and the press boys would buzz around us like
wasps about broiled lobster and another country might get
news of it, if some one of them isn't working along the same
line now. You'll have to check up on the tests. We'll work out
a plan so that no suspicion of your real destination will get
around. It's lucky you're a licensed pilot."

"With Washington alive with secret agents it seems incredible that we can keep our experiment off the record."

"Why not? The inventor is not a Government technician.
He has his own workshop. He swears that you, who trained in
the same flying field as he, are the only person he has told
about it, and you, only because he thought you could bring it
before the Government. You are convinced of his honesty and
patriotism?"

"Or I wouldn't have turned the proposition over to you,
Senator. Boy, what heat. What dust. These horses must be
hardened to it but they're moving like a slow-motion picture.
Now that the U.S.A. owns eighty thousand square miles of
country at the Antarctic why didn't we have our rendezvous
there?"

"We'll try it for the next one. Speaking of secret agents . . .
Political life without the challenge of foreign and domestic
intrigue, plots and counterplots, would be like salad dressing without acid, a dull and pepless affair."

"I'll bet we get it not only plenty acid but hot with Tabasco
if a hint of what we've put across today leaks out, Senator."

"Not afraid to carry on with me, are you? I may have to
put through some queer deals. Not dishonorable, you understand; just—just screwy."

"And can you do it! You're telling me. Shoot the works.
I'll go the whole way with you. I like a fight. There is no
one but myself to be hurt if I take a licking or two."

"No sweetheart or wife you mean? Why not? You're thirty-four, Duke, tops in your profession, and you own Argyle House which makes even the most blasé cave-dweller sigh with envy. Maybe it's your auger-eyes which warn the gals to look before they go off the deep end. They make even me wait for the green light to flash GO before I make a proposition to you."

"I'm too busy to fall in love, Senator. When I'm tied up on a legal case, and I mean tied, I think of nothing else. Women won't stand for that. Besides, I've never met one whom I've been sure I'd like to face across the breakfast table each morning for the rest of my life."

"That's an unnecessary worry in this year of our Lord. Most of the women of whom I hear breakfast in bed. Some day, though, you'll meet a girl and suddenly it will be all over with you. You'll have to have her. You're that type. But —it suits me to have you a bachelor. I'd hate to have the responsibility on my immortal soul of adding another widow to this already overstocked country. . . . I'll see you in Washington next month. I'm opening the house early to get Thalia started in school. My sister Kitty will be with me this winter as my hostess. You understand that even your partner Ben Jarvis is not to know of this expedition?"

"I do, Senator."

"You're my right hand, he's my left. There are times, this is one of them, when I don't want my left hand to know what my right hand is doing." He chuckled. "That goes for the other way round too. . . . By the way, speaking of hands, a distant cousin will arrive in a couple of months to swell my list of secretaries. He's been in Consular service abroad and is eager to get back to this country. He's the son of the man who gave me my first boost. I couldn't turn him down when he asked for a job; besides, his foreign experience ought to be valuable to me. Here's the crossroads. Good luck, Duke."

"The same to you. Don't let 'em get wise."

"Not from me. From now on I keep a large supply of red herring on hand. I'll be seeing you."

Tremaine touched his soft hat in reply. He sat motionless on his drooping horse till the Senator was a mere speck in the dusty distance.

"A large supply of red herring," he repeated under his breath. "He'll need them to draw across this trail he's blazing. He was right when he said we had rung up the curtain. The Show is on."

I

FAITH JARVIS caught her reflection in a large mirror as she crossed the Union Station in Washington with a bag-laden porter at her heels, a dark-haired girl in a rich red hat and matching skirt with a short mink coat. She couldn't see the girl's eyes but she knew they blazed with eagerness, she could feel the unsteadiness of her lips and the *thump-thump* of her heart.

The first week in December . . . It was also the week in which she had returned to the United States after eight years in Europe. Much as she had longed to come home she hadn't realized that the mere stepping from the train would be so thrilling. It tightened her throat, sent curious little shivers along her nerves. She was on her own for the first time in her life. What lay ahead? Whatever it was she could take it, she was tingling to meet it.

She eagerly scanned the faces of the crowd waiting. Ben had wired her on the arrival of the ship that he would meet her here with his car. Where was he? She hadn't seen him since he had come to Rome for their mother's second marriage three winters ago, but one certainly wouldn't forget one's own brother's face in three years—even if he had married during that time.

The expectant crowd had thinned. Where was Ben? Suppose something had happened to him on his way to meet her? Her throat tightened. Silly, why think of that? He might have been detained for any one of a dozen reasons besides an accident. Should she wait or would she better—

Who was the well set-up, tall, bronzed man who was frowning at the stragglers behind her? It couldn't be . . . ! It was! She dashed forward, caught his blue coat-sleeve.

"Duke! Duke Tremaine! Don't you remember me? I'm Faith! Faith Jarvis. Ben's sister!"

She smiled radiantly up into clear, clean gray eyes, eyes cool at first then flaming with a light which brought blood burning to her cheeks in response. He put his hand over hers.

"So you are Faith Jarvis? Pretty dumb of me but I was looking for a little girl. Forgot for a minute that you had grown up since the days your house was my second home."

"You, if anyone, should realize I've grown up. You sent Mother a cheque to spend for my birthday present each year I've been abroad."

"Did I? Careless of me. Must have forgotten to take you off my mailing list when you went away."

How like him. He had always been such fun. She had adored him. Memory flooded her eyes with tears.

"Stop blinking those uselessly long lashes or I'll think you're sorry I met you. Ought to have known you, I've seen your photographs. Your hair is as satiny black, your eyes as much like dark velvet pansies as they were eight years ago. Same funny little dent at the corner of your mouth, too. Why were you in another part of Europe each time I went over and tried to see you? Why hasn't Ben told me you are the loveliest thing in the world?"

"Brothers are notoriously unappreciative. Where is Ben? Why are you here, Duke? Has—has anything happened to—to him?"

"Take it easy. He phoned me to meet you. Nothing has happened to him except that he has married a woman who holds the world's record for jealousy and stages a scene when she gets that way. Sorry. Shouldn't have said that but Irene makes me so mad sometimes—this is one of the times. Come on, let's go."

A hand touched her shoulder. A voice exclaimed:—

"Faith! What luck. I come here to meet a chap I knew abroad and I find you!"

Faith turned and incredulously regarded the gray-suited man who had hailed her. His skin was fair, his mouth sardonic beneath a clipped blond mustache. Fine lines radiated from the corners of his large, pale blue eyes. He emphasized his words with sensitive, nervous hands.

"Wayne Marshall! I thought you were in Europe!" Her voice was warm with pleasure.

"In Europe with you here? Not a chance. When last summer you mentioned in a letter that you were waiting for the right moment to tell your mother that you intended to come to Washington to get a job—and be with your brother—I did a little wire-pulling and now I'm secretary to a distant cousin, a Senator. I've been here long enough to settle into my stride and make plans, many plans for you. Darn sorry I can't take you to tea now, but I've got to meet my man."

"Put the gentleman out of his misery, quick, before he cries, Faith. Tell him you're going with me," Duke Tremaine suggested with exaggerated courtesy.

She looked from one to the other. The space between them was charged with animosity. Why? Had they met before?

"I am going with Duke, Wayne. He's Ben's partner. Mr. Tremaine, Mr. Marshall." The men acknowledged the introduction by the exchange of level glances with no movement of their heads. "We'd better start, Duke; that redcap is glowering."

"I've met Tremaine, he's the right-hand legal adviser of my boss. I'll be seeing you later, Faith." Marshall replaced his soft hat with a dramatic sweep and strode away.

"Don't stand gazing longingly after your boy friend. Come on," Duke Tremaine ordered curtly.

"I'm not *gazing longingly*. I was staring at the man with whom he's shaking hands. He was on the ship coming over. Kept by himself. Gossip had it that he was traveling incognito, that he was fleeing from one of those turbulent border countries, where they shoot-you-at-dawn and confiscate your estates while you wait. You may have heard of them."

"A rumor of the sort has reached this country. The guy looks like a ham actor to me, with that monocle and fur collar. Let's get going."

In the wake of the redcap's half-trot Faith took three running steps to each of Tremaine's long strides.

"Tell me more about Irene, Duke. I had planned to stay with Ben and his wife for the present but perhaps she won't want me."

"Forget it. Because I think Ben is the grandest man in the world, I may be prejudiced against his wife. He and I went to the same prep school. Same college. Made the same teams. Took the same law course and trained at the same flying field. Got our degrees and our pilot licenses on the same day. Then I went to South America to study Latin-American law."

"You were there when Mother decided that my education should be finished abroad, as if one's education ever is finished."

"When my father died and I succeeded to the law practice which had been founded by my grandfather Ben came from your New England to be my partner. He has become one of the tax experts in the country. I've specialized in that and South American law. We work together as smoothly as the blades of a pair of shears, he's the office and I'm the court man. Then on the ship coming from your mother's wedding he met Irene and went crazy about her. She had been living abroad six years. When she was a child she grew up in the estate next to ours. I almost had a nervous breakdown when

I met him in New York and he said he had asked her to marry him."

"You didn't like her, even then?"

"No. I hoped and prayed she would turn him down. She kept him dangling for a month before she accepted him."

"Did she suspect your disapproval?"

"I tried to be enthusiastic about the marriage after it was an accomplished fact, but I wasn't cut out for a diplomat. She can't bear to have Ben and me together. Perhaps you'll like her. She has glamour and social background, scads of it. Perhaps I'm the one who's jealous. I don't know why I'm boring you with this monologue, most of which you know. Glad to be back?"

"Glad!" Faith hastily swallowed a sob. "Now that I know Ben is safe I'm fairly bubbling with return-of-the-native emotion. Pretty nice of you to meet me. Hope you haven't been waiting for me long."

"Years too long. Any trunks?"

"Expressed them from the train. Ben wired that he would meet me with his car."

"That program still holds only it's mine instead of his. Here it is."

"Thank heaven! Do you always plunge through a crowd and leap over people in your way as if you were hurtling to a fire, old-timer? I'm breathless."

"Sorry. When I start for a place I want to get there. You've been so long abroad you're soft. Hop in and relax."

As Faith waited in the low-slung blue-black roadster while he directed the stowing of her bags in the rumble she regarded him thoughtfully. His hands, strong, sure and beautifully cared-for were so different from Wayne's nervous, restless hands. He hadn't changed much in the years since she had seen him. He looked older, of course. His gray eyes were sterner, they were the eyes of a man who looked responsibilities squarely in the face and shouldered them, his mouth was straighter, harder; there was a touch of white, faint as hoar frost, in the dark hair at the temples. As a child she had thought him the handsomest man in her world. He didn't suffer now from comparison with the men she had met in a larger world. He was so alive. His eyes met hers.

"Will I pass?" he asked and laughed.

His voice was rich and deep as she remembered it. That hadn't changed. If she hadn't been sure that the man who had met her was Duke Tremaine that question would have settled it. He always had had an uncanny knowledge of what she was thinking.

He pressed something into the hand of the black-faced red-cap—whose smile broke white as a wave against a dark reef—and slipped behind the wheel.

"We're off. It isn't far. Out Connecticut Avenue a way."

The long sleek car rolled smoothly into Massachusetts Avenue. The late afternoon sun set the ripples on the broad Potomac a-glitter. Beyond the white dome of the Capitol loomed the Virginia hills.

"How spacious this city is!" Faith exclaimed rapturously. "Such wide streets as they ray out from the Capitol! L'Enfant's plan has improved with the years, hasn't it? How stately the Washington Monument is and how beautiful reflected in the pool. The streets are thronged."

"We've got a mammoth ship-building and Air Corps matériel program on. Many are here for that, not all American citizens, we suspect, more to fight for something the other fellow wants, some to snatch at opportunity—to hold out their hands for a share of the billions which are being broadcast,—and a lot of them to do their honest best for their country regardless of money, or the restraining orders of those back home who sent them here. They are the thread of gold woven through what seems at times to be a pretty dark pattern. Do you realize that the eyes of the whole world are watching this city? That the ears of the whole world are listening to it?"

She nodded. Now that she had actually arrived she felt limp as a deflated balloon. She hadn't realized before that she had been tense from the moment in Rome when she had announced that she was going home.

"Find it hard to break away?"

She had thought Duke submerged in the problems of traffic.

"Horribly hard. Mind if I tell you about it? Sometimes my conscience pricks, and I wonder if I was heartless to leave Mother. I had to rely on my own judgment, but I'd like your opinion. I know you'll be honest. You never were afraid to tell me what you thought of me."

"No? Well, I'm afraid now. But I'll listen. Shoot. Proceed with the story of the Revolt of Faith Jarvis."

She told him of her growing dissatisfaction with the aimless life she was leading, of her interest in what some American women were accomplishing, of her determination to return and do something, be of some use to her own country. And she told him how she had kept her own counsel and laid her plans and waited until Ben had written that he had secured a position for her before she had dropped the bomb of her intended return.

"And it proved a bomb that almost blew to smithereens my determination to return to the more abundant life about which I was hearing. Mother's tearful protests rocked it like an anchored boat in a typhoon. At her threat that she would stop my allowance if I left her it almost dragged anchor. Father left his property in trust for Mother during her life. All the income I have is dividends from stock my grandmother left me and perhaps you know what a broken reed to rely on dividends have been during these last years."

"You're telling me. Go on."

"I said jauntily, 'All right with me,' but I thought, 'Suppose I don't make good in the position Ben has found for me? I'm not a college graduate. I've had three years of Red Cross training, I speak and read French, Italian, German, and am fairly well grounded in the English language and modern American, but that may not get me anywhere.'

" 'Don't be a quitter,' I prodded myself, and here I am with fifty dollars in my pocket, a year's supply of Parisian clothes, forty silver boxes, some of them bought with your birthday money, a position waiting for me and all melty with emotion that I'm at home again. If you'll assure me that I wasn't heartless to leave Mother, I shall be the happiest girl in the world, Duke."

"Heartless! You know darn well you weren't. She didn't consider you when she took on a new husband, did she? You and Ben moved heaven and earth to prevent her marrying Count Whosis, didn't you?"

"We did."

"And he has turned out to be as worthless as you suspected. But you're here now, all right and safe." He had the same heart-warming quality of tender sympathy she remembered.

There was a curious clarity to blue sky and bluer water which reflected the arches of the Arlington Memorial Bridge. Trunks and branches were motionless as if cast in bronze; white buildings were luminous as alabaster lighted from within; flags drooped; the horizon was banded with soft rose. from east to west; from north to south the world was as still as if it were a painted panorama. Faith drew a breath of utter content.

"Something tells me that even for Washington this is one day in a thousand, Duke. It has a dreamlike quality. I feel an irresistible urge to pinch your arm to make sure you are real. Remember how I used to trail you and Ben? One of my enduring memories is the vision of you two boys disappearing round a corner or through a doorway when you saw me coming."

"Did we? When I look at you now, I wonder how we could have been such brutes."

"When *I* look back *I* don't wonder. I must have been a frightfully awkward, unattractive child with my gold-banded teeth and long arms and legs. My heart was shredded to ribbons when Ben told me I made him think of a centipede. I was fifteen when you left for South America. I shed buckets of tears. I was sure you would be eaten by wild men if you didn't crash in a plane. I've been several persons since then. What is ahead, I wonder? Ben has secured for me a position as social secretary to the sister of Senator Teele. I hope I make good."

"You will. The Senator is our client. He lost his wife two years ago. The sister, Kitty, is—well, perhaps thirty. Grew up under the rule of an iron mother. Now she is at the head of a Senator's household and is scared to death by her responsibilities. She's charming. She's the type which makes a man want to pull off his coat and fight for her—knight-and-his-lady's-glove stuff. The kind of woman who keeps the home in homemaking. She might prove an irresistible temptation to a man who loves graciousness, charm and unselfishness in a woman."

His eyes had narrowed, his mouth set in a stern line. Was he in love with Miss Teele? Was he the knight who would fight for his lady? The suspicion was like a cloud dimming the brightness of Faith's homecoming.

"She sounds interesting and likable."

"She is. She has a problem in the thirteen-year-old demon-daughter of the Senator, who resents her presence in the household and has a line which would make strong men tremble. Senator Teele has pushed himself above the majority of his colleagues. He's been working for a bigger counter-espionage appropriation, hammering at the Congress to set our own house in order before we dip into foreign affairs; arguing that our industrial machine must be geared-up, that the people have a right to start new businesses, or take a job without being scared to death that it will fold-up under them. 'Economic security' is his battle-cry. Also, he's throwing his immense vitality into a fight to improve air matériel. Air strength can't be gained after war breaks out.

"What d'you know about this man Marshall?" he asked with a change of tone which brought Faith sitting up straight.

"Did my prophetic ear catch the chime of wedding bells? Planning to marry him?"

"I shan't marry anyone. At least not for years and years. I don't think much of marriage."

"Poor, disillusioned old spinster. Ben and I will have to see what we can do about that. Can't have you going cynical on us and scoffing at the honorable estate of matrimony."

"Ben wrote that you still live at Argyle House. Are you married, Duke?"

"No. Where did you pick up that crazy idea?"

"You are so passionately enthusiastic over the 'honorable estate'—for me—I thought perhaps you had a wife and I hadn't heard of it. I remember how horribly jealous I was of your current heart-interest when you came home with Ben for week ends. Why haven't you married one of those glamour girls?"

The color stole to the uneven line of his hair, his eyes darkened and deepened.

"I've asked myself that, many times before today, without getting an answer. Now I have a sneaking suspicion of the reason why."

II

A QUALITY in Duke Tremaine's voice sent a chill feathering through Faith's veins. Had he meant that with his analysis of Kitty Teele's character had come the realization that he was in love with her? She said quickly:—

"I hope Ben's marriage isn't a mess, Duke. I have tried to fool myself, but I've read a lot between the lines of his letters: they used to be such fun, but lately they have grown very serious. He is so sweet, so dear, so eager to help everyone, I can't bear it if he is unhappy."

"Don't worry. He has hours when he feels he has the world by the scruff of the neck. He's keen about his profession and any man who loves his work as Ben does has something disillusion can't wreck. We have a bunch of clients who need expert tax guidance. You'd be surprised how many of the upper-bracket boys have South American holdings. Having you with him will help him over the rough places at home. Has he written you that Irene's grandmother lives with them?"

"He hasn't. I wonder why? He knows I adore old ladies."

"Old lady! Wait till you see Madam Carr. Ben and Irene call her 'Nancy.' When Irene wishes to be particularly annoying, she calls her 'Grandmother' in a tolerant tone which reduces Madam Carr to a state of speechless rage. She opposed Irene's plan to travel abroad by herself. But at twenty her granddaughter had come into a small property from her deceased parents and away she sailed."

"It's rather curious that I never met her among the American groups abroad. I wonder why she returned to this country?"

"She had been living on her principal. When that was gone, her grandmother refused to finance her. I have known and loved Madam Carr all my life. She's an up-to-the-minute person—if she is a crossword puzzle addict—with an amazing, effervescing vitality. She's rich, she is intelligently conversant of domestic and world problems, and she's a snappy dresser."

"Does she approve of Ben?"

"Adores him. Always backs him in a marital row, which fact doesn't increase her popularity with her granddaughter. She's a crackajack business executive; used to own a string of newspapers which she sold last year. Sometimes I think that woman knows more of what is going on at Capitol Hill than many of the law-makers, or the lobbyists, themselves. She was born here. She's philanthropic, she's kind if she likes a person, but she has a barbed and brilliant tongue when she doesn't.

"Don't get jittery about Ben. Know what I used to think when he and I took you on tough fishing trips or egged you on to try hard games? I'd say to myself, 'That youngster has the heart of a winner. She never asks, *Can I?* She says to herself, *I'm going to win.*'"

"That's handsome of you."

"Have you been told before that you have an enchanting smile? Aha! I can see by your denatured smirk that my discovery is old stuff. Here we are."

The roadster swung into the drive before a stuccoed house set in lawns, which were, even so late in the year, emerald green. Ben Jarvis was on the steps. His fair skin was flushed, his brown eyes were eager. He impatiently swept back a lock of light hair and pulled open the roadster door.

"Here you are, kid! Am I glad to see you?

"Sorry I couldn't meet you, but Irene wanted me at home when you arrived. Don't bother with those bags, Duke. Amos will look after them. . . . Come along."

Faith disciplined a childish impulse to run as far and as fast as she could from what awaited her beyond that open door. Had Duke been trying to prepare her for what she would find? For one panicky instant she wished passionately that she had not left Rome. She slipped her hand under her brother's arm as they entered the house.

"I'm more anxious to meet Irene, Ben, than she can possibly be to meet me. Duke has been telling me—"

"Nothing good of your brother's wife, I'm sure."

The voice was cool. Brittle. It came from the brilliantly rouged lips of an auburn-haired woman at the threshold of the living room. Her eyes were thinly veiled with antagonism. A long holder with a lighted cigarette was in one hand.

The words struck Faith like a blow. She stopped so suddenly that her shoulder touched Duke Tremaine's chest as he followed close behind. He laid his arm lightly across her shoulders. The contact steadied her. Silly, why should she feel that her brother's wife was her enemy? She would make friends with her. She must. She loved Ben more than anything in the world. She wouldn't lose him because of his wife. She held out both hands.

"Irene dear, Mother and I adore Ben. We love you already because you are his wife. He wrote us that you were beautiful, but he didn't give us any idea of how beautiful you are."

That wasn't flattery, it was the truth. Her hair had the sheen of burnished red-gold, her large eyes fringed with long black lashes were green as the emeralds of the Agha Khan, her skin was as smooth and creamy as a gardenia petal, her face was heart-shaped. The only flaw was a tight, small mouth. Her simple silver lamé afternoon frock was the last word in smartness. Her slender figure was reflected and re-reflected in the tall fourfold mirror-screen in the room behind her which was all pale, clear colors and glinting mirrored surfaces. Not many women are lovely enough to risk living in a looking-glass room.

"Don't keep your sister standing in the hall, Ben." Irene's voice cut through the strained silence like chilled steel. She frowned at the Negro maid in the wistaria-color uniform which made her look like a black-faced pansy.

"Violetta, show Miss Jarvis to her rooms. When you're ready, Faith, come to the glassed-in terrace, it is still warm enough there for tea. We're having April weather in December. Can you spare time to join us, Duke?"

It wasn't an invitation. It was a challenge. The atmosphere bristled with antagonism. Faith fancied she could hear the swish of suddenly bared rapiers. Ben's face had darkened.

His brown eyes were fixed on his friend with a wistful appeal which tightened her throat.

"Always have time for tea here, Irene. Your snacks have those of the rest of the world licked to a standstill."

Faith released her breath in a relieved sigh. She hadn't realized that she had been holding it. Was life in Ben's home to be like this? A series of battles in which, because she loved him, she would have to hold back her fire?

Holding back fire when she was angry hadn't to date been her number-one virtue. "You don't have to stay if your disposition can't stand the strain," she encouraged herself as she entered the cool green-and-white bedroom.

"Here you is. I sure hope you stay with us a long time, Miss Jarvis."

"Thanks, Violetta. Tell Mrs. Jarvis that I will be down for tea in five minutes."

"Yes, *Mam*. I guess you knows already folks has to be on time in this house or there's ructions." The maid sniffed and departed.

She hadn't known but she was learning fast the ways of her brother's household, she reflected, with a little bitter twist to her lips as she faced herself in the mirror in the luxurious dressing room with its crystal-and-silver-laden toilet table, the streamlined tub with its gleaming shower curtain and huge green bath towels.

She critically appraised the dark-haired, dark-eyed girl looking back at her. The rich rose-red of her hat and frock, the sheen of silver beads, accentuated the vellum smoothness of her creamy skin. Her nose and eyes were exceptionally good. She was slender without looking as if she were in the last stages of anæmia. The deep dimple at the right corner of her mouth had its uses. Not glamorous like Irene, but not too bad. Had Duke meant it when he had said she was the loveliest thing in the world?

> "Magic mirror on the wall
> Who's the loveliest of them all?"

She wrinkled her nose disdainfully at the girl whose face had flushed a soft pink as she quoted from "Snow White." Vivid lips tilted-up at the corners revealed a flash of perfect teeth.

"Silly! Haven't you had experience enough to recognize a line when you hear one? You need a guardian."

Her smile faded. She needed more than a guardian. She needed a course in human relations if she were to live in Ben's home. Why were Duke and Irene so antagonistic? They must have been friendly when they were boy and girl. She had felt as if she had been hurtled into an armed camp when she had entered the hall. She brushed a dark curl back over her ear, pulled her red hat at the current rakish angle and went down the stairs.

There were periwinkle blue cushions in the chairs on the broad terrace from which you looked down into the garden. A golden bowl of yellow roses, a huge Sheffield tray with a steaming kettle and shining silver tea-things, exquisite cups and saucers were on the table at which her sister-in-law presided. A white-haired woman in black with a sensational double necklace of pearls was nibbling a pencil as she frowned at a crossword puzzle. The glass doors had been thrown back. The air which drifted in was spicy with the bittersweet scent from English box hedges. A butler with black skin and grizzled hair was passing a tray of sandwiches.

Duke Tremaine and Ben, perched on the stone parapet smoking, slid to their feet as Faith came through the open French window. Men are so fine, she told herself as she looked at them—forgetting that while in Europe she had begun to lose faith in the sex.

Her brother drew her toward the older woman and presented her proudly.

"Nancy, this is my kid sister, Faith."

The jewels on the large white hand Madam Carr extended were no more brilliant than her dark eyes.

"How do you do, my dear. I've heard a lot about you. I thought you might return from your years abroad a French fashion model with a European point of view. I'm monstrously relieved. You are outwardly Parisian but—I can tell by your straightforward eyes—inwardly American."

"Take this comfortable chair, Faith," Duke Tremaine suggested. "You must be tired after your long trip."

"Never suggest to a woman that she's tired, Duke," Madam Carr protested. "Believe me, you appear as fresh as a daisy, my dear. I felt the glow of your personality the moment you stepped to the terrace. How long have you been traveling?"

"About ten days. After the hours on ship and train this house seems like something in an iridescent dream, Irene. I saw your fine Italian hand in those mammoth bath towels, Ben. Remember how you used to rave because Mother didn't get them big enough?"

"Amos, bring the hot sandwiches. You should have had them here before this."

"Yes, Madam." The butler's voice was servile, the hate

in his eyes as he answered Irene sent little chills feathering through Faith's veins.

"How will you have your tea?"

Faith knew from the scrape in her sister-in-law's question that reminiscences of the years before his wife had come into Ben's life were taboo. Had she already commenced to edge between him and his sister as she had between him and his friend?

"Strong of hot water, lemon, no sugar," she answered lightly in spite of her smarting heart and eyelids.

Duke Tremaine presented a cup and saucer with one hand and a silver tray with the other.

"Here you are, Faith. Here's Amos with hot mushroom sandwiches. Try one of those slivers of toast spread with orange marmalade. I'll bet you've never tasted anything more delicious. You must be starving. Pretty dumb of me not to have stopped at the Mayflower for tea. It has been so long since I have welcomed a lovely returning native that I've forgotten the technique."

Irene Jarvis shrugged slender shoulders. Her laugh was shallow.

"Don't be deceived by Duke's You're-the-only-girl-in-my-life line, Faith. He does it well. Superlatively well. Marmaduke Tremaine, with his badminton court, his plane and his roadster, is the answer to every debutante's and every dashing widow's prayer. He hasn't become the city's number-one bachelor menace without having earned the reputation. But he has reduced side-stepping a matrimonial climax to an art."

Duke Tremaine's lips parted as if to give vent to a furious protest, closed in a grim line. Faith remembered that he hated the name Marmaduke.

"Your friend Wayne Marshall phoned this morning, Faith." Irene's voice cut in on the silence which had followed her fling at her husband's friend and partner.

"Wayne! Phoned you! Where did you meet him, Irene?"

"Why the stunned surprise? Everyone of importance or semi-importance who comes to Washington has a letter to me. You forget that my family has been here since it became the Nation's Capital. I told him I didn't know just when you would arrive and asked him to drop in this afternoon on the chance that you might be here."

"Why didn't you let us have the kid to ourselves for a few hours, Irene? It has been years since Duke and I have seen her. We want to hear what she has been doing in all that time."

"So sorry, I hadn't realized that your sister's return was such a heart-shaking occasion to you and Duke, Ben. Evidently you and I are *de trop*, Grandmother. We are intruding on this tender reunion." Irene pushed back her chair and rose. "Amos, take the tea-things to the living room."

Faith saw the butler look at Ben. Saw her brother shake his head. His shamed, apologetic eyes hurt her intolerably. Had her coming made life harder for him? Why, why had she come home? Home! That was a joke. This house didn't know the first letter of the word.

Violetta appeared at the French window. Her enormous black eyes rolled knowingly.

"Mr. Wayne Marshall is here with another gen'man, Madam," she announced.

In her passionate relief at the interruption which had saved the smoldering situation from bursting into flame, Faith eagerly extended both hands to the man who appeared behind the maid. She had always liked him, had even had moments of wondering if she were not really in love with him; now he seemed like a heaven-sent messenger of reprieve.

"How marvelous to see you so soon, Wayne!"

The color of his face deepened and accentuated the curious lightness of his eyes. He held her hands close in his.

"This welcome repays me for chucking that swell assignment in France that I might be near you, darling." He drew her closer.

"Ben, you might mention to Mr. Marshall that we also are among those present," Duke Tremaine suggested coolly.

With a lingering pressure Wayne Marshall released Faith's hands. He stroked his small mustache with a finger adorned with a massive intaglio ring. The expression in his eyes as he regarded Duke frightened Faith. She felt caught in the undertow of dislike which surged from one man to the other; it was so strong as to be almost a tangible thing.

"Sorry to have annoyed your brother's partner, Faith," Marshall apologized suavely. "I'll tell you what I think of your welcome later. I've brought a friend who has just arrived from abroad with a letter to you, Mrs. Jarvis. May I present Count Carrilski?"

The man who had greeted him in the Union Station, minus the fur-collared coat, stepped from the dusk of the living room.

Irene sprang to her feet. Her outflung hand hit the steaming kettle. It toppled. Its scalding contents poured over the tray.

III

AT IRENE'S startled cry Ben and Duke Tremaine sprang toward her. Madam Carr rose hastily. Faith quickly righted the alcohol lamp and the kettle.

"Did it scald you, Irene?" her husband inquired anxiously.

Colorless but smiling she shook her head. Her eyes were as dark as malachite.

"No. No. Please forget it. The water spattered, that's all. See?" She held out her hand which showed a few red pindots. "I don't understand how it happened. Sorry to have made a scene just as you were presenting your friend, Wayne. The name was?"

She was enchanting, gracious as she smiled at the tall man with squared shoulders, smooth blond hair and inscrutable dark eyes which seemed to have receded deep into his head. Color crept back to his white face as he adjusted his monocle. He clicked his heels and bowed from the waist.

"Carrilski, Madam. I am desolated that on this, my first viseet to your city, my sudden appearance should have frightened you, should have caused what might have proved a serious injury." His guttural voice with its foreign accent was not without charm.

"Your appearance had nothing to do with the accident, Count. I was startled, not frightened, when the kettle overturned. I've never been afraid in my life." She named the Count to her grandmother, Faith, her husband and Tremaine.

"I have great pleasure seeing Mees Jarvees on the ship crossing, though I did not meet her. I was too what you say, 'low,' to be an entertaining companion. She was the, I believe the pictures call it, the romantic lead on the ship, She—"

"Amos, stop fussing with the tray and take it out." Irene cut in on the Count's tribute to another woman. "I'm sure that Wayne and his friend are perishing for something to drink, Ben. Please everybody sit down and relax and stop looking as if we'd been on the verge of tragedy."

"I'll take off my hat to Irene's nerve. She might have been terribly burned or scalded," Faith said in a low voice to Duke Tremaine as she perched on the terrace wall beside him. His eyes were on Count Carrilski. "You'll have to admit that she was a grand sport."

"Who, Irene? Sure, she's a sport of sorts. Where did you say the Count hailed from? I wonder—" he broke off the sentence as Wayne Marshall approached.

"It's a break, Faith, that you and I are to have the same boss. I am Senator Teele's secretary," he announced.

"One of them," Duke Tremaine corrected blandly.

"His confidential secretary," Marshall reminded in his turn. His shrug was of the very essence of Gallic insouciance. As if that explanation were the statement to end all statements, he apologized suavely:

"A thousand pardons, Madam Carr, for not having seen you before, but our entrance was so distracting that I forgot my manners. How are you today?"

"Fit. Superbly fit as I was yesterday and shall be tomorrow. Don't inquire for my health as if I were an octogenarian."

"You'll learn, before long, that Grandmother is edgy about her age, most elderly people are, I find," Irene Jarvis purred "Do come and sit by me and the Count, Wayne. Here comes Amos with the sherry."

Irene's voice made Faith think of honey, smooth, golden, sticky honey. Was she being so overpoweringly sweet to Wayne because she had sensed the fact that Duke disliked him? Why did he dislike him? She had felt his antagonism from the moment they had faced each other. Behind his inscrutable eyes what was Count Carrilski thinking about this American household? He appeared like a man who had seen everything there was to see, or was his touch of world-weariness a pose?

Madam Carr crossed the terrace and stood framed by the casing of the French window, an imposing figure in sheer black, against which her pearls gleamed softly. Her regally held head was crowned by silky white hair coiffed in the latest fashion.

"Irene has me wrong, Mr. Marshall," she corrected sweetly. "I'm not in the least edgy—edgy, what an expressive word!—about my age, because I'm never aware of it." She smiled at Faith.

"Come to my rooms, my dear, when you want to escape being drawn between hostile forces. Your soft, low-pitched voice with the sparkle in it is a joy to hear. This is my contract evening, Irene. I am dining out. Count, I hope you will find our country interesting. It has its points—to a foreigner. Good afternoon, everybody."

Faith's eyes followed her erect figure till it faded into the dimness of the living room. They came back to Irene. Her mouth was pinched in a bitter line. She might be waspish, selfish, but not stupid as so many selfish people were. Far from stupid. She was a person to watch surreptitiously for danger signals.

"There goes the brainiest, most valiant woman in Washington," Duke Tremaine declared with heart-warming sincerity. "She knows more facts that are off the record than the majority of the high-up boys on Capitol Hill."

"I can well believe it," Count Carrilski agreed. "She has that, that—how shall I say it—that air of absolutism—ees eet not?—which I have seen in women who were the power behind a throne."

Faith drew a deep breath of relief. She hated contention. She felt as if she had been trying to beat her way out of a thicket of nettles since her arrival at her brother's house. Duke's enthusiasm was bound to clear the atmosphere. Her peace was short-lived.

"Really, Duke! *Grandmother* the brainiest and most valiant woman in Washington? You've forgotten the charming, blond sister of Senator Teele who, gossip has it, is the inspiration of your days and—"

"Irene!" Ben Jarvis' voice was hoarse with anger.

Did Miss Teele mean so much to Duke? He had spoken of her with warm admiration. The malice in Irene's suggestion left Faith shaken as if something cruel and cold had touched her. She felt suddenly adrift.

"Irene, you've missed your vocation," Duke Tremaine declared lightly. "You should be a writer of radio skits; think what you could do with the material to be dug up in Washington, the life stories of some of the citizens. I'm sure that in a very short time Marshall, in his confidential position, will be able to help you."

"What do you mean by that dirty dig?"

"Mean, Marshall? Nothing to make you grit your teeth. You look to me like a man who will accumulate gossip as a rolling ball picks up snow, a born chatter columnist. We have gossip and intrigue in this country, Count, if we have no courts with a power behind the throne."

"I understand, Meester Tremaine. A sly word here, a whisper there and the credentials of an ambassador crumble to powder or the seat of a senator breaks beneath him. That is your meaning, ees eet not?"

"In a nutshell. It was a remarkable summing-up for a person on his first visit to this country, Count."

"I *said* to this city, Meester Tremaine. But it is also my

first viseet to your country. Already I am speechless from
its size."

"And you haven't seen the half, yet." Tremaine turned
to Faith. "What are you doing tonight? Too tired to step
out night-clubbing? There's a Russian *bistro* here which is
the high spot for the moment."

"Tired! Of course not. I—"

"I'm glad, Faith," Irene Jarvis intercepted hastily, "because I accepted an invitation for you and Ben and me from
the Browns for dinner and the theater."

"That just about washes up my suggestion, I take it. I'll
be seeing you. Don't let them pad your engagement book
against me, Faith."

Tremaine nodded to Irene, to the men beside her and
entered the living room. Ben went with him, hand on his
shoulder. Why had she let Irene dispose of her evening Faith
asked herself. Was she developing an inferiority complex so
soon? Why hadn't she told Duke that she would step out with
him? It wasn't too late. She would tell him now.

As she approached the hall she heard voices. Perhaps Duke
and Ben were conferring about business. Perhaps this wasn't
the strategic moment to interrupt. As she paused she heard
Ben say:—

"Marshall's a stuffed shirt but what else have you chalked
up against him, Duke?"

"Against Marshall? Nothing. Haven't spoken to him half
a dozen times since he's been with the Senator. Who's this
Count Carrilski? Marshall said he had a letter to Irene. Saw
him at the station when I met Faith. Looked like a male
movie menace out of a job. How's the 'confidential secretary' fitting in at the Teeles' socially?"

"Kitty doesn't like him."

"Has it arrived at the Kitty stage with you, Ben? Look
out, boy. She's a terribly sweet person."

Faith saw Duke drop his hand on her brother's shoulder
before he closed the front door behind him. What did it
mean? Were they both in love with Miss Teele? Duke was
free. He could love whom he liked—but for Ben . . . Hadn't
fate given him a mean enough break when he had married
Irene? Would his unhappiness with her tempt him to love
another, a sweeter woman?

Hours later, in a satin lounge-coat shaded like luscious
ripe nectarines, over matching crepe pajamas, she leaned
against the frame of the open French window in her bedroom and looked down at the warm dusk of the shrouded

garden, from which rose the moist night-breath of box hedges, the lazy stir of rustling twigs and branches. One! Two! The boom from a distant spire floated in on the scented breeze. Two o'clock. Only two? It seemed years since she had seen Duke waiting at the Union Station.

Hands thrust into the pockets of her coat, head dipped back against the frame of the window, eyes on the celestial glory of the stars that blinked like golden lids warding off sleep, she reconstructed those hours. One by one she visualized the events since she had arrived at her brother's house with all the persons she had met parading through her technicolor memory. It was like walking in a gallery hung with portraits—No, it was more like Madame Tussaud's waxworks peopled with the figures of the afternoon and evening.

A knock? Wasn't her first day at home over yet? She opened the door. Her brother, still in evening clothes, put his finger to his lips. Whispered:—

"Duke is on the phone. Wants to speak to you. Take the call here."

He closed the door. She ran to the telephone on the stand beside her bed. Spoke into it eagerly.

"It's Faith, Duke. What is it? What has happened?"

The wire faithfully transmitted his low laugh.

"Can't tell you all that's happened—yet. Couldn't sleep until I knew you were safe and happy."

"Of course I am. Where are you?"

"At home. I'll give a party to introduce you to Argyle House some day soon. That wasn't all I called you for. Want you to know that if you are unhappy at Ben's you can always marry me."

"Can I? *Marvelous*. You are self-sacrificing."

"You're laughing at me. Your voice rippled."

"How can I help laughing? That's what I call an anyport-in-a-storm proposal. Thanks a million but I don't want to marry anyone."

"Sure you won't be tempted by a title?"

"A *title!* One in the family is enough, thank you."

"Then that's all right—for the present. I'll keep my fingers crossed, though. Ben and I won't let that man Marshall carry you off either, remember."

"Why don't you like Wayne, Duke? I could feel your antagonism."

"Maybe it's his ring that gets me down. Huge rings on the male lead's hand annoy me. Perhaps it is the possessive way he looks at you which makes me want to fight. I didn't like that 'darling' either. Good night. I'll be seeing you."

"Good night. Thanks for calling."

Seated on the edge of the bed, Faith thoughtfully regarded the cradled phone as she pulled off a silver mule.

Of course there was something more than annoyance at a ring behind Duke Tremaine's aversion. What was it? Wayne had been furiously angry. Had he anything to hide which he thought Duke knew? Of course he hadn't. He didn't take life and responsibilities very seriously but that didn't necessarily mean that he was a double-crosser, did it? She visualized him as he had talked to Irene. Had he changed since he left Europe or was it the different setting in which she had seen him this afternoon that gave an impression of slickness she never had noticed before?

Duke's face flitted across the hazy no-man's-land between consciousness and sleep; with it drifted the faint echo of his voice saying:—

"You can always marry me."

"I wonder—I wonder what marriage to Duke would be like?" she said softly. "Heaven for a woman who loved him and safety for all time. But, as it happens, I don't love him. He doesn't love me."

She reached for the lamp and snapped off the light.

"And the afternoon and the evening were the first day," she paraphrased drowsily; "and what a day!"

IV

DECEMBER had gone out wreathed in holly, with oaks, pines, crape myrtles and sycamores frosted with light snow, to the echo of gay Christmas bells. January convened Congress, set lawmakers busy laying political wires, members fighting for chairmanships, lobbyists emulating the ever busy bee; opened important houses; set hotels humming with life, embassies alive with envoys; sent people in evening clothes thronging the night clubs, started the social top spinning. Also, it saw Faith Jarvis established as secretary to Kitty Teele.

Duke Tremaine was thinking of her as he stood at his office window, hands thrust hard into the pockets of his gray coat. He wondered if she were happy in her job, remembered his assurance to the Senator that wilting day on the desert that he never had seen a girl whom he would be content to see across the breakfast table for the rest of his life. And the Senator's reply, "Some day you'll meet one and suddenly it will be all over with you. You'll have to have her." It had happened just like that.

Why hadn't he realized that her charm and sincerity had lain in his mind wrapped in a silky cocoon of memory across the years, only to burst its chrysalis and emerge his one and only love?

He grinned at his high-flown comparison. That was going some for a problem-logged lawyer like himself. He was just back from South America. He had taken Faith out but once before he left the city. He had hated like the dickens to go, with Marshall not only *persona grata* at her brother's home but working where they would be thrown together constantly. She had appeared so thrilled to see him that afternoon at Ben's.

He couldn't explain to himself why he disliked the man, everyone else seemed to think him God's gift to Washington society. He distrusted him. Distrusted him so much that before he left the city he had written to a foreign correspondent for Marshall's dossier and that of Count Carrilski. As yet he had received no answer. He had not mentioned his reaction to the Senator, who appeared to think his confidential secretary one of the boy wonders of the consular world.

Beneath him the streets billowed with people. Above them loomed the sun-tipped Washington Monument. The tidal basin, with its border of dogwood which later would burst into pink and white glory, reflected the clear blue of the sky. Pennsylvania Avenue stretched ahead: a tree-bordered canyon, thronged with taxis. White buildings gleamed in the clear air. Men trundled flower carts patched with colors gay as a harlequin's coat. Birds were chirping and hopping on the iron-railed balcony outside the office window. Hard to realize that the month was January, with this April weather. He answered the burr of the interoffice phone.

"Madam Carr? I will see her at once."

What had Nancy Carr on her mind, he wondered. Ben was her adviser though he helped her straighten out business tangles when his partner was away.

"Good morning, Duke." She entered, looking in her black frock and regal furs like a fashion drawing of the smart older woman. "You couldn't appear more surprised if a ghost from your past had bobbed up in this office. Cheerio. I may be the ghost from some man's past but not yours. It's the present I want to talk about."

"Sit down. Better throw off that expensive-looking silver fox jacket." He laid it over the back of a chair before he seated himself across the desk from her. "What's on your mind, Nancy Carr?"

"Two things. Serious ones. I wouldn't take your time in business hours otherwise. You may send me a bill for the conference at your usual exorbitant rates." Laughter twinkled through the anxiety in her dark eyes. "I can't talk to you at the house, you don't come there; every ear is a dictaphone at social affairs in this city, where a world-shaking decision may be made by two men drinking tea. So I came here. I'm worried about Ben. It's getting me down."

"Ben! What's the matter with Ben?"

"I'm not sure anything is, but, I have a horrible suspicion that he's falling in love with Senator Teele's sister."

"Sure you're not suffering from an acute attack of imagination, Nancy Carr?"

"I'm not. I know human nature from A to Z. I can read faces, I knew from yours when I just dropped what I thought was a bomb that you're as uneasy about him as I am. It's a natural that it should happen. The Senator depends on Ben. He calls him his left hand, everyone knows that you're his right. While you were away he had him at the house constantly. More decisions are made in that home study of Joe Teele's than in his office at the Senate Building."

"You said something then."

"Certainly, I said something. I never make mistakes. I make corrections." Laughter flashed in her eyes and was gone. "Kitty Teele with her shyness and charm, her smooth unhurried voice is a lady—Ben is old-fashioned enough to like a lady and Irene is—you don't have to be told what Irene is. Except for the six years abroad you've known her since she came to live with me at the age of eight. We don't any of us know what happened over there. I watched her trying to 'vamp' you, that was the word in my mouth, in the month between her return and her engagement to Ben. The rush of color to your face confirms my suspicion. Didn't want her, did you?"

"I didn't want my house done over by her. She returned from abroad with an interior-decorating fixation. Insisted that the dining room chairs should have zebra-striped coverings. I ask you, can you see them in strictly Georgian Argyle House?"

"I can see that you're a master hand at turning the subject. We'll lay that question on the table. I never was more susprised in my life than when Irene accepted Ben. He isn't her type. I love him as if he were the son I always wanted and never had. He's such a dear. Amos, the butler, thinks he's an angel from heaven, and he isn't far wrong."

"That's because Ben proved that Amos didn't choke his wife to death. Boy, how we worked to follow the only bit of clue we had as to the real criminal. We got our man."

"And Amos was free. He would walk over red-hot coals for either of you boys. Irene is jealously aware of that. If Ben falls in love with a woman not his wife and that woman a Senator's sister, I wouldn't blame him if he did, and she loves him, it will ruin his career and he is on the way to a brilliant future."

"It wouldn't help the Senator's onward and upward climb, either. It would give his opponents an opportunity to take a few hefty cracks at him. Perhaps you've observed that indirect but notable efforts are being made to stop the favorable publicity his activities have been bringing him."

"I have." Her voice was grim. "To return to Ben . . . What can we do to stop his growing love for Kitty Teele?"

The unsteadiness of her usually firm mouth, her anxious eyes hurt him. She was such a valiant person, her gay courage stimulated every life it touched.

"Nothing. We'll have to trust to Ben's honor."

"What is honor?"

"Honor? What is honor? Can it be defined exactly? I suppose it has a different meaning for each person."

"The dictionary defines it as 'a nice sense of what is right, conformity to a high standard or to accepted rules of conduct.' For a man to leave his wife for another woman has, unfortunately, become a blinked-at and all too common 'rule of conduct.'"

"Nancy Carr, visualize Ben, remember his patience with Irene, his unfailing courtesy, his tenderness. He won't let his wife down. If what you suggest is true—mind you, I'm not admitting it—do you think Irene has an inkling of his feeling for Kitty Teele?"

"Irene! You know her as well as I do. Would she suspect that she couldn't hold any man—but you? Perhaps you are right about Ben, perhaps he is temptation-proof, but, I confess that for the first time in years, I'm frightened. I lie awake at night thinking of it, fearing that he will wreck his life because he thinks he can't live without a certain woman only to discover, as so many others have discovered before him, that forbidden fruit no matter how sweet, grows bitter, unbearably bitter to the taste. Will you—will you speak to him about it, Duke? He would listen to you."

"No. You don't catch me barging in on another person's life."

"My only excuse for asking was that to me he is a son, a splendid son. I might talk to Faith."

"Why make her anxious?"

"Perhaps we won't have to, perhaps she'll sense the danger. She's keen, Duke, she's a mixture of sweetness and sophistication. She not only has charm and sparkle and that elusive human quality which we call, for want of a better word, 'personality,' but she's a crackajack executive.

"I know what that smirk means. You're thinking, 'Nancy Carr's discovered another paragon.' I'll grant that some of my swans have turned out to be geese, but Faith is different.

"She knows the world yet the knowledge hasn't tarnished her spirit or her belief in the best. One can't call her innocent, because there is no longer the ignorance of life we used to call innocence."

"Perhaps not, but there's a lot, a whole lot of decency, which takes its place. Decency, standards, and a sense of moral responsibility which guards against cheapness."

"You're right, Duke. I wasn't really dropping a tear to the memory of the young person who knew nothing of the so-called facts of life. It's better for them to know the world in which they live. But, I'm troubled about Faith, as well as Ben. I don't like her intimacy with Wayne Marshall. He's taken her dancing and to the theater, has been her shadow since you've been away. Sometimes I believe she's in love with him. Women as intelligent as she have gone squishy over his type before this. It's the mustache. When he strokes it with his ringed finger and looks at me from beneath his sensational lashes, it gives even my simonized heart a thrill. What do you know about his pal, Count Carrilski?"

Her shrewd eyes were boring into his. Did she suspect him of knowing more about the visiting foreigner than he admitted?

"Nothing. Absolutely nothing more than you know, Nancy Carr."

Apparently she had not suspected, as he had, that Irene had pushed the kettle to cover her frightened surprise the afternoon Marshall had brought the Count to the terrace. The man had been almost as white as she. They had met before undoubtedly. That was one reason he had sent for a check-up of Carrilski's title and estates.

"That's convincing. I'm always suspecting that you and Joe Teele are holding out on me. The Count claims to be a Pole, but he adjusts his monocle like an Englishman, springs to attention like a German, devours caviare like a Russian, presses his lips to a woman's hand with the ador of an Italian and sounds his vowels like a Frenchman. When he's off guard he has the boyish charm of an American, the best type. Have you noticed that last trait, Duke?"

"No. I've been away since he reached town. Haven't seen him since the afternoon on the terrace at Ben's. From your description I'd say he would qualify for the International Set. Did you see the letter he brought to Irene?"

"Yes. The signature was so full of s's and z's it sounded like a sneeze. She said it must be from someone she'd met at an embassy, she had met dozens of attachés. She couldn't understand, though, how the writer had known her married name. Seemed quite disturbed about that."

"Carrilski." He scrawled the name on the green blotter. "What else have you on your mind?"

"Marshall again. There is no mistaking the fact that he is in love, as deeply as a self-centered man can be, with Faith; but he flatters Irene, takes her night-clubbing. Why? Answer: To get himself and his friend the Count into the Army and Navy set, especially the aeronautic branch with which she is on drop-in-at-any-hour terms."

"Has Ben noticed their attention to his wife?"

"He's used to seeing Irene's tame cats about the house. They hover around Faith too. These two men are different. What are they after?"

"A good time, I'd say. Irene travels with a high-power crowd. You're not getting a spy fixation about them are you, Nancy Carr? Remember you've been rallying your friends, the Senators, to help Joe Teele fight for an increased appropriation for counterespionage."

"If more Americans had a spy fixation I'd breathe easier. There are several thousand propagandists operating openly in this country and only their masters know how many under cover. Washington is the key city of the world today. Secret agents . . . Foreign spies behind every tree—and you'll admit there are plenty of trees. Wayne Marshall gave up an excellent appointment abroad, with every chance of mounting fast and high on the Consular ladder, to come to Washington; I've discovered that. Curiously enough, he arrives to take a position as secretary to Joe Teele at the time the Senator is the supreme agitator for that extra air-research appropriation, is backing a new attack-bomber, the design and specifications of which he guards with his life, figuratively speaking. He doesn't intend to have it sold to foreign democracies no matter how friendly."

"How do you know so much about that bomber? I thought the Senator's possession of the design was off the record."

"It is, but Joe told me and I supposed of course you knew about it. He tells you everything, doesn't he? To return to Marshall. Why didn't he stay in France?"

"I heard him tell Faith that he came to be near her. I don't like him; when he held her hands that day at Ben's I had to remind myself that a perfect gentleman didn't sock a man because the expression of his eyes annoyed him; but I don't believe he is here as a spy. He's an American citizen. Why should he spy in his own country?"

"Because someone has the power to bring pressure to bear on him. Who could get information of our air bases, our naval strength, our ammunition factories better than the confidential secretary of Senator Joe Teele, who is a fighter, who has the backing of the strongest, most constructive men in Congress? Men have been known before this to be traitors to their country."

"Have you told the Senator of your suspicion of Marshall's disloyalty? I'm sure he likes him."

"No, because it is only suspicion, only a hunch. But remember, my mental observation and deduction scout has been on this Washington merry-go-round for years, long before the Government departments discovered the alphabet; it ought to get results. Having accomplished what I came for, to shake you up, I'll go."

As she slipped into the silver fox coat Tremaine held for her she asked:

"Like Faith Jarvis a lot, don't you?"

His grave eyes met hers steadily.

" 'Like' hardly expresses what I feel for her, Nancy Carr."

"Then, my boy, look out for Irene. She'll stop at nothing to break you with the girl you love."

V

DUKE TREMAINE gazed unseeingly at the door he had closed behind Madam Carr. She had charged him with indifference. Little she knew of his anti-spy activities. She mustn't know. No one must suspect that a quarter of his time was devoted to charting the source and following the course of subversive propaganda. Even Ben didn't know. Only Senator Teele. He worked under his orders.

His thoughts switched back to the present. Was Faith in love with Marshall? Nancy Carr had been right about a bomb, but it had not been her suspicion as to Ben's attraction to Kitty Teele which had rocked his mind by its impact. It had been her summing up of Faith's emotional response to Wayne Marshall. "Sometimes I believe she's in love with him," she had said. Was she?

A fool question like that wouldn't get him anywhere. He'd better stop wondering and swing into action. He caught up the phone and spun the dial; told Sam, the butler at the Senator's that he wished to speak to Miss Jarvis. He drew intricate curlicues on the immaculate green blotter as he waited.

"Faith Jarvis speaking."

The lilt in her voice came across the wire as clearly as if she were in the office. He didn't need television to see her velvety dark eyes, her ardent mouth with the adorable dent at a corner of her vivid lips.

"A man by the name of Tremaine calling."

"Duke! You're back! How marvelous! It seems ages since you planed away to South America."

"Miss me?"

"Frightfully. Missed talking things over with you. You have a way, you always had, of untangling my problems. So much has happened since you left."

"What?"

"If you snap like that you'll bite the phone wire in half, old-timer."

"Sorry. What's happened?"

"My job, of course."

"Like it?"

"Love it. Miss Teele is a dear if she has an inferiority complex the like of which I've never seen. We ride, the bridle paths through the woods are perfection, exercise at the gym; give two mornings to Red Cross work, and attend social affairs by the glamorous score. We go to church, too. We get a lot of fun out of the same things. Then there are the charities, and a discussion group where we are instructed as to the why, wherefore and for what the Government departments exist, and how to take an intelligent part in politics. That is one of the things I came home to learn but I haven't progressed far."

"Don't be in such a hurry. You've been here a little over one month. Sounds like a success story to me. Like the Senator?"

"He's a grand person. *Bon viveur.* Gay, with a boyish charm·at times and the next minute with a grand manner before which I *almost* bend the knee. His daughter, Thalia is— Well, I haven't made much progress with her, either. I've tried. Sometimes I walk to school with her. She has acquired a duck who resides in the garden, whose euphonious name is Jemima; that creature, and Snubs the Boston bull, follow at her heels when she's at home. Mary's little lamb has nothing on those two. The incessant quacking and barking have reduced her aunt and yours truly to the verge of a nervous breakdown."

"Thalia's all right. She's lost her way in an emotional maze, that's all. She'll straighten out. She's a clever kid, so full of vitality that her daily routine doesn't use up her pep. She's a bit slow in studies, especially English, but she'll catch up. I didn't call you as an adviser for the adolescent. Dine with me tonight, will you? I'll be on the jump every minute today. Won't have time to dress for one of the night spots. We'll drive into the country to a chicken-and-waffle place in which I'm interested. Okay?"

"I'd love it. Unless the Teeles are entertaining my evenings are my own. I'm still making headquarters at Ben's, though I'm rarely there except to change my clothes and sleep."

He had a curious sense that a third person was on the line. It couldn't happen in his office. He was using a private wire. Could the listener be at the Senator's? . . . "Look out for Irene. She'll stop at nothing to break you with the girl you love." . . . Nancy Carr's warning echoed through his mind as clearly as if amplified by a mike. He was getting screwy. Irene wouldn't be at the Senator's at this time of day.

"Where are you, Faith?" he asked sharply.

"In Miss Teele's sitting room."

"Anyone else there?"

"No. What time shall I be ready?"

"I'll be at the Senator's at six. You won't mind if I come for you there instead of Ben's, will you?"

He would have taken his oath that a phone was gently cradled. He no longer felt that third presence on the wire.

"Are you listening, Duke?"

"Sure. What made you think I wasn't?"

"I—I felt it. Of course I won't mind if you come for me here. Think I have forgotten the verbal fireworks your last call at Ben's set off, because you had 'lured,' was Irene's word, Ben to a class dinner the week before? I wish you and she were better friends. She can be charming and believe it or not there are times when I suspect that she loves her husband. I know it isn't your fault that you don't get on together. You are mighty nice to her; she's the one who won't do her part. What started the feud, Duke?"

"That old debil of a green-eyed monster, jealousy, I presume. Let's sign-off on Irene and—"

"Good-by."

"Hey, what's the rush?"

"You said you would be on the jump every minute today, didn't you?"

"I'm not so busy I can't talk with you."

"If you are not, I am, old-timer. Miss Teele is waiting for her invaluable secretary."

"Okay. Business before pleasure. Until six, lady. My love to Thalia. I'll be seeing you. Good-by."

He spun the phone dial and ordered two perfect gardenias sent to her. Hands thrust into his coat pockets, he paced the office. Back and forth. Back and forth, trying to set in some sort of order Nancy Carr's troubled confidences and suspicions.

Was she right about Ben's attraction to Kitty Teele? Right or wrong, whatever Ben felt he was too honorable to upset the woman's life by letting her know he loved her. Love? Nancy Carr had dragged into the open a word he himself had had to force into the background whenever he had seen Kitty Teele and his partner together. She had asked him to speak to Ben.

He couldn't, he wouldn't do it, even though he knew his best friend was heading straight for tragedy. He was betting heavily on Ben's sense of honor, but with a shrew like Irene at home would honor save him if he discovered that Kitty Teele returned his love? She wouldn't let him know, ever. Shy and unsophisticated as she was, she filled her position as her brother's hostess with beautiful dignity. Perhaps she didn't love Ben. With which cheering thought he would pigeonhole the Jarvis-Teele complication. He glanced at the clock. He was milling over romantic problems when he should be digging out law for a brief.

At his desk he pulled a heavy book toward him, saw the scribbled name on the green blotter. Carrilski. Had he and Irene met abroad? He remembered her face when the man had stepped from the dusky living room to the terrace—his stunned surprise. If they had, it had been more than a meeting. The sudden appearance of a casual acquaintance wouldn't turn a sophisticate like Irene into a ghost.

Could there be grounds for Nancy Carr's suspicion that he and Marshall were up to deviltry? Was Irene being forced into their scheme, if it were a scheme? That was a thought which would bear following up.

He slammed the book shut. He couldn't concentrate with a procession of questions and conjectures marching through his mind. He would drop in on Ben. Nancy Carr had confessed that she had blown off steam to him also. To what extent?

As he entered the office his partner was standing at a window, staring at the birds preening and hopping on the iron-railed balcony.

"What's on the little mind, Ben? You've brushed back that blond lock of yours twice. Did Nancy Carr drop in on you too, waving a Stop–Look–Listen signal?"

"*Too!* Did you see her, Duke?"

"I did. Much as I admire my old friend and your grand-mother-in-law,—she's a swell person,—I wish she had selected another day to warn us of danger ahead. I've got to brief the Arnold *vs.* Arnold case and I'll be darned if I can nail my attention to it after her visitation."

Ben Jarvis' brown eyes were as expressionless as bronze eyes, his face was colorless.

"What did Nancy Carr tell you?"

Did his brittle voice mean that he suspected he and Kitty Teele had been the subjects of the interview?

"International note. She's all het-up about Count Carrilski. She intimates he's a phony. Got any views on him?"

He could feel Ben's relief. He watched him cross the room, perch on the corner of his broad, flat desk, saw the color steal back to his face, the sparkle to his eyes. Good old Ben! Wasn't it enough that he had drawn a matrimonial blank—wrong word: nothing blank about Irene, "a powder magazine" was better—without plunging him into love with a woman he couldn't have? It sure was a cockeyed world. Cockeyed, maybe, but inexorable. If one made a mistake Life saw to it that one paid. He had tried, how he had tried to make Ben realize the sort of person Irene was; but he had been madly in love with her and wouldn't listen.

"Views about Count what's-his-name, Duke? Can't say I have. He's at the house, more or less, but he hasn't registered with me. Lord, where do these afternoon tea and cocktail boys find time for the social merry-go-round? He is one of Faith's stag-line. It's a long one. She has found some old friends, attachés of embassies, who are giving her a rush. If I say it who shouldn't that kid sister of mine has what it takes."

"She's no longer a kid."

"Sez you—like a whip snap. To return to Nancy Carr and

her red flag of danger. Whether she's right or wrong we'd
better keep our eyes and ears wide open. Shall we pass her
suspicion on to the Senator?"

Ben mustn't mix into this. Suppose the Count proved to
be hectoring Irene? He might go haywire and get himself
into a tragic mess.

"Pass on suspicion to Joe Teele? He doesn't need it. That
man imagines a spy behind each pair of eyes his meet.
You'd better keep out of it for the present. Let me handle
the Marshall-Carrilski axis. From this minute I'll leave no
stone unturned until I've proved Nancy Carr's hunch true or
false."

"If Marshall and the Count do belong to the espionage
school of thought, the devil help them, no one else could, it
they have you on their trail, Duke. But, watch your step.
If they are a couple of spies with a foreign government behind them they'll stop at nothing to break you."

"Now that's queer."

"What in thunder are you grinning about? I'm not being
funny. I'm in dead earnest. What's queer?"

"That very warning was shot at me not half an hour ago
—about a different person. Life is a battle, Benjamin,
unless one is content to drift with the masses. Looks to me
as if I had the fight of my life, ahead. I haven't had a real
one for some time. I'm just raring to go. The finish may
not rate a burst of rockets and a brass band but I'll let
you in on it. Come on. Let's eat. Then I'll get back to work."

"Just a minute while I wash my hands." Ben Jarvis opened
a door and a light sprang on. "Even if you do own this
building, sometimes I think we ought to move into one of
the modern ones, Duke, but boy, I like our windows opening onto balconies and where would we find a closet big
enough for a small office like this?"

"With everything in it but the kitchen range. What's the
idea keeping that bunch of scarfs hanging there? Must be
a dozen. Going in for haberdashering or breeding moths?"
Tremaine raised his voice above the gush of water from the
faucets.

"You needn't shout. I'm not deaf. I keep them here because if I took them home Irene would give them away,
pronto. They're old, they're shabby, but I love 'em. Every
scarf brings back a memory of a good time. You can lose
almost anything but you never can lose the fun you've had.
Following which sparkling gem of philosophy— Hullo, Marshall. What can we do for you?" Ben Jarvis asked as he
dried his hands.

"Nothing thanks, they don't stint you in closet room here,

do they? Count Carrilski has rented the office next to this.
I came with him to help settle so dropped in here for a
minute."

"Count going into business?"

"Nothing like that, Tremaine. He's handling family affairs
here. There's quite a fortune to invest, I understand. He
needed headquarters. I hear him in the hall now. Come and
say, 'howdy,' will you?"

"Sure. Come on, Ben."

The Count was standing in the doorway of the office beyond Jarvis'. He clicked his heels and readjusted his monocle.

"It is a coincidence and a pleasure that we are to be
neighbors, friends I hope, ees eet not? Perhaps at some time
I may be of use, be able to repay the charming hospitality
of the Jarvees home." There was a touch of mockery in his
bow before he followed Marshall into the office and closed
the door.

Jarvis and Tremaine looked at its unlettered glass panel.
They grinned at each other and walked along the corridor
to the accompaniment of the click of innumerable type-
writers.

"Cut us off before we could say, 'Welcome to our building,' didn't he?"

"An office next to yours, 'Family affairs'; I wonder? Something tells me that it is not a 'coincidence.' Which one is
the lead and which the stooge in that build-up, Ben?"

"Listen, Duke. If you continue to look at Marshall as if
he were poison, you'll not get anywhere in finding out.
And if you don't find out, the Senator may land in a nasty
mess that will break him. Get that?"

"Righto. From now on I will be 'friends, I hope, ees eet
not?' By the way, don't mention the fact that I own this
building. Something tells me that you and I will get those
guys if they are crooked, Ben."

"If they don't get us first. Come on. As you suggested
some time ago, let's eat."

VI

FAITH cradled the phone as Kitty Teele entered the boudoir
and snuggled girlishly into a deep chair. The room was
wholly unsuited to her. Too much baroque in the décor;

too many ivories, crystals, figurines littering shelves and in-
laid tabletops, too much color in the chair and couch coverings; too much richness in the damask hangings.

She had nothing to fear from the strong sunlight that
poured over her, if it did bring out the lines a not too happy
life had etched at the corners of her eyes. It turned her fair
hair to minted gold, rouged her delicate skin and the rosy
curve of her tender mouth, deepened the violet-blue of her
eyes which were intent on the warm, lazy sway of tree
branches. When it shone through a crystal ball in its path it
sent little rainbows dancing on the sheer white wool of her
frock.

What was she thinking about? Faith remembered Duke's
remark. "She's the type which makes a man eager to pull off
his coat and fight for her, knight-and-his-lady's-glove stuff."

He was right. She had been Kitty Teele's secretary but a
month and already she was eager to help her in any way
she could. If only she would assert herself more. Her supine-
ness at times was maddening. Why didn't she soundly
smack her disagreeable niece? Charge it up to adolescence,
as apparently Duke did and as a child specialist would; the
fact remained that Thalia had the most hateful line a youngster could possibly think up.

"Every guest you invited for the Sunday supper has accepted, Miss Teele," she announced. "Senators by the dozen,
oodles of representatives and, hold your breath, one member
of the Cabinet. That last is a feather in your cap. With such
a company, nation-shaking decisions may be made in your
drawing rooms or the Senator's study."

"The Senator's study is holy ground. The person who en-
ters there uninvited, enters at the peril of his life." Kitty
Teele rose and stretched her arms. "I believe those swaying
trees hypnotized me. Your voice roused me from the trance.
Mind if I say I love you in that spruce-green wool frock?"
She looked over Faith's shoulder.

"It is an imposing list, isn't it? The feather is in your cap,
not mine, Miss Jarvis. The Sunday night supper was sheer
inspiration. How did you happen to think of it?"

"You said you dreaded a formal dinner because you
couldn't speak the languages of some of the persons your
brother wanted to entertain. You needn't have worried. They
all speak ours. I thought an informal party would be worth
trying. If it is a smash-hit we might make it a weekly affair,
Miss Teele."

"Would it be a tragic breach of Washington etiquette, if
you called me Kitty? I would love it, but, being what the
newspapers dub 'a child of nature from the cow-country,

wholly unaccustomed to the Washington merry-go-round,' I really wouldn't know the social rules."

"Hooray! If the reporters could hear that snap in your voice, they would reconstruct their graphs of your character. You may be Kitty to me and I'll be Faith to you inside this room. Outside, perhaps it would be wiser to stick to formalities."

"I wish you would decide to live here, you are such a wonderful tonic. There is a suite over this which would be perfect for you. The Senator gave me permission to have it done over. I loved planning it. Only last night when he met you going home late as he was coming in, he remarked that it would be a great saving of your time and strength if you would make your headquarters here. We won't infringe on your free time, I promise. Think it over. It would be such a joy for me to have you in the house. You give me courage, belief in myself."

Faith was shocked at her sense of relief at the suggestion. What a chance to escape from the disagreeable atmosphere of her brother's house! She mustn't think of it. Ben wanted her, needed her.

"I would love it, but it wouldn't do," she said quickly before she could yield to temptation. "Ben would be frightfully hurt. And he is hurt—" she caught back "enough." Why parade a family skeleton?

"Your brother adores you, doesn't he?"

"We have always been pals in spite of the fact that he is ten years older than I. He and Duke brought me up in the way I should go until I was fifteen, then Mother tore me away. Hear that bird-call! 'Cheer! Cheer! Cheer!' What is it?"

Kitty Teele joined her at the window.

"A cardinal. There it is! Perched on that rhododendron. Isn't he gorgeous with his red feathers and his ruff of black around the bill going up to the peak of his crest?"

"Gorgeous is the word. Look! There's another bird. All soft buff tinged with green and faint rose."

"That's the woman in his life. She doesn't sing. She—"

The door banged open. A girl stalked into the room. She was perhaps ten pounds too heavy for her age, three inches too tall. Her brown frock was the exact shade of her eyes, which were magnified behind bone-rimmed spectacles. Her nose was of classic perfection; if ever her mouth grew up to them her large white teeth would be lovely, at present they gave a fierce, I'll-grind-your-bones effect to her expression. Her short chestnut hair stood out like a floor-mop gone mad when she shook her head for emphasis—which gesture occurred on the average of once a minute.

Her face was dark with anger. The Boston bull which had dashed into the room at her heels playfully caught the hem of Kitty Teele's frock and began to chew it. The white duck which waddled in the wake of girl and dog quacked incessantly.

"I'd like to know what you mean by telling Cook not to give me snacks between meals?"

"Thalia, take that creature out of this room." Kitty Teele ignored her angry question. "It is bad enough to have it everlastingly quacking in the garden. I have told you repeatedly not to bring it here."

The girl swooped on the duck and cuddled it in her arms. "What's the matter with Jemima? You don't want me to have anything I love, do you, you old meanie? First it's eats and now it's pets. You masticate my father, then barge in on this house my mother furbished, change it and—"

"Furbished is right! Masticate! Don't speak of the Senator as if he were a lamb chop, my dear." Kitty Teele's laugh was like a note of shaken music. "Really, Thalia, is that what you mean? Isn't it 'fascinate'? You should study words. If you are ambitious to use those of more than one syllable it is quite important that you use them correctly. Perhaps though, if you did, you wouldn't be nearly so amusing. My friends are in stitches, fairly in stiches when I repeat some of your howlers."

The girl stared at her aunt with amazed eyes. Her face flushed crimson.

"What's happened to you? Picked up some spirit somewhere, haven't you? In stitches! Your friends laugh at me, do they? Have you ever told Duke Tremaine what I say? Has he laughed at m—me?" the last word ended in a gulp.

"I can't really remember, Thalia. There have been so many," Kitty Teele answered calmly, though Faith noticed that she quickly clasped unsteady hands behind her back.

"I don't believe he laughed at me. He wouldn't. The next time I see him, I'll ask him and if you've been lying about him there are a few things I'll tell my father about you that won't be lies. I know what you're up to. Come on, Snubs! Stop chewing that skirt!" She glared at Faith.

"You're her accomplishment in this, I'll bet. You've pepped her up. You'd better watch your step, Miss Jarvis, or you'll lose your job, if you are the sister of my father's solicitous. That's all—for now."

She stalked from the room with the duck quacking in her arms and the dog barking at her heels.

Kitty Teele closed the door behind her and leaned against it. Her face was white, her eyes were like larkspur petals under tears.

"She's right, Faith. You have pepped me up, made me realize what a spineless person I've been. How far does a spineless person get in this age? Nowhere! She can hold neither respect nor love. I hated to hurt Thalia, but—but Ben— your brother, told me either to tell her father or to try ridicule the next time she treated me to one of her outbursts. I won't tell her father so I tried the other way."

"I'll say Ben's prescription worked to a charm. Wasn't she mad? I came in for my share of the hurricane."

"It was the thought that Duke Tremaine may have laughed at her that hurt the most. He never has and I shouldn't have let her think so; she adores him. But when she accused me of influencing her father and barging in on this house, which I think is a horror in some of its furnishings—I haven't had the courage to tackle this so-called boudoir,—I went a little crazy." She paused to clear her voice of tears.

"My brother begged me to come here as his hostess. It seemed at first as if I couldn't give up my own plans. I had been on leash so many years. Mother dominated my life. With freedom and some money, I had planned to travel. That doesn't mean that I'm sorry I decided to come to Washington to help Joe. He really needs me. Before he married he and I were as near and dear as you and your brother. I have grown to love the city. I was terrified at first, but since you came I am no longer jittery. I'm beginning to believe in myself."

"Don't worry about what Thalia thinks Duke thinks, Kitty. I have just been talking with him. He likes her. You were right to smack her, figuratively speaking. There are times when endurance becomes a sort of cowardice. Perhaps we are too critical of her. Perhaps in reality she's a Cinderella crouching in her own emotional ash-heap."

"Please find her and assure her that never to my knowledge has Mr. Tremaine laughed at her. That's only being fair to him. When you come back we will drive to the Capitol. The Senator is to introduce one of his bills today and asked me to be present. We'll lunch in the Senate dining room."

"After that I'll stop at Ben's to dress. I'm to dine with Duke tonight."

"You see? If you were staying here your clothes would be upstairs. Do change your mind and live with us."

"Not yet—perhaps later."

If I am convinced that Ben would be happier without me,

Faith told herself, as she ran down the stairs in search of Thalia, who at this hour was likely to be regaling herself with forbidden snacks in the pantry.

It was wonderful to have Duke back. She had met men who had amused her, men who had interested her, men who had loved her, but never a man who had thrilled her till the afternoon in Union Station when his eyes had looked straight into hers and he had said:—

"Why hasn't Ben told me you are the loveliest thing in the world?"

"What's the big idea standing staring into space as if you were in a trance?" Marshall demanded from the hall below.

She laughed as she took the last two stairs in a jump.

"Starting a little 'Information Please' clinic on your own, Wayne? Now I'll ask a question. Isn't it time you were at the Senate office building?"

"Stopped to complete some notes the Senator wanted and to tell you that he will meet you and Miss Teele at the reception for the new Senator's new bride this afternoon at the Mayflower. He'll make it at about six. You are to wait there for him."

"I can't go, Wayne. I have another date."

He shrugged, stroked his mustache with his heavily ringed finger and smiled with the engaging charm which warmed her eyes and curved her lips in response. She liked him. Very much. He had been a gay, stimulating companion during these last weeks when she had felt like a stranger in a strange land, the sort of friend he had been abroad. Curious that on the day of her arrival she had sensed a change in him. Imagination due to her emotional excitement, doubtless . . .

"Better think it over, darling." His voice recalled her thoughts to his announcement that she was to attend the reception. "Senator Teele wants the new man's support for his pet bill, and his being at the reception won't count a nickel's worth if the women of his family aren't there too."

"I'm not his family. I'm hired help and I wish you'd stop calling me 'darling.' "

"Why? Does Tremaine object?" As her lips parted in indignant denial he returned quickly to his argument. "You were hired, weren't you, because your brother's wife and her grandmother are tops socially? You are counted in with them. You'd better go. It's part of your job."

"Sure of that?" she asked in troubled uncertainty. What would Duke think when she phoned him she couldn't keep their date?

"Couldn't be surer. I've been in consular service since I

left college, but Washington has all the places in which I've
served licked as the center of intrigue and world importance
today. Careers have been made at teas like the one you're
trying to sidestep, and more often broken because some brainless woman thought she had been slighted. No one knows that
better than Senator Teele. He'll be there. I have been instructed to escort you and his sister. Going?"

"*Going?*" Faith felt as if she were being pushed to a decision. "*Going? After that burst of eloquence? Of course I'm
going.*"

VII

FAITH took her seat beside Kitty Teele in the gallery reserved
for Senators' ladies at the Capitol with two gardenias fastened
to the shoulder of her jacket. It was maddening that Duke
had been absent from his office when she had phoned to tell
him that instead of being ready to go out with him at six
she would be at that poisonous reception. Only she hadn't
used that adjective when leaving the message with his secretary. She had said, "Tell him the Senator's orders changed
my plans, that I must attend a tea at the Mayflower."

She tried to shake off the mist of disappointment which
hung over her spirit. Evidently he had ordered the flowers
to be sent before he had been told that she couldn't keep her
date with him. She forced her attention to her surroundings.
Senators were strolling into the chamber, by twos and threes,
some laughing, some frowning, some appearing bored. Page
boys darted about. Green baize doors swung. Visitors' galleries were filling and, in the seats reserved for the ladies of
the Diplomatic corps, foreign exotic-looking women shrugged,
chattered, raised lustrous, soulful eyes to heaven and rouged
glamorous lips. In the press gallery, reporters scribbled or
leaned across green tables to talk with confrères.

Irene had taken a seat in the gallery. What had brought
her? This was the last place in which one would expect to
see her. She didn't care for the executive and legislative side
of Washington, her interest lay with the Army and Navy.

Count Carrilski loomed in a doorway. "Distinguished" was
the word for him. Gossip had it that he was enormously rich
and heir to a near-royal title. He was an entertaining com-

panion. Evidently he hadn't seen Irene, for he was sitting down several rows behind her. He had said that this was his first visit to the United States. What would he think of the free and easy manners of the men who were lounging, arguing, laughing, at the desks on the floor of the Chamber? Which ones were the threads of gold which Duke had said were woven through what at times seemed to be a pretty dark pattern? Each time she had visited the Senate Chamber she had remembered the simile and had wondered.

The Vice President mounted the rostrum. Conferred with two men who had been waiting for him. Pounded his gavel. Members settled into their places. The buzz of voices stilled. The Chaplain offered a prayer. A moment of silence. The business of the day began.

Faith's eyes flew to Senator Teele. He was frowning a little. She caught his swift look at his sister beside her, saw Kitty's tender mouth widen in a smile. She felt the current of sympathy between them. He straightened his broad shoulders. A man rose, droned on and on. Another spoke and then another. Time was flying. Would the Senator get his chance today?

She drew a quick breath of excitement as he rose, a fastidiously groomed and tailored figure. He was recognized by the Vice President and began to speak.

"I honestly believe that war is on the way out of the world. That belief isn't super-optimism, it's anti-defeatism. I believe, also, that if this country is adequately prepared to meet aggression, war as a means of settling international quarrels will be given a hurry-up shove toward extinction."

He looked like a man who knew where he was going, who was relentlessly on his way. He sounded like a man who was fighting for a measure in which he passionately believed.

There were no interruptions. Faith wondered if that were a good omen. She watched the men behind the desks on the floor; men who had been sent there by voters, who had been boosted into their high place by fiery speeches and red-hot campaigns. Were they worth the effort it had cost their constituents to put them there and taxpayers to keep them there? Two had mistaken the Senate Chamber for a restroom and were asleep. One was filing his nails. Some were scribbling on pads—notes for an attack? Others were listening intently and nodding approval at salient points.

Senator Teele finished and sat down. He mopped his brow with a huge white handkerchief. Members rose and asked questions to which the author of the bill responded briefly. Some were dull. Some were brilliant. Some were impassioned.

Some spoke in so low a voice as to be barely audible in the gallery. Most of the queries came from the opposition. There would be no rubber-stamping of this bill. Through it all the men of the Press scribbled madly, came and went. Occupants in the galleries bent forward in tense interest. Two Senators rose and hurled invectives at each other. The thump! thump! of the gavel restored order. The rollcall began. The Clerk droned the names. When it ended the bill had been defeated by three votes. The Senate recessed.

Faith relaxed. She had been tense with excitement. What impression had Count Carrilski received from the session? She glanced toward the gallery where she had seen him. He was leaving. Irene had gone. Bored, probably. Why had she come?

The members drifted out in arguing groups. The men at the Press tables rushed from the gallery or thrust papers at others who grabbed them and dashed out as if shot from a gun. A stout man, with a bald spot smooth as a billiard ball, had linked his arm in Senator Teele's. They were laughing. Laughing after the defeat of a bill for which he had been passionately pleading? Incredible. How could he do it?

After that, lunch in the Senate dining room, with important men stopping at their table to speak to Kitty Teele . . . Black-faced waiters hovering . . . Luscious oysters, big and plump . . . More senators appearing to pay their respects to a distinguished colleague's sister . . . Kitty, with her recently acquired confidence, gaily replying to their compliments and sallies . . .

Later Faith stood at the top of the steps of the Capitol. Broad highways rayed in all directions like the spokes of a giant wheel. Broken they might be by intersecting streets or the blue Potomac, but always they picked up their design and went on and on to hills, to the sea, to towns and wooded slopes. The slanting sun was plating the city with rose gold and capping the Monument with flame. Straight ahead, down Pennsylvania Avenue, the White House gleamed like a massive pink pearl set in an emerald lawn which had defied the threat of winter.

She glanced at her wrist watch. She had better start if she intended to walk part way to Ben's. She descended countless steps to the street. Glorious afternoon. Gorgeous world. Sky, blue to the zenith, clotted with downy white clouds with fluffed gold edges. A tangy breeze rustled bronze twigs and branches, swayed evergreens for all the world like a stylist calling attention to the latest models in smart winter-wear for trees. Marble buildings had been conjured into rosy-gold

palaces and topaz towers by the reddening sun. From a taxi
drifted a radioed voice singing Schubert's Serenade:—

> "Through the leaves the night winds moving
> Murmur low and sweet . . ."

She détoured to Constitution Avenue, and entered the
Smithsonian for a glimpse of the Spirit of St. Louis. The
sight of the small plane always fired her with the determination to make good. If a man could fly across the Atlantic in
that toy why should she fear to attempt any difficult thing?
Answer: She shouldn't.

As she approached, men, women and small boys were
looking up at the plane. A woman separated from the group,
hurried away. Faith hadn't seen her face but she walked
like Irene. The bit of hair visible from the back was the
color of Irene's. It was coincidence, that was all. Mrs. Ben
Jarvis would consider it provincial for one of her social importance to visit a place like this.

"Good afternoon, Mees Jarvees."

Faith turned with a start. Hat in hand Count Carrilski
was smiling at her. For an instant her heart was as still as a
robin listening for a worm, then it settled into steady drum-
ming. That had been Irene! Had the two met in the Senate
Chamber by arrangement? Had she disappeared a moment ago
because she was afraid of being seen with him? Did the quick
narrowing of Carrilski's eyes mean that he suspected she had
recognized her sister-in-law?

"So you come here too, Count?" She struggled to keep her
voice light. "Are you wondering how a man ever flew in
that—'crate' is the word for it. Looks like something which
had been knocked together in a back yard, doesn't it? When I
come here I remember how I lay awake and in imagination
flew every mile across the ocean with Lindbergh the night he
started."

"You are an emotional person, are you not, Mees Jarvees?"
the Count asked with the amused indulgence one would show
a child. "You are a-tremble with excitement over an exploit
which I grant was heroic. That winged thing above us ees
like a mosquito compared with the gigantic planes which
fly from continent to continent now. Your Senator Teele
argued today for even greater ones for the Army; he has
plans already for them, ees eet not?"

Faith's watch-your-step scout tapped her shoulder. Why was
the Count asking these questions, which no one outside the
air arms of the Army or Navy could, or should, answer?

"Better query someone else about that, Count. I'll confess that construction and plans and specifications leave me quite cold. I have neither a mechanical nor a scientific cell in my brain. Good-by. I must go if I intend to reach my brother's in time for tea."

"I am desolated. Some day perhaps you weel show me the wonders under thees roof and in the city? There are many, ees eet not? I know so little where to look, and a guide-book—" he shrugged disdain. "I so want to know your country. Will you present my respects to Madam Jarvees? I hope soon to call. She ees an enchanting person. *Au revoir.*"

That was bluff, pure bluff, Faith decided, as disturbed by her certainty that Irene had met the Count clandestinely, she hailed a taxi to take her through the center of the city. If Irene were at home when she arrived, she would know that her sister-in-law had left the Senate Chamber by herself, that the likeness to her of the woman she had seen at the Smithsonian had been coincidental, that Count Carrilski really had been there to see the "wonders" as he called them and not to meet Irene.

Why should they meet in such a public place? Its very publicity was a safeguard, wasn't it? It was a pretty safe bet that none of Irene's friends or acquaintances would be sight-seeing. The Count and Irene! He was attractive. He was credited with great wealth and a glittering family background. While she had talked with him she had felt that behind his foreign manner was a man she might like. Had Irene felt his charm? She was extravagantly fond of money. Would she be tempted by that and a title, or would it mean an adventure into extramarital territory?

Not that. She thought too much of her social supremacy, she'd never risk it for an emotional experience. There were too many who wanted her place, who would be avid to pull her down. Did Ben know that the Count and his wife were meeting? She, herself, didn't *know* it, did she? She'd better walk this thing off her mind.

She dismissed the taxi—drew a long breath of the frost-tinged air. She loved it. It sent doubts and anxieties sprinting out of sight, quickened her pace, made her feel as if her spruce-green turban and black pumps had sprouted little wings like those on the cap and heels of Mercury, that light-footed messenger of the gods.

She walked more slowly as she approached her brother's home. No Mercury-like wings on her feet now. She hated to go in. She was on edge every minute she and Irene were together for fear she would say something that would rouse her sister-in-law's jealousy or anger, the immediate result of which would be that Ben would be hurt and that the servants would be nagged into suppressed revolt. Was she worried by something about which the other members of the family knew nothing?

What a way to live! What a spineless, senseless way for Faith Jarvis, who had left Rome for freedom from her mother's despotism, to live! It was as spiritually uplifting as burrowing in a clump of nettles would be, and about as comfortable. She had made her headquarters at her brother's house long enough. He would be bitterly hurt when she left, but she would explain that living at the Teeles' would make her work easier. She wouldn't tell him that, also, it would be easier to see her friends. Duke wouldn't object to calling there for her.

She would be on her own at last. Freedom! Wings on her feet again! She ran up the steps of the Jarvis house, opened the door with her key, greeted the grizzled-headed butler in the hall with a friendly, "Hulloa, Amos!" His face crinkled into a welcoming smile in response. With the sense of being on top of the world she entered the living room.

Irene, at the tea-table in a green afternoon frock, seemed to have the sharp, bright surface of the mirrored room behind her. If she had been with the Count she wouldn't be dressed like that, would she? Faith's buoyancy burst like a rainbowed soap-bubble in a puff of cold wind as she noted her sister-in-law's lowered eyelids and sulky mouth. The "enchanting Madam Jarvees," the Count had called her. He should see her now. Ben was standing with one arm on the mantel. Madam Carr, in a smart black hat and frock, was drinking tea.

A bowl of pink snapdragons flanked the big Sheffield tray. The air was fragrant with the scent of flowers, the tang of burning wood, the aroma of Orange Pekoe—but heavy, depressingly heavy, with a woman's mood.

She tried desperately to think of something to say, something gay, casual, that would clear the atmosphere of the temperamental fog, but her mind drew a blank. I'm sunk, she thought, just plain sunk, and swallowed a nervous chuckle. Instantly she reminded herself that this was not the moment to register mirth even if going mentally dumb had its funny side.

"Why are you grinning like the Cheshire Cat, Faith?" Irene Jarvis demanded. "If you know anything amusing for heaven's sake give us a break and tell it. Nancy Carr and Ben have had me on the carpet because I night-clubbed with Wayne

Marshall. He isn't especially interesting, but if Ben will work evenings what am I to do? I'm bored stiff. I want to go to New York, I need a change; but neither of them will finance the trip."

"Was I grinning, Irene?" Faith ignored the complaint and replied to the question. "I shouldn't be. I should be registering grief. The Senator's bill was defeated. Did you know it, Ben?" Her brother nodded. "Then I made several détours. One to see the Spirit of St. Louis." She surreptitiously watched Irene's face. No change of expression or color. "It's a gorgeous day, perhaps that fact was tilting up the corners of my mouth. Miss Teele didn't need me this afternoon so here I am, home early. In time for tea."

"Getting off early seems to be a family characteristic. Ben sneaked in a few minutes ago. As he never has time for tea here I presume he is planning to meet Duke Tremaine for badminton. It's always Duke! Duke! *Duke!* I hate the name: Ben would rather be with him any time than with me. If he worked longer hours he could give me the money I asked for. He—"

"What's the matter with you, Irene?" Madam Carr interrupted her granddaughter's petulant complaint. "You sound hysterical. You've been behaving lately as if your nerves were raw. I'm ashamed of you."

"And why—Grandmother? Why should you be ashamed of me because I want money for a trip to New York? Ben won't let me accept an allowance from you, he insists that I must get along on what he can give me. All right then, why shouldn't I expect him to provide luxuries? He's a plodder. The Senator could give him tips to make money, big money; why doesn't he take advantage of them? Other people do it."

"Irene!" Ben Jarvis' voice was hoarse, his face livid.

For an instant the weird stillness that precedes the bursting of a shell brooded in the room. Then Madam Carr, with a whisper of taffeta, rose. Red spots burned in her cheeks. Her eyes were black diamonds.

"Irene! *Irene!* Do you never stop to consider where your abominable temper is taking you? I know you can be charming," she conceded, as her granddaughter's lips flew apart; "that's what makes the situation tragic. But, the charm spells are becoming less and less frequent. Only the most beautiful woman in the world can stand looking angry, and even she would be lovelier with a smile. Think it over."

She crossed to the door, turned at the threshold. Countless times the mirrored room gave back her tall black figure, the sheen of her pearls, the scorn of her mobile mouth.

"On second thoughts perhaps you can't think, or long before this you would have taught yourself to control jealousy if it killed you. Perhaps you are equipped with one of those mechanical brains that can do everything except think. I'm fed up with your tantrums. I'm fed up with the constant change of servants. I won't be here for dinner. I'm going upstairs now to tell my maid to pack my trunks. I'll be glad to get away from these mirrors which ring up my age with the inhuman accuracy of a cash register every time I pass them. I shall move to the Mayflower."

"You can't, Nancy Carr. This is your house. You've got to help—"

Irene's furious protest drifted out into a hall quite empty of human life. She whirled toward her husband.

"She can't leave us like this. She promised to finance this place. She's furious because I said that about Duke Tremaine. She adores him. She loved him much more than she loved me when we were children. So do you, Ben. I'd hate to be shipwrecked with you and Duke, if you had to choose which one of us you would rescue. *Duke!* Why am I wasting time on him? Will you, or will you not, give me five hundred dollars for a trip to New York?"

Ben Jarvis' face was chalky. His eyes burned.

"I've told you I can't just now, Irene. Money's tight."

"Money! Money! *Money!* Everybody talks about money! If you hold out on me, I'll get it some way. I'm going to New York. I've *got* to get away. I—I—must have a change."

VIII

"I MUST have a change!"

It seemed to Faith that she stood for years mute, stunned, with her sister-in-law's hysterical voice echoing through the charming room. For no reason at all she was suddenly convinced that Irene had been with the Count this afternoon. Was she running away from or with him? Ben looked as if he had reached the limit of endurance. She'd better escape before the marital storm burst.

"Ben, listen to me a minute, please," she begged breathlessly. "I'm moving to Senator Teele's. Kitty wants me there. It—it will be much more convenient for me. You won't mind, will you?"

Her brother looked at her as if her shaken voice had summoned him from a far country.

"You have the right idea, kid. You'll be a darned sight happier there than here."

He had approved her suggestion so promptly that she regarded him with a slight touch of resentment. While she had been piling up a mountain of dread as to the effect of her leaving, it was evident that life would be easier for him if she were not here.

"Then I'll pack at once. *Au revoir*, Irene. Thanks for all you've done for me." She struggled to keep her voice light and dashed to the hall.

In her room she locked the door. Sobs tore at her throat. She put her hand over her eyes as if by covering them she could shut out the memory of Ben's livid face as Irene had flung that hateful taunt about a "plodder" and "big money."

She filled two week-end cases, one with silver boxes, they were the darlings of her heart. She would return later to pack her trunks. She changed to a black velvet frock, adjusted her gold lamé and ruby velvet turban, pinned the gardenias to the fox collar of her gold-buttoned velvet jacket. The flowers had come through the last hour better than she had. She put money into a bag of the size and shape of a brief-case which matched her turban, and she was ready to leave her brother's house.

She phoned for a cab. Opened the door cautiously and peered into the hall. She couldn't, she wouldn't meet Ben or his wife. Had they made up the quarrel? Had Irene succeeded by blandishment in getting five hundred dollars? The house was still. Only the ponderous tick of the clock on the landing, the snap of the living room fire and the faint, far resonance of an automobile horn broke the silence.

She bumped down the back stairs with a suitcase in each hand. Ran into Violetta in the hall. The maid stifled a shriek which had been born lusty.

"You sure give me a start, yes Mam, you did. I done thought 'twas a bandit stealin' up behin' me. Guess I got nerves. The Madam come in a little while ago an' give me a ter'ble dressin' down cause I didn't get her housedress out quick. She sure was in a hurry. Seems as if she didn't want no one to know she'd been out." She rolled black eyes at the bags. "Mah goodness, you ain't goin' for good, is you?"

"I'm off for a visit."

"Glory, dat French maid of Madam Carr's she tole me she leavin' for a visit too. Look lak dat Ex-*o*-dus de Bible tell

about had struck dis house. Does de boss and de Madam
know youse goin'?"

"Of course. There's the taxi. Take these bags out for me."
At the curb she pulled a bill from her purse. "Here's some
movie-money. Good-by."

She stepped into the cab, closed the door quickly, softly
with the panicky sense that if she didn't use speed and caution the evil spirits of anger, jealousy and deceit which had
been rampant within the house would sneak out and follow
her.

Irene had been at the Smithsonian. Violetta's statement
as to her hurry to dress proved that. Did Ben know she
was meeting the Count? Was the man making love to her
or was he using her as a tool to advance schemes of his
own? Why not try to find out? She had returned from Rome
determined to be of use to her own country. Was this her
chance? If he were snooping for a foreign power she might
block him. He was a man of the world. She had met many
like him. Was she enough of a sophisticate to lure him from
Irene and save Ben more heartache? She'd have to frequent the movies and study the technique of the glamour
girls on the screen.

Less than two hours later she was in the midst of a
crush of envoys, reporters, socialites, senators, congressmen,
their constituents from the sticks and wide-eyed women who
were seeing Washington for the first time. The sound of music melted into the hum of voices, the scent of spring flowers mingled with exotic perfumes.

"You look like Chanel and a Paris fashion show, Faith."
Wayne Marshall's eyes smiled warmly into hers. "You're al-
ways keen for a Strauss waltz. 'Roses from the South.'
Dance?"

"Love it!"

She turned to Kitty Teele who was talking to Ben, eagerly, earnestly. His face was as expressionless as a white mask.
Where was Irene? Had she refused to come after the battle
of the afternoon? Were she and Carrilski together?

"Come on. Miss Teele won't even know you've gone—
now."

Something amused, a hint of malice in Wayne Marshall's voice sent her startled eyes to his as they moved in
rhythm to the music.

"What do you mean by that cryptic remark?" The center
of the maelstrom of dancers was hardly the place to make
such an inquiry but she couldn't let the innuendo about Ben
pass—Ben, than whom there was no straighter, more honorable man in the world.

"Mean? Are you blind?" His laugh was worldly-wise, indulgent. "I mean that those two are mad about each other. I wonder how Tremaine is taking it? He was picked by the Senator as an escort for his sister when he, the Great Man, was too busy to do the social act. He has been so attentive that everyone thought he was caught at last. You remember that your sister-in-law referred to his devotion to Miss Teele. But, he's been away. He said he went to South America, I wonder if he did?"

"Why should he say he was going if it weren't true?"

"Diplomacy, sweet child, diplomacy. You've got a lot to learn about the world in which you're living."

"Perhaps, but I don't intend to learn it here." His last bit of gossip pricked like a splinter in her heart. "Let's get out of this crush."

They found seats near a window in the brilliantly lighted foyer. With every current of air a massive palm waved its green fronds above them like a punka.

"We'll settle this once and for all, Wayne!" Faith announced indignantly. "You and I are working for the same people. It's pretty low-down of us even to think scandalously, much less talk about them."

"Loyal soul, aren't you? So am I, loyal. If I seem crabbed charge it up to the fact that I've got the jitters about my boss. I'm convinced that he's being double-crossed by someone he trusts. I intend to follow every possible clue until I run the man to earth."

Someone he trusts. The words echoed disturbingly in Faith's mind. She thought of the Count's question about Senator Teele's plans for greater planes and wondered if she'd better tell Wayne of her suspicions that there had been a motive behind his casual query. But, the Senator didn't trust Carrilski especially, did he?

"You'd better give Miss Teele a tip that she's playing with fire to have an affair with a married man." Marshall's low voice went on: "A man whose wife's social position would crack every front page in the country if there were a scandal. You might tell her, also, that enemies of her brother are watching her as a cat watches a mouse. One misstep of hers and the Senator will be smeared, a great paw will descend on him, squash his bills and his career flat. They'll do it smugly, on a safeguarding-the-country's-morals issue. Opportunists or politicians, they're waiting for a chance."

"Affair with a married man! You can't mean my brother? I don't believe it. Kitty Teele is as straight and fine as a woman can be. As for Ben—" her voice failed as his face as she had seen it a few moments before flashed on the screen of memory.

"I can see you've noticed it. He's cursed with a scolding wife. What man wouldn't escape if he could?"

"*Escape!* You talk about the smearing of the Senator by his enemies! Would you call it *escape* for Ben to involve the sister of his valued client in a scandal? That would be smearing and then some. What has Irene done to you that you criticize her? She has introduced you and your foreign pal, Count Carrilski, to her friends; pretty nice of her, if you ask me. I think you're disgustingly ungrateful and if there is any one trait I despise, it's ingratitude."

"Don't get me wrong. I admire Mrs. Jarvis enormously. Through her I've met people whom it will be useful for me to know that I may be of more help to the Senator. Understand that whatever I do, I do to help him."

A hint of panic in his voice. Apparently Irene's good will was of immense importance to him. Faith appraised him speculatively. He was extremely good-looking, he had charming manners, he had a positive flair for saying the right thing at the right moment, he was supposed to have an income, quite independent of his salary. A playboy, perhaps, but a gay companion. With all those assets, why did he need Irene to put him in touch with people who would be of use to Senator Teele, a man who, in influence, in power, in political backing, towered head and shoulders above her social set?

"If you're so anxious to help the Senator you'd better stop spreading scandal about his sister," she suggested gravely. "I like you Wayne, but—"

"I love you. I'm on my way up. This secretary job with the Senator is a mere way-station on my road to diplomacy. Marry me and you'll go places, darling," he declared with impassioned assurance.

"You sound like a United States Navy poster, 'Join the Marines and see the World,' or an ad, 'Buy a trailer and tour the country.' I don't want to go places. I've been going places for the last eight years. I intend to have a home with a garden in summer and window plants, lots of them, in winter, and shelves for books that I can *own* and read and reread. Up to a few months ago, when I bought a book and loved it I'd have to present it to a library when we moved on. It isn't the garden and plants and bookshelves in themselves, it's what they stand for: safety, stability." She laughed. "What started me on that tirade, I wonder?"

"Merely my remark that you would marry me. We'll take the matter up again at length. Here comes Miss Teele with two satellites, the Count and your brother. She's a pretty

clever woman for a shy, country girl from the cow-country.
She—"

"Don't say it, Wayne! Apparently Washington doesn't
agree with you; it is sharpening your tongue, and believe
me, a sharp tongue will cut off your diplomatic career in the
very flower of its youth. I don't wonder Miss Teele makes
friends. She is so lovable."

Kitty Teele and the two men were laughing. She wore a
hat consisting largely of a white rose and yards of blue
veil. The sapphire velvet of her simple frock brought out
the gold in her hair. Her eyes were as brilliant as sea-
water in the sun as she looked at the Count who was bending toward her with an air of devotion.

"Wayne," Faith asked impulsively, "have you ever thought
that Carrilski might bear watching?"

"Ssh! Whatever you think, or suspect, forget it. If you
want to help me, *forget it.*"

She was right in her suspicion of the Count, or Wayne
wouldn't have whispered that warning. The man appeared
absolutely carefree as he laughed with Kitty Teele. Her
heart gave a frightened leap as she noted her brother's eyes
as they rested on the woman beside him. It was the look
of a man deeply in love. His guard was up so quickly that
she wondered if her imagination had played tricks. She
thought of Irene's expression as she had seen it last. How
could he help comparing the two women? One so sweet and
tender and the other so—so—

"Here you are, Faith," Duke Tremaine's voice cut into her
disturbed reflections. "Turned me down for a handsomer
man, I see. How are you, Marshall?" His greeting was cor-
dial. Wayne Marshall's eyes narrowed speculatively. As she
noted their expression for a breathtaking instant Faith had
the crazy thought that Duke was the man Wayne suspected
of being false to the Senator.

"I tried to make it clear over the telephone, Duke, that I
was under orders," she explained, "but that bossy secretary of yours was so short and businesslike that I felt as if
she were checking off my words as a taxicab clicks off miles."

"Gowan hasn't much social what-have-you, I'll admit, but
she's a swell buffer. She told me you were coming to this tea
so here I am to warn you that you can't play fast and loose
with me, lady."

"I'm a witness to the fact that she was in a dither because she had to," Kitty Teele championed. "She and I
were ordered to appear here under pain of death and here's
the Senator to swear to it," she added, as her brother detached himself from an arguing, gesticulating morning-coated

group of men with red carnations in their lapels. "You did order Miss Jarvis and me to attend this function, didn't you, Joe?"

"Order you to come here, Kitty? You know I never interfere in your social plans, you are perfectly free to go or come as you like. Where did you get that foolish impression?"

Miss Teele looked inquiringly at Faith, who challenged:

"Wayne, that question is up to you." If his eyes could scorch she would shrivel to a crisp. Why?

"I assumed, Senator, that you wanted Miss Teele and Miss Jarvis to attend this reception, that it was important for you. The host can be—"

"Important!" The word was like the growl of a lion whose sore paw had been trampled. "You assume too much, Marshall, when you assume that I need to cling to the skirts of my womenfolk for influence." His smile was warm and friendly as he turned to Faith. "You see, I already count you as a valued member of my family, Miss Jarvis."

"Thank you, Senator for—for—for liking me."

"I believe I've embarrassed you." His eyes twinkled. "Duke, explain to the lady that it is just my politician's line, make it statesman's if your conscience will permit. By the way, just back from South America, aren't you? Did you finish up that business of mine?"

Faith detected a note of restrained eagerness in the question. Duke Tremaine shook his head and laughed.

"Not this time, Mr. Senator. 'Hurry' is your middle name but that South American bunch doesn't know the first letter of the word. However, I pushed it forward. Everything's under control."

"*Hmp!* Kitty, my apologies for talking business here, but it's almost as hard to get hold of Tremaine as to arrange for a conference at the White House. Count, you look distressed at my breach of etiquette. I saw you in the Senate gallery today. Getting an earful of my eloquence on the need of air research to send to the boys back home?"

"Joe!" Kitty Teele protested softly.

"I am learning much, Senator Teele." Carrilski's expression was inscrutable. He bowed stiffly and walked away.

"Guess I trod on the Count's toes. I must cut out the old rough-diamond manner and watch my step with these foreign lads, they don't understand humor—American style. Kitty, we'll pay our respects to the new wife of the new senator who is fighting one of my bills tooth and nail. Come along, Wayne, I want you to send a cable. Ben, as my lawyer, I need you to prevent me from slipping my head into a legal noose."

Faith watched the four as they walked away, Marshall conspicuously lagging. Her eyes came back to Tremaine.

"What made you so suddenly friendly to Wayne, Duke? When you and he are together I feel as comfortable as I would if two huge bulldogs were preparing to clinch. Why the change?"

"Oh, Ben warned me I was getting crabbed, that I didn't try to like people. So, I'm trying to like the Senator's cousin."

"Trying to appear to. You can't fool me, old-timer. I wish you really liked him. He is devoted to the Senator's interests. Just before you appeared he was telling me that he suspected that his boss was being double-crossed by someone . . ." She stopped as Marshall's expression as he had looked at Duke flashed in her memory.

"Go on. Never start a sentence you're afraid to finish."

His voice and implacable eyes set her heart beating like a metronome gone mad.

"I'm not afraid. He said 'someone the Senator trusted.' "

His laugh was obscurely disturbing.

"That wouldn't be the shattering discovery your bated breath implies. Men in high office have been betrayed by supposed trusties before. There are forces at work against Joe Teele, so insidious, so underground that Ben and I can't lay a finger on them. If they'd only attack in the open! They're too shrewd. They know if they did, thousands of voters who never had heard of him would become Joe Teele conscious. That's politics."

Faith remembered Wayne's insinuation about Ben and Kitty Teele. Could those rumors be at work to undermine the Senator? Ben and Kitty! Irene and the Count . . . What a mess! What a tragic mess!

"What's drained the color from your face, Faith? The Senator's troubles? You mustn't take them to heart. This is Washington, girl, Washington. The news that makes Page One today will be plowed under by the sensation of tomorrow. Is it true that you've moved to the Teeles'?"

"Bag, baggage and forty silver boxes."

"How did Ben take your running out on him?"

"He gave me the shock of my life. I thought he would be bitterly hurt, but he seemed glad to have me—g-go."

"Hey, don't blink those long wet lashes. I can't bear it." He cleared his husky voice. "Couldn't stand Irene, could you? The fact that Marshall is on location at the house a large part of the time didn't also figure in your move, did it?"

"Don't be absurd. Why should it? We're both busy at our

jobs. He is there only in the morning, when he works in the Senator's study."

"At the house in the morning. Oho! I see light, a blaze of light. When did he deliver the Senator's order that you and his sister were to come here?"

"Just after you phoned and asked me to dine with you."

"I wonder if the telephone in Kitty Teele's boudoir is on the same hook-up as the one in the hall? . . . That was what is called a rhetorical question. You needn't answer. Any reason why you and I can't dine at the chicken-and-waffle place now?"

"It's a date."

"Then we'll do a quick fadeout. Get your coat. I'll tell Kitty where we're going, otherwise she might set the F.B.I. on your trail. Make it snappy. I'm starving."

IX

FAITH's dark eyes were brilliant with appreciation as she entered the great room paneled with pine, at the Inn.

The brick wall in which the fireplace was set rose from hearth to ceiling, broken only by a huge time-darkened oak beam which served as a shelf for burnished copper platters and mugs. Their shining surfaces reflected the wavering flames of white candles in tall, slim sticks. Two iron kettles swung over a heap of gray ashes crowned by glowing red coals. A mammoth ham hung against the bricks on one side of the opening; ears of corn, brown, yellow, white, skillets and ancient frying pans on the other. Strings of dried apples and onions were festooned from the sturdy smoke-stained rafters. Three Negro fiddlers seated on a platform were talking in low voices. Uncovered tables were set for service.

The tall man at the door, black as obsidian, with grizzled hair and squared shoulders, bowed with the dignity of a king in exile. His teeth were white as the whites of his eyes.

"Got your message all fine an' dandy, Mistuh Duke. Smell de chicken fryin'? Just you slip off dat top-coat.

I'll tak' it. It sure is gran' to see you? Been away, hasn't yo'?"

"Yes. I'm glad to be back, Zeke. How's business?"

"Fine! Fine! Mo' parties comin' later. Sophy!"

In answer to the call a portly woman, with skin as ebon as the man's, in a white turban and an enormous white apron that almost covered her ample polka-dotted red dress, banged open a swing door. She bustled forward smiling and chuckling, her big gold earrings swaying.

"Ah sure is glad to see yo', Mistuh Duke. Seems lak years since you done come to see us. Let me tak' dat coat, honey-girl." She pulled out cane-seated ladder-back chairs at a pine table set for two in a bay formed by the curve of lattice windows.

"Here yo' is, Mistuh Duke, yo' fav'rite place whar yo' kin see de fire. Zeke saved it fo' you. Dis house is yo's w'en yo' come."

"Thanks, Sophy. I brought Miss Jarvis to have some of your chicken. The poor girl has been living in Europe where the cooking isn't like yours."

"Mistuh Duke he's a great joker, ain't he, honey? Co'se I know's I'se a good cook. You's not Mistuh Ben's sister, is you? *Hmm?*"

Faith admitted that she was.

"I sho' is glad to know yo'. Next to our Mistuh Duke I think he's de finest man in Wasin'ton, an' I know heaps of de big pol'ticians who come here, I sure do. Mistuh Ben, he wuz out fer chicken an' waffles las' week. He brought a lady, light complected as hisself, she sure was a sweet pusson, I never seed her befo', had I? *Hmm?*"

The eyes she fastened on Duke Tremaine were two interrogation points. Who was the woman? Faith wondered with a panicky sense of apprehension. It couldn't have been Irene, she was neither as light "complected" as Ben nor could she by any stretch of the imagination be called "sweet."

"How should I know whom you've seen, Sophy? About that dinner? I'm so hungry I could eat raw dog and I see the glassy stare which precedes starvation in Miss Jarvis' eyes."

The black woman's deep-throated chuckle was like the rumble of distant thunder.

"Ain't no glassy stare in dat honey-girl's eyes. Dey's soft as de black down on a ducklin's breast, dey is. Don' yo' worry, dat chicken an' waffles dey'll be along quick. Don' yo' mind if I talk much, honey. Mistuh Duke wuz mah child w'en he wuz little an' I haven't seen him fer a month. Yo' wouldn't think to look at him now, wif dos se'rous deep lines between his nose an' mouf, dat he wuz a case, dat boy."

Faith laughed in sympathy with the mirth that shook Sophy's broad shoulders.

"Yes, Mam, he sure wuz a case. 'Member, Mistuh Duke, when yo' ma used to mak' yo' go over to de Carr place an' 'pologize lak a little gent'man 'cose you slapped dat Irene-chile's face, after she come runnin' ober to our house an' say you daid? *Hmm?* I knowed you didn't do it, but Missy Tremaine she made you go an' say yo' wuz sorry, jus' de same. She never would have no quarrel wid her neighbor, no suh."

"Sophy, suppose you sign-off on the story of my dark and devious past and produce that chicken."

"Yo' sure don't lak to have me talk 'bout you, Mistuh Duke; I won't no mo' 'cept to tell yo', honey-girl, dat my child, dere, was de han'somest boy in de county, noble-lookin' from de day he wuz bo'n."

"Sophy! Will you go back to the kitchen or must I carry you?"

"I'se goin', Mistuh Duke. I'se a-goin'. Ob co'se yo' want Virginia ham an' corn puddin' wid de chicken? Yo' lak de same, honey-girl? Hmm?"

Faith said Thanks, she would, and the woman went away.

"She's the first Southern mammy I've ever met. So you were 'de han'somest boy in de county.' Amazing how life can change a face, isn't it, Duke?"

"No accounting for tastes, but there are persons who think it's not too bad now," Tremaine boasted grandiloquently. "As you may have gathered Sophy is a privileged person. She was my mother's maid for years and when she married Madam Carr's butler, Zeke, we set them up here. They do a good business considering they have no liquor license. This Inn is a Tremaine heirloom. We can't let it degenerate into a hot night spot like the one up the road."

"It's adorable. How beautifully those Negroes play!" She hummed "Way down upon the Swanee River" in a sweet husky voice, to the accompaniment of violins. "The music switches-on my imaginaton. That must be the very fireplace beside which a girl named Cinderella dreamed jeweled dreams and watched the fairy godmother step from the chimney to grant her wish."

"Suppose the fairy came now? What would you wish, Faith?"

She thought of her brother, of the look in his eyes when they rested on Kitty Teele, of the "sweet lady" whom he had brought to this Inn.

"That Ben and I may take life on the chin and not fold-up under temptation. If she would grant two, I'd wish to be one of those gold threads in the country's pattern you spoke of the other day."

"You don't need a fairy godmother to have both of those wishes granted. Knowing Ben and you as I do, I'd say that the first is already in the bag. As for the second, you're more than a thread, you're a whole strand of gold, now. Having that point nicely settled we will turn our attention to more mundane things. Did you get that whiff of fried chicken and broiling ham when the door opened? Believe it or not, here it comes."

A mulatto maid, in a linen dress as pink as the petals of a Perfection rose, wheeled up a serving table laden with a platter of fried chucken in delectable gravy garnished with waffles and plump sweet potatoes; another, with crisp slices of ham and corn pudding, was flanked by a deep dish of sliced apples baked in butter and brown sugar.

"How's the world treating you, Magnolia?" Tremaine asked as he selected the choicest pieces of chicken for Faith.

"Fine, Mr. Duke."

"Pass that plate to Miss Jarvis. Business been good?"

"Sure. That friend of yours, Mr. Marshall, has come here a lot. He brought other men. One was a fine foreign-lookin' fella, said he was a Count. I bet them two's just rolling in money. Zeke had to make change for a hundred dollar bill. *A hundred dollars*, when they paid their check. They think a lot of you, Mister Duke, awful interested in what you do. Asked if you flew to South America often and questions like that."

"Which I hope you had the good sense not to answer?"

"Don't you worry about me answering questions. If Zeke sees customers trying to make conversation, he pretends he thinks they're complaining of the food or service and is beside me before I have a chance to open my mouth. He's too snooty, Zeke is. Afraid someone will start gossip about a politician and it will be traced back to the Inn and ruin business. Just as if money wasn't money where-ever it comes from. Believe it or not, the high rollers have it an' it makes a place exciting."

"Life will be plenty exciting for you if Zeke hears you voicing those sentiments, Magnolia. Run along. I'll ring when we're ready for nuts and coffee."

"So, Marshall is a friend of mine," he reflected aloud as the maid left the room. "I wonder why he's interested in my South American trip?"

"He asked me if you'd really been there."

"He did? Looks as if I'd have to bore some of my friends with the colored movies I snapped in points south. I wonder what attracts men like Marshall and the Count to this quiet Inn?"

"How could a person help repeating, if he'd once been here? It's fascinating, Duke."

As they ate at the candle-lighted table, Tremaine, encouraged by Faith's eager questions, described headline personalities in Washington, those who had convictions and fought for them, those who stood for principles, not parties, those who were merely rubber-stamp legislators; talked about bills before Congress, foreign affairs, the anti-aircraft defenses and the air arms of both the Army and the Navy, referred to a recent violation of the Espionage Act.

"Just what does that mean, Duke?"

"It may mean photographing our fortifications; securing plans of our air bases showing the location of anti-aircraft batteries; the number of pursuit, bombardment, attack and observation planes, recent improvements of same, the size of the Personnel. Research plants particularly. Airplane quality is more important than quantity to the United States at present. In fact, any information which would help an enemy country in time of war."

"Much of it going on here?"

"More than citizens outside this city realize. Our counter-espionage budget was three hundred thousand dollars annually as against Great Britain's three millions. You may conclude from those figures that spying is quite an industry. Why think of that? This is a party. In that square collar of coarse white lace you look like a girl in a Flemish painting, Faith."

She abandoned the impulse to tell him of Count Carrilski's question about Senator Teele's plans for greater planes for the Army. After all, she might have imagined significance where there had been nothing more than the give-and-take of conversation.

"It is, and what a party!" she responded gaily. "I could die eating this cream gravy." The candle flames set little motes of gold dancing in her laughing eyes. "This is my dream inn, Duke. Rosy light from the fire filling the dusky corners. Swaying shadows. Stars twinkling beyond the lattice windows. The moon dangling in the sky as pale and cool as a slice of honeydew melon. Fiddlers playing and Magnolia singing. Listen."

> "Sleep, Kentucky babe . . .
> Close yo' eyes in sleep,"

the mulatto girl crooned.

"I don't wonder the place is popular. It is full now."

"We'll have the table cleared and then we'll talk."

"Talk! What have we been doing?"

"I mean about ourselves, you and me."

A boy, with shining black eyes and teeth, white as his spotless smock, rolled away the laden service table and returned with a copper bowl heaped with pecans and walnuts, and a tray with coffee pot and cups.

"That all y'all want, Mistuh Duke?"

"That's all, Clem."

The boy threw a log on the fire and departed. Scarlet and yellow flames danced and writhed up the great chimney, set grotesque shadows flickering on the pine walls, splinters of light glinting on every shining surface.

Faith had the curious feeling that Duke and she were in a world apart, a little world whose silence was broken only by the crack of nutshells and an occasional sharp snap from the fire. The singing of violins, the murmur of voices, seemed remote and unreal. He pushed a saucer of nut-meats across the table.

"There you are. That, with coffee, is the perfect ending to a perfect dinner. Smoke?" he offered his silver cigarette case. She shook her head.

"No? Do you realize how little I know about you, the grown-up Faith, I mean? This is only the third time I have talked with you since you returned to the land of the free and the home of the brave."

"And each time your eyes have bored into me as if you were determined to find out what made me tick." She loved his low, rich laugh.

"I'm only wondering how much of the little girl I knew is within your lovely self. You're such a cool, sophisticated young person sometimes that I'm afraid of you. What's on your mind? Something has been troubling you ever since we left the reception. You were hurt or sorry. You said I helped. Try me now," he urged tenderly.

"It's Ben."

"Ben! You mean that he is unhappy because of Irene? Don't worry. It's got him down at present, but it won't keep him down."

"Does that mean you think he'll *divorce* her?"

"Don't you believe in divorce?"

"Of course, under some circumstances, but can two persons who have been married really be divorced? In Europe I met so many ex-marrieds, oftentimes guests at the same dinner. As I saw them laughing and wisecracking with each other, I used to wonder if, under their gaiety, remembrance of the hours they had lived together as man and wife wasn't drawing them with almost irresistible force, if memory wasn't a bond no court of law can break?"

"I have a lot to learn about you, haven't I? You are grown-up, aren't you?"

"Don't laugh at me, Duke."

"I'm *not* laughing at you. I'm adoring you."

His tender voice, his eyes with the disturbing light in them, set her pulses quick-stepping.

"I'm sufficiently grown-up to have felt frightened when I saw Ben with Kitty Teele this afternoon. There's no mistaking the look in a man's eyes when he loves a woman. I can tell."

"Can you? Forewarned is forearmed. I'll be mighty careful to guard my eyes when you're around, Miss Jarvis."

He was laughing but his color had mounted. She shouldn't have said that Ben was in love with Kitty Teele. It might hurt Duke horribly. Hadn't Irene and Wayne intimated that he was devoted to the Senator's sister? She drew a breath of relief. Fortunately she hadn't said that Kitty was in love with Ben.

"We've been looking all over the place for you," an impatient voice announced.

Irene Jarvis and Wayne Marshall were standing beside the table. Duke Tremaine rose. He glanced at the man in white tie and waistcoat, red carnation in his lapel as revealed by his thrown-back Inverness, at Irene's gold-braided white serge wrap and the misty billows of coppery tulle below it. Out for the evening, obviously. Why had they stopped at the Inn *en route?*

"Don't tell us that you are carrying out the Senator's orders *again*, Marshall," he observed urbanely, "that *he* sent you for Miss Jarvis."

X

WHAT'S his game? Duke Tremaine asked himself. How did they know we were here? . . . The answer to the second question was easy. Marshall had been present when he told Kitty Teele that he was taking Faith to the Inn. Granted that the man was in love with her,—his every look attested that,—that he was jealous of any man who took her out, was that a reason for him to follow her like a sleuth in a Class B movie?

And just where did Irene Jarvis fit into the scenario? It wasn't surprising that a newcomer to Washington like Marshall would be dazzled by her beauty, by her social importance, be flattered by her invitations; but the catch was that he should feel it necessary to show her quite so much attention, when the political and diplomatic world swarmed with charming younger women and girls of equal social importance and influence. Had Nancy Carr been right when she had suggested the possibility of a subversive plan behind his attention to her granddaughter?

"Just why have you been looking for me, Wayne?"

Before Marshall could reply to Faith's crisp question, Irene laid her fingers on his coat-sleeve. Her long enameled nails shone like jewels against the black cloth.

"Let me answer," she begged sweetly. "I must tell you how sorry I am about this afternoon, Faith. I admit I have a beastly temper. My blow-up because Ben wouldn't finance a trip to New York was what sent you bag and baggage to the Teeles', wasn't it? I told Wayne I couldn't face my husband again, that I wouldn't sleep a wink tonight until I had asked you to come back. He was an understanding dear, and offered to help me find you."

"Sweet of him to personally conduct your conscience-purge, Irene. Thanks for asking me, but I can't change my residence again. I don't want to. Life at the Senator's is thrilling. Also, it's heavenly peaceful."

"Don't be so hard. I've said I'm sorry. If you won't return to stay, won't you please go back to the house *now* and explain to Ben why you prefer to live at the Teeles'? He's on the verge of a nervous breakdown. When I entered his den before I left the house, his face was chalk-white as he fussed round his desk. He jumped as if he'd been shot when I spoke to him. Then he began to pace the floor and accuse *me,* his wife, of having driven you out."

"She can't go," Tremaine intervened lightly. "She is out for the evening with me, and I never permit a party to be broken off in the middle."

"Really, Duke, you amaze me. I would have thought you would agree to anything that would ease your adored Ben's mind."

"Better keep your voice down, Irene," Faith suggested. "You're attracting attention. The guests behind you are looking at us. Shall we go to Ben, Duke?"

"We shall not. Here's Sophy. Irene, you remember her, I'm sure. Sophy, you haven't forgotten Missy Irene, have you?"

The black woman's smile exposed white teeth back to the gaps left by extracted molars.

"Glory, co'se I hasn't forgotten Missy Irene, Mistuh Duke." Her broad shoulders heaved with laughter. "Don't I 'member de time she catched de mumps an' give 'em to ebery oder young 'un in de neighborhood? She knew she had 'em, wanted all her playmates to enjoy 'em too. She allus wuz an angel child. Den she went to Europe. What yo' doin' all dat time in dat strange place? *Hmm?*"

Irene Jarvis' face flushed and as suddenly paled.

"None of your business. You always were a meddling old nigger, Sophy. Wayne, we'll go. Apparently Faith thinks more of remaining in the present company than of easing her brother's mind. I'm leaving for New York tomorrow. At least she might stay with him while I'm away."

"I'll see you in the morning at the Senator's, Faith," Wayne Marshall reminded. "Remember what I told you this afternoon? I've struck the trail! I'll need your help." His eyes were brilliant, his voice was exultant. His fingers clenched and unclenched in nervous excitement. "Come, Mrs. Jarvis. Good night."

Tremaine watched them as they crossed the room with Sophy like a ponderous rear-guard stalking them. Irene passed the respectfully bowing Zeke at the door with her chin in the air. What had Marshall on his mind? Why had he been inquiring about the South American trip? He was as charged with excitement as a live wire with electricity. Why should he take the domestic differences of the Jarvis family to heart? Irene was going to New York while the Washington social season was in full swing. Why? What was the answer?

"So that is that!"

He turned at Faith's exclamation and sat down. She rested an elbow on the table and her chin in hand. "Where do we go from here, Duke?"

"Not to Ben's house to relieve his mind, or rather Irene's. Where would you like to go? Dance? A movie? It's too late for the theater."

"Let's stay here and talk. The musicians have gone. Is it closing time?"

"No. They play for dancing at the roadhouse beyond here. Who turned on that confounded radio?"

"I rather like the soft music. Do you believe that Ben is on the verge of a nervous breakdown because I left his house, Duke?"

"*No.* You told me that he seemed glad to have you go didn't you?"

"I did. Irene has driven first you, his friend, and now me, his sister, from his home. That should satisfy her. Knowing her for what she is, how could you let Ben marry her, Duke?"

"*Let* him! Ever tried to argue with a man in love? You might as well attempt to persuade a brook to turn round and run uphill. That doesn't mean that I didn't try. Trouble is, that when Irene is good, she is like the little girl with the curl; she's very, very good. She can turn on charm, buckets of charm, till a man would honestly believe he was in love with an angel!"

"Did you ever feel that way?"

"Never. She was always poison at the box office to me. She knows it, knows that I tried to turn Ben against her. An incident is never closed, is it? It sends out tiny feelers of consequences which may spread and spread and develop into serious conditions. Your mother's marriage was that kind of incident, if one can call marriage an incident. Had Ben not crossed the ocean for that, he wouldn't have returned on the same ship with Irene. Had he met her under different circumstances he might not have fallen in love with her."

"*Ooch!* What a shivery suggestion, that an incident is never closed! It sends icy inchworms looping up my spinal column."

She couldn't tell him that a stab of apprehension as to the consequences from the incident of her meeting with the

Count this afternoon was what had started the loopers looping.

"While we are on the subject of incidents, what did Marshall mean when he said he'd struck the trail?"

She reminded him that she had told him of Wayne's suspicion that the Senator was being double-crossed.

"I got all that, but why does he want your help? Why drag you into the mess? Keep out of it. Promise me that you—"

"News flash!" The radio announcer's voice set the air vibrating. *"While the family was away late this afternoon the home study of Senator Teele was entered and the safe rifled."*

"Away! Wasn't anyone in the house while you were at the reception, Faith?"

"Only the servants. Kitty's maid was to take Thalia to a supper at dancing school."

"Let's get going. I may be able to help."

As he drove the roadster toward the city his thoughts reverted to Marshall. What had he meant by "he had struck the trail"? What trail?

"Why so grim, Duke?"

"Look here, stop watching me."

"Oh, but 'yo' have such a fasc'natin' face, wif dos se'rous deep lines between yo' nose an' mouf. Yo' sure am a case, Mistah Duke."

He resisted a passionate impulse to close her laughing lips with his. Nothing doing. She would think he'd lost his mind. To him she was the girl he loved. To her he had been but a memory for years.

"You're wasting your talents as a social secretary, you should be doing imitations," he declared, and sent the car ahead in a burst of speed along a highway turned to ribbons of black mirror by the lights from passing automobiles.

His thoughts switched back to Senator Teele. Had he kept a record in his home study of the invention which had been discussed that day in the desert, an invention on which a man was working under tremendous time pressure and secrecy in a remote workshop? He wouldn't do it. He was too keen about keeping it secret. Perhaps it had been the design and specifications of the new and deadly bomber he was recommending which had been taken. That loss would be serious too. The Senate commission on aeronautics hadn't seen them. Joe Teele had a leak psychosis. His fear that a foreign agent would hear of these aviation research finds of his was an obsession. Only Ben and he, and apparently Nancy Carr, had been let into the secret of the bomber.

Had Marshall found out in some underground way? It couldn't have been he who had robbed the safe. He had been at the Mayflower, after which he must have dressed to take Irene to dinner.

Carrilski had bowed himself away early from the reception. Marshall had practically ordered Kitty and Faith in the Senator's name to attend it, and Joe Teele had indignantly disclaimed the command. Was there a chance that the "confidential secretary" had cleared the house to make the way easy for the Count?

"How the fields glisten! Hoar frost, isn't it?" Faith commented softly. "This country we're racing through is so calm, so cool. It's hard to believe that part of the world has gone cockeyed with power. I know you're in a hurry to reach the Senator's, Duke, but wouldn't we be more useful if we were to arrive whole?"

"I'm sorry." He drove more slowly. "I'm trying to figure out why anyone would break and enter Joe Teele's study."

"Would he be likely to keep valuable papers there that his opponents might want?"

"You never can tell what boners these crazy big-shots will pull, but it's a wonder that a man busy as the Senator doesn't pull more. He's on the jump every minute of the day and most of the night. Bills. Hearings. Interviews. Long distance conferences with his state. Besides which he likes a game of cards and is the perfect answer to a hostess' prayer as a dinner guest. The lamps on the Memorial Highway look like enormous moonstones. That rosy sky means the city."

"Isn't the floodlighted dome of the Capitol beautiful? Why are the two flags flying there now? I thought they were furled at sunset."

"They are, everywhere else, but during the World War it was decided that there should be one building over which the Stars and Stripes never ceased to wave. The Capitol was selected as being typical of the United States. Great idea, isn't it?"

"It is. It tightens my throat. One never can realize what that flag means till one sees it floating far away from—"

Her voice was drowned by the roar of a truck as it passed on its way to the city market. The scent of fruit trailed back from it. A bus ambled by. Taxis scooted around corners. In the glare from passing headlights, Tremaine glanced at her serious face.

"Relax, Faith. Don't try to settle Ben's problem; that's what you're thinking of now, isn't it? Smile. You have a lovely smile. Smiles and laughter are what the world needs terribly at present."

"You're right, Duke, about the uselessness of trying to settle another person's problems. I wouldn't want anyone to attempt to arrange my life. After all, the more one's mistakes hurt, the less apt one is to repeat them. Here we are.

"Every window lighted. Looks more like a party than a robbery," she whispered as she and Tremaine raced up the steps.

"Oh, there you is, Miss Jarvis." The butler's usually black face was a dirty yellow as he opened the door. "Turrible things has happened. Turrible, Mistuh Tremaine, suh."

"Anyone hurt, Sam?"

"No, suh, nobody hurt, suh, 'cept Mr. Senator's study. Dat looks lak a hurricane done go through it."

"Anything missing?"

"I don' know suh. I didn't get no partic'lars."

"Is the Senator here?"

"Yes, suh! He come home shortly after de buglars busted in. Don't know 'zactly w'en dat wus. Missy Thalia, she come in from dancin' school an' went to de pantry. Den Mistuh Ben Jarvis, he came in to dis hall wid Miss Kitty. After a few minutes I hear de front do' close. I wus busy in de dinin' room w'en de bell ring, an' w'en I answered dere wuz Mistuh Ben agin. He said as how he'd forgotten something the Senator told him to get in his study. I needn't wait, he say. Soon I hear de do' open an' shut agin but I was busy, didn't notice special, thought it wuz Mistuh Ben goin' out."

"You don't know that it was Mr. Ben?"

"No. I jus' reasoned 'twas him, Mistuh Duke. Was you thinkin' dat might have been de buglar?"

"No, no, Sam. Burglars don't come in front doors—usually. What happened next?"

"Next thing I knows the Senator was in dis hall yellin', 'Sam! Sam! I'se been robbed. My room's all busted-up!'"

The butler drew his hand across the drops of sweat on his forehead.

"De boss may think I did it. I swear to God, I didn't, Mistuh Tremaine."

"Of course you didn't, Sam. Where is Mr. Jarvis?"

"I don' know. Last I see of him he was goin' toward dat room. De perlice say dey want to know where he is, too."

"Duke. They don't think—Ben—"

"No. No! Faith. They only want to question him."

"Tell the police I'm here, Sam," Ben Jarvis announced.

"I heard the news of the break over the radio. Seen the

study, Duke?" His brown eyes burned with excitement.
"No. Faith and I just came in. Sam said—"

"That I was the last person seen going toward that room.
I heard him. Come on in. Let's find the Senator. He's there,
isn't he, Sam?"

"He sure is, Mistuh Jarvis. Miss Kitty, she there too. De
Senator, he shooed-off de perlice. Said dey'd better get
busy following dem buglars, instead of stan'in' roun' lookin'
at his room."

<h1 style="text-align:center">XI</h1>

"BUSTED-UP" is the word, Faith thought as she entered the
study paneled in pine, with heavy crimson velvet hangings
drawn across the two windows. Every light in the room was
turned on. Drawers of a filing cabinet had been pulled out,
the door of a wall safe swung open. On the glass top of a
huge flat desk papers had been scattered. From a tray in
the midst of them the diamonds in an old-fashioned sunburst
winked a thousand iridescent eyes, rainbows of color shot
from the gems in a scatter of rings. Senator Teele and his
sister in a turquoise-blue dinner gown were bending over
them.

"Thank the Lord, you boys have come." He straightened with a groan. "I've been checking up on these gew-gaws
till my back's broken."

"Anything missing?" Duke Tremaine asked tensely.

"My memoranda of the specifications of the demon bomb-
er. Both you boys warned me not to keep them here, but
I thought they were safer in this room than anywhere in
Washington."

"This wasn't forced, Senator. Someone knew the combination!" exclaimed Tremaine at the safe. "Who, besides—"

"You, Duke; Ben; myself and—Kitty."

"That rather puts it up to Ben and me, Senator."

"Forget it, Duke. I would no more suspect either of you
of stealing them than I would suspect myself. What would
be the object? You can see them whenever you want to.
Someone, in some miraculous way, discovered the combination. I'm infernally sorry, now, I let anyone know the safe
had been opened."

"Did you tell the police?"

"Like an idiot I did, Ben. I was so surprised when I came into this room, I guess I lost my head. I didn't suspect that anyone knew I had those specifications. Whoever has the memoranda now must know that he has the working formula from which a technician who knew his job could construct an attack and defense bomber that's bound to revolutionize air warfare. They'll be hustled out of the country quick."

"Do you think an agent of a foreign country stole them?" Faith's question was little more than a strained whisper. Had Wayne meant this when he had said that he was on the trail of the person who was double-crossing his boss? He had vibrated with excitement. Of course not. How could he have known about it?

"Who else would want them?" Senator Teele's voice answering her question broke into her troubled surmising. "The plane is something absolutely new, an engine of terrible destruction. Through me, our Government was to have been given the first chance to accept it. I hadn't submitted it. I had it up my sleeve to spring when my bill for additional air research appropriations went through. I hope and pray we'll never have to use it, but the fact that we have it will help stave-off war."

"When did you discover this mess, Senator?"

"When I returned from the Mayflower reception, Duke. Ben brought Kitty home and I hung around to talk over my bill with the gentleman from Illinois. Instead of going directly upstairs to change for dinner as is my habit, I came here and found this. Ben, did you come into the house when you and Kitty returned?"

"I did, Senator. I not only came in with her but after I said good night, I came back. I remembered that at the reception you asked me to pick up the rough draft of the counterespionage bill you had left on this desk, check it, and deliver it to you tomorrow."

"Did you get what I sent you for?"

"Yes, sir. Just where you had left it."

"That's a break. I wouldn't want that floating round the country—either. The robbery must have happened between the time you left and when I came in. Quick work. Sugar, where have you been?"

He smiled indulgently at his daughter, who entered nibbling a huge wedge of rich fruitcake. Dressed in a full-skirted pale blue frock, with a matching ribbon binding her short chestnut curls, she was almost pretty. Her eyes, which looked enormous behind the strong lenses of her spectacles, widened.

"Gosh, what a mess this room is! Who's been throwing a fit here? Where have I been, Pop? Can you tie that! To that hidjous dancing school, of course, I should think you'd remember what a fight I had with her about going." She nodded in the direction of Kitty Teele. "She's always taking the joy out of life."

"Stop it, Thalia!" The Senator's command was a roar. "Your Aunt Kitty gave up her own plans, her own life, to come here to look after you."

"That's too bad, because I don't want her. She'd better go back to her old plans. She'd better marry that man she was kissing in the hall tonight."

"Thalia!"

Kitty Teele's stifled exclamation sent Faith's heart to her throat. She looked from her white face to Ben's whiter one, then at Senator Teele whose skin had turned a deep crimson. She heard Duke's laugh.

"Snooping, Thalia?" he asked.

"I wasn't snooping!" she denied furiously. "I didn't even wait to see who it was. I just saw a man's back and heard him say 'darling.' His voice made me feel queer all over and I beat it."

"And you didn't stop to say 'Howdy' to me. I wouldn't believe it of you, Thalia." The pallor of Duke Tremaine's face belied the lightness of his voice. "Haven't you suspected that your aunt is my girl? Righto, Kitty?"

Above the crash of her senses, Faith heard the low answer:—

"Righto, Duke."

"Thalia! Go to bed," the Senator thundered.

"But, Pop—it wasn't my fault when I saw—"

"Go to bed! If you repeat what you said a moment ago about your Aunt Kitty, we'll chop the head off that Jemima duck of yours, eat it, and give away the dog. Get me?"

"But, Pop—" the last word was a heartbroken wail.

"I mean it. *Watch your tongue*. Now go to bed."

Faith slipped her hand under the girl's arm.

"Come on, Thalia. We're the younger set, we can't listen-in on the old folks' conferences. Do you know what that silly Jemima was doing this afternoon? I almost—" and the door closed behind them. Their laughter drifted back from the hall.

Duke Tremaine tried desperately to shut Faith's shocked

white face from his memory. Couldn't she realize that he had made that declaration about Kitty on a crazy impulse to save Ben? If she hadn't, the moment he cut loose from this room he would find her and make her believe it. That meddling child . . . If she had kept her mouth shut he wouldn't be in this jam. His indignation cooled. The cause went beyond Thalia. If Ben hadn't—

"I'm sorry about this." The Senator's grave voice switched his train of thought. "Ben, you'd better stay away from the house at present. You were the man with Kitty whom Thalia saw in the hall, weren't you? Duke's dramatic announcement didn't deceive me. I haven't been blind. We can't have gossip started about Kitty and a married man, not only for her sake and your wife's, but for mine. My opponents in the Senate would seize it as a starving dog snatches at a bone."

"Joe! It was just—just—"

"It never happened before—I swear. I—" Ben Jarvis interrupted Kitty Teele's shaken attempt at explanation.

"I believe you. I'm not blaming you, boy—but it must not happen again. Duke, you'll have to pay for your quixotic gesture of shielding Ben. Play gigolo to Kitty for a while and let your other girl friends slide. What's a kiss usually? Nothing, but in this case it might cause great unhappiness in Ben's family, might cost me my bill. A little concentrated devotion on your part will scotch any gossip about her and Ben. You'll agree to that?"

"I agree."

The hectic session in the study had had one good result, Faith concluded, as she walked toward home after leaving Thalia at school. The girl had clung to her last night. Before they had started out this morning, she had raced through the conservatory, down the steps into the garden, to make sure that her adored Jemima had not been decapitated. When the duck waddled toward her quacking and shaking its wings she had caught up the creature and hugged it.

Grand morning. In spite of last night's frost, still April-like weather. She was glad of this chance to get her mind calmed down. It whirled as if it had been chucked into an electric fan going at full speed. One excitement after another yesterday had culminated in Duke's announcement that Kitty was his girl.

Why had she been so shocked at his declaration? Hadn't Irene intimated that he was in love with her? Hadn't Wayne said that Duke's world had decided that at long last she was sufficiently in love to marry? Hadn't the memory pricked like a sharp splinter in her mind ever since?

Why, why did her heart ache and smart intolerably when she thought of it? Had she thought of much else? Why? Because she loved him. The answer came with the blinding suddenness of a flash-bulb. Was that the reason no man ever had stirred her to more than friendship? Why he made the other men she knew seem colorless and boyish? Her pulses had shaken her with their throbbing when his eyes had looked straight into hers that first afternoon as he demanded:—

"Why hasn't Ben told me that you are the loveliest thing in the world?"

Now his attraction for her lay in something far deeper than kindling eyes, lean bronzed face and firm-lipped mouth which could soften in a boyish laugh, or in a voice which could be gaily disturbing or authoritatively stern. It lay in the soul of him which no bludgeoning of adversity could cripple or crush.

Last night at the Inn his voice had been possessive. She had imagined it, of course. She had taken what Irene called his "line" seriously. Only a short time after, hadn't he admitted that he loved Kitty Teele? Suppose he did love her, he might retain the affection for the girl he had seen grow up, mightn't he? If that same girl had hoped it was something deeper, she was out of luck. Someone jostled her.

"Look where you're going!" an impatient voice reminded.

"I'm sorry," she apologized and realized that she had been absolutely absorbed in thought.

It was like coming out of a dream to find that automobiles and taxis were rolling up and down the Avenue, that men and women were passing her. Now that she was aware of them she noticed they were smiling broadly. Was it because the sun was shining and plating the world with gold? That wouldn't make them turn and look back, would it? What did they see?

She walked faster. If there was anything funny going on, she was all for it. A passing voice chuckled, "If it ain't Donald Duck in person!" What *was* that white thing ahead? It couldn't be! It was! Jemima waddling toward her in the middle of the sidewalk. Thalia must have forgotten to fasten the door of the pen. A delivery boy probably had left the garden gate open.

Could she catch the creature? She must. The girl would be brokenhearted if anything happened to her pet. If she were to return the duck unharmed she might win Thalia's

confidence and in time influence her to appreciate what her
aunt had done for her. She hated being conspicuous, but
she hated more Thalia's injustice to Kitty Teele.

"Jemima. Nice Jemima!" she cajoled. The duck saw her
coming and squatted. She clutched futilely. It spread its
wings. Flew. Ran on the tips of webbed feet.

The next few minutes moved with the speed and color
of a pantomime behind a gauze screen, the gauze being
her unbelief in their actuality. She was angrily aware that
she was making a spectacle of herself as the duck squatted,
flew, pranced on tiptoes and she raced, clutched, raced and
clutched with no success to the accompaniment of chuckles,
cheers, guffaws, shouts of good-natured derision from persons passing. Duke had said that the world needed laughter.
Thanks to the act that silly duck was putting on, it was getting it this morning—plus.

Jemima, fagged but undefeated, flew between the open
gates at the East Entrance of the White House grounds. A
guard lunged for her and missed. With a quack of achieve-
ment, the duck landed in the fountain pool.

"I presume you think you're a born comedian. I could
wring your neck!" Faith declared furiously.

"Boy, oh, boy! The chase was better than a three-ring circus. Shall I wade in after the critter?" a breathless voice
asked. She turned. It was Carrilski. Hatless. His monocle
dangled by its ribbon. From the sidewalk a grinning crowd
looked on.

"How long have you been trailing us, Count?" she demanded.

"For two blocks. What a sight! What a newsreel! I'd
have given my ears for a camera." His voice was broken
with laughter. "Lost my hat in the chase. Shall I wade in?"
he repeated.

"Good heavens, no. Don't you know where we are? In
the White House grounds. We may wade into the hoosegow,
if we aren't careful." She smiled at the two guards.

"Will you catch the duck for me? The little girl to whom
she belongs, Senator Teele's daughter, would be brokenhearted if she were lost, otherwise I never would have
chased her in here."

"We'll get her, Miss. Lucky the bird didn't run down the
highway. I suppose you'd have followed and not given a
hang about traffic or the jaywalking law," the guard, with
amazingly blue eyes, observed with a friendly grin. He
waved at the crowd. "Move on, folks!" Chuckling, laughing,
they moved.

Faith breathlessly watched him as he pursued the duck round and round the pool. He reached. Caught a web foot. Slipped. Lost his balance. Splashed into the water. Dragged himself out with Jemima dangling by one leg.

"That bird sure knows how to hit the high spots. Ain't nothing good enough for it to swim in but the White House fountain pool, seems like. Here it is, Miss."

"Permit me, Mees Jarvees. The wetness will be bad for your charming costume." The Count seized the quacking duck round the middle. "I weel carry Mees Jemima. It ees a quite nice name for a duck, ees eet not? Are we walking?"

"I am." She turned to the guards. "I can't thank you enough. Senator Teele can do it better than I. Are you really going through with this ridiculous stunt, Count?"

"It is I, or you, ees eet not, Mees Jarvees? I could not permit a lady with whom I am promenading to carry a burden. Thees duck may weigh eight pounds—an' live eet ees more. If eet ees embarrassing for you I weel call a cab."

"Not for me. If you are game I am."

"Your voice, eet ripple with laughter. May I not have the fun also?"

"I was thinking what a choice morsel this exploit would be for the Chatter Column of the evening paper. Something like this:

" 'The sensation of the week: Count Carrilski, the bachelor darling of post-debutante circles, with a Pekin duck—wired for continuous sound—clutched in his arms, taking a constitutional with Miss Jarvis, Faith looking very up-to-the-minute in canyon-green hat and jacket, and the latest word in pleated plaid skirt.' Think you could bear up under that, Count?"

"The Carrilski can—what you call eet—bear up, under reedicule or tragedy. Some day, I weel tell you what eet has endured."

Faith's conscience pricked. Each time she had met him a doubt as to the validity of his title had flashed through her mind. She had been unfair. An impostor would not speak with such conviction of his family. If he were in Washington as an observer for a foreign government as she, and apparently Wayne Marshall suspected, it might be his way of serving his country. Patriots had given their lives in such service. She tried to make up for her doubt by friendliness. From their animated conversation one might have thought that walking with a quacking duck was the latest fad in the best social circles.

She opened the front door of the Teele house with her

key. Through the hall, into the fragrant conservatory with its towering palms and yellow clouds of acacias, the duck-laden Count followed her. Down the three steps to the garden, and the runaway was securely fastened in the pen.

"That seems to be that! Thanks a million for your help," Faith acknowledged fervently.

"Eet was nothing. The—the duck—chase makes us friends, ees eet not?"

"If that experience doesn't, nothing can. Won't you come in and have something to drink or smoke after your strenuous exertion?"

"Thank you, no. Eet ees too early in the day to intrude upon Mees Teele. May I not leave by thees garden gate?"

"Yes. It opens on a narrow street which cuts into the Avenue."

"Then I weel go thees way." He clicked his heels. "*Au revoir*. When you are in need of a duck-hunter—I am your man, ees not that Americane?"

He opened the gate—looked back at the house as if to impress every detail on his memory. The door of the conservatory was open, the broad steps with ornate iron railing which led up to it were as yellow with sunlight as the branches of acacia visible within.

"Charming! Charming," he said, and with another bow closed the gate behind him.

Hands in her jacket pockets, Faith looked up at the house. She never had really noticed it from this angle before. The garden, the steps, the terrace and conservatory had been designed to give the impression of space and spread. One never would think, from the sedate brownstone front, that the back had this *al fresco* effect. She wouldn't have suspected that the Count had such an appreciation of artistic perfection.

Queer, that of all the men she knew in Washington, he should have been the one to help with the three-ring circus she had put on. What a sight they must have been parading along the Avenue.

"Three-ring circus!"

The words clanged through her mind like a fire-alarm gong. The Count had said that exactly as an American would have said it. Not a trace of accent. Queer. Very queer. Was it likely that a foreigner would lapse into English in a moment of excitement? Wouldn't he exclaim in his own language? Would he say "Boy, oh, boy!" ?

She looked down at the duck squatting as contentedly in a pan of water as it had in the White House pool.

"Jemima! Jemima! Have you been of some use, after all? The incident of your get-away is not closed. I can see a whole brood of consequences. But, they are off the record at present—understood?"

The duck quacked response to the girl's excited voice and began to oil the downy feathers on its breast.

XII

THE old-fashioned bigness of the drawing rooms of the Teele house appeared to stretch to accommodate the guests who poured in for supper. Walls, ceiling and swaggered curtains were the same pale blue. Voices were gay in badinage; muted in confidence; unleashed in argument. On a small table near the fire a great silver bowl of rich, creamy eggnog broadcast an enticing aroma.

Beyond in the dining room Georgian silver coffee urns on serving tables hissed and bubbled. Oysters and oyster crabs, with diced celery and a *soupçon* of onion in the cream sauce, sent up appetizing steam when silver covers were lifted. Platters of cold smoked turkey were garnished with little piping hot sausagss.

Graceful decanters and wine and champagne glasses, unbelievably thin, had a buffet all their own. The fragrant breath of yellow roses in bowls, white lilac and lilies in tall vases scented the air. From the hall above drifted the muted music of harps playing Strauss's "Joys of Life."

Duke Tremaine caught sight of Faith in a shimmering sheath of violet satin, clouded with untold yards of shell-pink tulle. A diamond butterfly fluttered sparkling wings on her left shoulder. Its mate shimmered and quivered in her dusky hair. He remembered that his grandmother had worn one. Hair-ornaments had completed their cycle and were in fashion again.

He hadn't seen her since the night she had stood as if turned to stone and heard him declare that Kitty Teele was his girl. That had been three days ago but the three days had seemed a century. He had kept away from her because he had promised the Senator not to revoke on that announcement. Why wouldn't Ben talk, explain to him where he was when the safe had been opened? All anyone could get out of him was that he had found what he wanted in the Senator's study, had left the house and gone home.

Was Faith worrying over his silence? She must know that the Senator attached no blame to her brother for the robbery. There was a hint of strain about her lovely mouth. Did she care that, so far as she knew, he and Kitty Teele were engaged? She was smiling now at Marshall, who looked as if the weight of the world rested on his shoulders. He had lost some of his gloss. He didn't seem so assured. Was the Senator making him feel that he was under suspicion? Joe Teele could skin the hide off a man without raising his voice when occasion demanded.

What had the confidential secretary meant that night when he had told Faith "I've struck the trail"? What was he saying now to her, to which she answered with a negative shake of her head? Apparently he had argued her into consent. She was leaving the room with him.

"Here you are, Duke!" Senator Teele's voice, the Senator's hand on his shoulder, stopped his pursuit of Faith. "Been looking for you and Ben. They're all here, my friends and enemies from Capitol Hill. Kitty and Miss Jarvis did the trick. Great girls, but you know that. Want you to meet a couple of my constituents from the home town. They're in need of a tax expert and I recommended you. Come to my study in about five minutes."

"Thanks, Senator. Any clue as to who showed an undue interest in your safe?"

"No. I presume this city is crawling with men, and some women, who would sell their souls to secure the specifications of the latest super-super demon of the air. As for the press boys—they're living in my outer office."

"It will be pretty serious if those memoranda are already leaving the country."

"Don't look so worried, Duke. Hunting down the thief isn't your job, it's Ben's. Keep *your* hands off. I think he's on the right track. He suspects—"

"Good lord, Senator. Keep *your* voice down! If anyone should hear—"

"You're right, boy, you're right. Bits have been appearing in the papers that have amazed me, items I've never given to the press. Leaks. Leaks. Where do they come from? All in my favor, to be sure, all build-ups, but I don't like it. Someone's lapping up news as stealthily as a cat steals cream. Suppose the snooper ferrets out the reason for our conference in the desert last summer? Think of the headlines." Deep creases slashed between his nose and mouth,

regret darkened his blue eyes. "We've lost two planes and
one pilot testing that invention. I hope to God our man
makes good without another crash."

Duke watched him as he walked away. His low voice had
been profoundly moved. The loss of a life would cut deep.
There was something nearer than the experiments in a distant workshop to be concerned about at present. Had he told
anyone else that Ben was on the trail of the memoranda
which would practically provide working plans to a man who
could understand them? If the news got on the air Ben's life
would be in danger.

"Come back to the party, Duke." Madam Carr tapped his
shoulder with a silver fan.

"What do you mean by creeping up behind me like that,
Nancy Carr?"

"I didn't creep. I swished with taffeta."

"My mistake. You're a snappy number in that silver gray
with the soft pink fichu and pearls, Madam Carr."

"Flattery, sheer flattery, but I like it. Irene says I believe
every compliment paid me. Why not? Why not enjoy the
applesauce of life? It is so easily digested. My granddaughter
went to New York the day after the safe break, I understand. She didn't tell me she was going. I wonder where she
got the money. She was almost hysterical when I refused to
give it to her unless she told me why she wanted to rush
away in the midst of the season here. Do you think the attraction is a man?"

"*No.* Perhaps she wanted new clothes. Perhaps she was
fed-up with the social round. A little bird told me that you
had engaged an apartment at the Mayflower, right?"

"Right. That same little bird must have had a busy three
days and a hoarse throat spreading the news. Every person
I've met in these rooms has commented on my move. I only
hope that I haven't hurt Ben by walking out. He looks like
death and destruction, I saw him today. Is he worrying
about this safe-cracking business, or is it all Irene? Is Marshall here?"

"He is putting on a good show playing assistant host."

"That young man has lost a shade of his *savoir faire.*
Anything more heard about the rifling of the Senator's study?
I have a feeling that there is something phony about it, a
touch of Hollywood melodrama. Found out yet where Count
Carrilski comes from? 'One of those border countries' doesn't
tell me much. He was standing quite near you and the Senator when you were having that heart-to-heart a moment

ago. I could see his ears stretch to hear what you were saying."

Tremaine remembered the Senator's admission that Ben was hot on the trail of the memoranda of the specifications. He said as lightly as he could with possible consequences to his best friend chilling his blood:—

"If the Count is in this country on an espionage assignment, Nancy Carr, he was wasting valuable time listening to the Senator, who was asking me to come to the study to meet a couple of his home-town men." He laughed. "Having finished your cross-examination of me what are you going to do now?"

"Shoot the first person who says, 'I hear you've moved to the Mayflower.' If I'm locked up for murder I'll engage you for my defense counsel, Duke. Will you take the case?"

"Sure. I'd do anything for you, Nancy Carr."

She patted his arm tenderly. "I always feel as if I'd been sitting in the sun, when I've been with you, my dear. My heart is warmed through and through."

His eyes followed her as she crossed to the door. A grand woman. Was she right? Had Carrilski been listening to his talk with the Senator? He tried to believe that Joe Teele's voice had been so low it couldn't be overheard, but he knew he was fooling himself. The Senator had said that Ben was on the track of the missing papers. In case the Count was interested in their disposal Ben must be warned.

He was on the lookout for his partner as he made a slow progress through the rooms. His troubled thoughts were constantly interrupted by a touch on his shoulder, a voice speaking his name, a hand held out in greeting. It seemed as if every person he knew socially or politically in Washington was in league to detain him. To avoid more delay, when he reached the study, he opened the door, closed it quickly and backed against it in surprise. Faith was perched on the broad flat desk, her gauzy pink skirts billowing about her. One silver sandal rested on the green blotter as if ready to step off. He could see her lovely bare back, not her face. Marshall stood before her. His face was strained and colorless.

"I hate to tell you but you ought to know, darling, that—" He interrupted the sentence to look up as Duke Tremaine stepped forward. "It is an ancient, but still honored custom to knock at a closed door," he reminded suavely.

Tremaine restrained a furious urge to plant a short smash to the jaw.

"Having been sent here by the Senator for a conference

I hadn't expected to find his private room in use for a sentimental twosome."

"Duke!" The intensity of Faith's protest, her surprised dark eyes, increased his anger. She slipped to her feet. "This isn't a twosome and it *isn't* sentimental."

"No? My mistake."

The room was so still he fancied he could hear time tossing off the minutes, sending them pelting after one another like balls in a bowling alley. Why had he snapped like that at the girl he loved?

"Don't give it another thought, *Mister* Tremaine," she flouted airily. "It was our mistake. Maybe we have intruded, maybe the gentleman is here to meet a lovely lady before the Senator appears, Wayne. Come on."

She crossed the room with head high, in her indignation apparently unaware of the sandalless condition of her foot. On the threshold Marshall looked back.

"Shall I tell the lady you're waiting? I've heard rumors," he added with malicious emphasis before he closed the door.

In the hall he and Faith came face to face with Senator Teele and two men.

"Did you come out of my study, Marshall?"

"Yes. Miss Jarvis and I went there to escape from the crowd for a few minutes. I had important news for her and—"

"After this, find some other place in which to confide important news. I've had all the intrusion, the breaking and entering my room I'll stand for."

"You're not accusing me of robbing your safe, Joe, or are you?" Marshall was white with anger.

"I'm not accusing you of anything. I'm telling you to keep out."

"It was my fault, Senator," Faith admitted hurriedly. "I've been standing for hours. My sandals were so tired that I sneaked in there to slip one off. My goodness, I've just remembered I left it on your desk!"

"That's all right, Miss Jarvis. See anything of Tremaine? I told him to meet us there."

"He is waiting for you."

"That's what I admire about him," the Senator confided to the men as he herded them toward the study. "Dependable. Mark my words, he'll be in Congress before long. He has what it takes. He has been a close student of political science, besides having an unusual training in tax and Latin-American law. That last is why I recommended him . . ." The closing door shut off his voice.

"We certainly were unfair to Duke." As no answer came to Faith's regretful remark, she turned. Wayne was standing with head bent. Was he trying to hear the end of the Senator's sentence?

"Giving an imitation of a listening-post, Marshall?" inquired Ben Jarvis, who had come up behind him.

"I was considering whether I dared return and salvage Faith's sandal. The Senator is in one of his raw-meat eating moods, champagne does that to him. Perhaps you are going in and will—"

"Perhaps I am and perhaps I'm not. Better go up and get another pair of shoes, kid. It would be a social blunder to run around in even *one* stocking foot in this distinguished company."

"Thanks for the etiquette hint, *Emily Post*." Faith flung the sarcastic retort at her brother before she charged up the stairs in a swirling mist of shell-pink tulle.

XIII

SHE dashed into her room and slammed the door as if to shut out the smarting, stinging memory of Duke's eyes as he had said "I hadn't expected to find his private room in use for a sentimental twosome."

She incredulously regarded Madam Carr seated at a small table, pencil in hand, frowning at the page of a newspaper.

"How did you get here?" she asked.

"My dear, is it your custom to enter a room in the manner of Eliza with the bloodhounds at her heels? I came to escape the crowd. I'm worn out lying about my reason for moving to the Mayflower. My car won't be here for a half-hour. So, like Goldilocks, I tried different rooms till I found one that suited. I like an open fire. I like soft yellow walls and delicate blue chintz. I have a couple of East Indian silver boxes which I'll add to your collection. I found the crossword puzzle page of the newspaper so here I am and with your permission, here I stay."

"I hope you will, you dear." Impulsively Faith pressed her lips to Madam Carr's cheek and felt it warm under their touch. "I came tearing up for a pair of sandals."

"What happened? A Cinderella act? Did you lose a slipper fleeing from the Prince?"

"Nothing so romantic. Wayne and I were in the Senator's study, when in stalked Duke Tremaine looking like a thunder cloud all dressed up in black tie and dinner jacket. He intimated that we were intruding on private domain, and we were, because when Wayne and I came out, the Senator with two cronies was on his way in."

"Joe Teele can't drop his Bills even on an occasion like this. I presume you were a perfect lady and apologized prettily to Duke for your intrusion?"

"I didn't. I was furious with him for assuming—he didn't assume, he brazenly accused Wayne and me of being there for sentimental reasons. Wayne had heard something he said I ought to know. He had just begun to tell me when Duke appeared, so I don't know now what it's all about."

"Beware, my child, of the person who is eager to tell you 'something you ought to know.' There's bound to be a thorn in it."

Faith crossed to the window and pulled aside the sheer curtain against the glass. Would there be a thorn in what Wayne had to tell her? His eyes had burned with excitement, his face had been white.

"Don't you love the gold-capped Monument at night, Nancy Carr?" she asked in an effort to forget his voice, which had set a premonition of disaster shrilling through her mind like a faint, far fire-siren. "I adore this city. It is so gay, so beautiful, so drenched with tradition, so inspiring. It has everything desirable."

"It has, my dear," Madam Carr agreed gravely.

"Smooth runs the water where the brook is deep.

A Mr. William Shakespeare thought of that first, but it always simmers to the top of my mind when I think of Washington. The surface is stimulating, shining, mirroring high ideals, brilliant plans, honest thinking and endeavor, but underneath, the current of temptation runs strong and deep to sweep men from their feet, the temptation to use power and prestige and the trust of fellow workers for self gain. There are treacherous holes in the bed of this brook, to trip the weak, the unwary. One of the most tricky is espionage. So, watch your step, my dear, don't lose your heart to a glamorous foreigner. I've noticed that you've rather fallen for that handsome Carrilski."

Faith laughed. "Which reminds me that I had the funniest

experience with him, on my way home from Thalia's
school . . ."

The incident of the runaway Jemima lost nothing in her
dramatic recital. Madam Carr's low laugh bubbled an accompaniment to the girl's vibrant, charming voice. She dabbed
at her eyes with a film of pink chiffon that matched her
fichu.

"My dear, I haven't laughed so much in years! Of all the
screwball situations! I can picture the Count, eyeglass and—"
Her exuberance fell flat as a skipping leaf deserted by a
breeze. "Did he—did he say anything, make any exclamation
that would betray his nationality?" she asked sharply. "You
know, Faith, I may be unjust, but I'm suspicious of every
foreigner who comes to this city."

He had betrayed himself, but until she found out more
about the man she wouldn't admit it, Faith decided.

"We were so excited over that darn duck, we neither of
us knew what the other was saying. Someone's knocking.
Kitty has missed me. I should be downstairs helping instead
of holding a giggle-fest here with you." She opened the door.

"Here's your sandal," Duke Tremaine said. "Thought
you might need it."

His eyes, his steady, dangerously cool eyes, set her pulses
thrumming. She thought of his voice as he had asked:
"Haven't you suspected that your aunt is my girl, Thalia?"

Jealous, wasn't she? Jealousy—what every woman knows,
terrifying if you loved, degrading anyway, distorting your
judgment, tearing your heart to tatters—she caught a glimpse
of her strained expression in the mirror—and tarnishing
your beauty, if you had any.

"Thanks a million, Duke. Tell Kitty I'll be down in a
minute."

He didn't go. Instead he looked at Nancy Carr, who
smiled and nodded.

"You needn't say it, Duke. I'm fairly intelligent. I understand. What's a five letter word which means hurry?
Scram. I'll give your message to Kitty, Faith."

"Wait! I'll go with you."

"Not yet." Duke Tremaine blocked the way. "I didn't
come with a message from Kitty. I want to talk to you.
Thanks a lot," he said to the woman at the door. As she
closed it behind her he dropped the silver sandal into a
chair.

"What was Marshall saying to you in the Senator's
study?"

There was steel in his voice, or iron—Faith couldn't re-

member which was the more unbendable. She kept her lashes
lowered. If she looked at him she might betray the fact that
she loved him, might forget that by his own admission Kitty
Teele was his "girl."

Suppose she were? Why shouldn't he love the Senator's
sister? He still thought of Faith Jarvis as a little girl, would
be amazed if he suspected she loved him. What was love,
anyway, that she was making such a tragedy of it? Something here today; gone tomorrow. Hadn't she seen that dem-
onstrated time and again? Duke had said she had the heart
of a winner. Would she let love beat her?

"Answer my question." His voice was low and controlled
but every nerve telegraphed to her brain, "Watch your step!"

No time to think. She must escape with banners flying.
She smiled. It was quite a nice smile. One mirrored wall
gave it back to her, gave back her eyes shining like jewels,
the dent at a corner of her vivid lips.

"Really, Duke, how crude. What a question to ask of a
girl in love!"

"What do you mean? In love? You're not in love with
Marshall, are you?" He turned as a knock was followed by
the opening of the door. "Thank the Lord, here's Ben. Now
we'll get somewhere. Ben, Faith intimates that she's in love
with Marshall."

"Marshall! With that stuffed shirt! Is he in the habit of
paying the check with a hundred-dollar bill when he takes
you out stepping, kid? Believe it or not, he flashed one at
Zeke's and Sophy's, the other night. You're crazy. I won't
let you marry him."

"That's just too bad. You've no right to speak like that,
if you are my brother. First Duke roars at me, then you.
Won't you and he ever realize that I've grown up? First I
had Mother everlastingly checking up on me, now you boys
begin. I'll remind you that I'm free, white and twenty-three.
You didn't either of you consult *me* as to the person you
intended to marry, did you? Who knows, I might have given
you some Stop—Look—Listen advice."

She saw the tremor of Duke Tremaine's lips before he
closed them in a hard line. Behind him stood Ben, his eyes
burning, his face white, and behind Ben the mirror gave
back the flicker of firelight on the silver boxes on the
shelves, the soft yellow walls, the motionless figures of two
men in dinner clothes and a girl in a bouffant shell-pink
tulle over shimmering violet satin.

"You haven't answered my question, Faith," Duke Tremaine reminded. "Are you engaged to Wayne Marshall?"

"She can't be. I won't permit it," Ben Jarvis protested.

"Are you engaged to Marshall, Faith?"

"And if I am?"

"Don't be so darn flippant when Duke asks you a serious question, kid," Ben Jarvis protested. "If a girl can love a man like Marshall she isn't worth wasting breath on. Here's where I do a blackout. Promised to look in on another party. You handle this, Duke." He left the room.

"You haven't heard the last of this, Faith, but I'll bide my time." Duke Tremaine laughed. "Don't look so tense. This isn't a tragedy. Sit down while I put this on." He slipped on the silver sandal. "But, you'd better tell Marshall that there's likely to be trouble if he doesn't stop calling you 'darling.' There you are, now we'll go down. Kitty'll think you've run out on the party if you don't appear pretty quick, Miss Jarvis."

He was so like his old friendly self that Faith's heart stopped pounding. She could even laugh.

"What a fuss you and Ben worked up over nothing. I feel as if I'd been caught in the Great Blow of September Twenty-first. I'm ready."

As she entered the drawing room she was surprised to find that the party was over except for the presence of Count Carrilski. He made her think of Robinson Crusoe on a desert island. He clicked his heels and pressed his lips to her hand.

"At last I find you, Mees Jarvees. I have not the pleasure of seeing you since the day of the duck hunt. Eet was amusing. I am desolated that I am tardy. The guests they have gone and there were many what you Americans call the Big Shots here, ees eet not?"

His accent had taken on a new high. Apparently he didn't know that for a few moments, a few betraying moments on that "amusing" occasion, he had forgotten it. Who was he? Why was he in Washington? She intended to find out. Should she have told Duke of her suspicion? No. Not yet.

She looked naive and young, quite like a school-girl begging her movie idol for an autograph as she smiled up at him.

"The Jemima hunt was grand fun. We made giant strides in friendship, didn't we, Count? I've been looking for you all the evening. I was so *afraid* you wouldn't come." She felt Duke's quick glance at her. "I wanted to tell you how sorry I was that I had to hurry away the afternoon at the

Smithsonian before I told you that I would love to personally conduct you about Washington."

"I am enchanted, Mees Jarvees. Eet ees an omen of good that I should hear such news immediately upon my arrival, ees eet not?"

"Just arrived!" Duke Tremaine's voice registered courteous surprise. "I was sure I saw you here half an hour ago, Count. Must have been someone from an Embassy. You attachés are typed, as they say in Hollywood."

"But I am not an attaché at present, Meester Tremaine."

"My mistake. Faith, have you had anything to eat?"

"No, and I'm starving."

Kitty Teele approached them.

"The servants are setting small tables in the conservatory. We'll have our supper there. You'll stay—Duke?" A lovely color tinted her face as she said his name.

"Of course, Kitty. Count Carrilski has just arrived and has as yet had no supper."

The deftness of his suggestion made Faith think of a magician skillfully forcing a card from a pack, but—why should Duke wish to force a comparative stranger on the little supper party? Was he also on the trail of the man's activities?

"You will join us, Count?"

"Eet will be the greatest pleasure, Mees Teele, to remain. Here comes my good friend who has made eet possible for me to meet you, his interesting compatriots. I was just telling Mees Teele how much I owe to you, Wayne," he added as Marshall joined the group.

"Thank the letter you brought to Mrs. Jarvis, not me. Here's the address of the Personal Service Bureau. They'll supply a girl for part-time work. Tore the page pulling it from my notebook, but it's all there." The Count thrust the slip of paper Marshall offered into the pocket of his dinner jacket.

"Supper is served, Madam," the butler announced.

At the threshold of the conservatory Wayne Marshall caught Faith's arm.

"Don't go in yet. Got something to tell you," he whispered.

"The same world-shaking item you lured me to the study to confide?" Faith's voice was gay but her eyes stung, her throat tightened as she saw Duke seat Kitty Teele at a small white table in the shadow of a spreading palm. He motioned the Count to a chair beside her. More symptoms of friendliness to the man he had apparently disliked! She had seen his quick glance at the slip of paper Wayne

had given the Count. Did he suspect that it meant more
than an address?

She heard the surprised twitter of parakeets, saw the flame
and flash of a goldfish in the pool beneath the fountain, the
lazy sway of yellow sprays of acacias, and thought: I'll
never smell hothouse earth and fragrance again without
seeing Duke bending over Kitty Teele.

"World-shaking! You'll think it is." Marshall's tense voice
brought her startled eyes to his, set little chills feathering
through her veins. It must be important. His face was colorless, was etched with new lines.

"What is it?" she whispered.

"I know who broke into the safe."

"Really! Have you told the Senator?"

"*Schss!* Keep your voice down. Not yet. It's up to you
whether I do or not."

"To *me!* What have I to do with it?"

"A lot. It was your brother!"

XIV

"COMING?"

Kitty Teele's gay voice shattered the silence which lay
like a heavy fog between Faith and Wayne Marshall.

"We can't talk here," she whispered. "Meet me—meet me
tomorrow afternoon at four near the Lincoln Memorial. I
don't believe you—but—" She broke off to answer Kitty.

"I'm coming! The aroma from those creamed oysters
makes me ravenous."

Only one episode stood out clearly after that. Duke had
knocked over a full goblet of water on the table. Even in
her preoccupation she had thought, How unlike him to be
clumsy. . . . While he had fumbled for something with which
to sop it up, the Count had pulled a handkerchief from
the pocket of his dinner jacket, had checked the rills and
trickles before they could drop on Kitty's glittering black
frock.

While the others talked and laughed a sentence kept going
over and over in her mind: "It was your brother!" Why
couldn't she forget it? Why couldn't she laugh off Wayne's
statement as an absurdity? Whenever she tried, Irene's

words at the Inn burned red in her memory like a Neon sign:
"When I entered his den his face was chalk-white as he
fussed round his desk. He jumped as if he'd been shot when
I spoke to him."

If Ben had opened the Senator's safe for a dishonest purpose he would be chalk-white, wouldn't he? But of course
he hadn't. She was disloyal to believe it for an instant. As if
drawn by a magnet she met Duke Tremaine's intent eyes.
Why was he looking at her? Had she answered someone at
random?

She asked herself the question again at midnight as, still
in her evening frock, she paced the floor of her sitting room.
No sense going to bed. She couldn't sleep with "It was
your brother" overriding every other thought. As Wayne
had said good night he had added casually:—

"Tomorrow at four. Lincoln Memorial."

Duke had spoken to her immediately after. Had he heard
the reminder? Suppose he had. When Kitty Teele didn't
need her she was constantly making dates with men friends
to walk or ride or fly, wasn't she?

If only she could have spoken to Wayne alone for just a
minute. No chance. He had left with the Count for a late
party. The Count! The speed and thoroughness with which
Wayne's bomb had blown from her mind all that glamour-
girl stuff about luring him away from Irene would be funny,
if she could see humor in anything with her heart aching
like a tooth with an exposed nerve.

She pulled aside the curtain and looked out. The almost
three-quarter moon rode high. Its brilliance paled the stars
and lighted a cloud formation which loomed like a Max-
field Parrish castle, its impenetrable walls and conical towers
faintly luminous.

A sound penetrated her absorption. Jemima was quacking, quacking like mad. The duck must have escaped from
the pen. In spite of heartache, memory warmed her eyes
with laughter. She had been just fourteen when she con-
ceived the idea of becoming a capitalist by raising ducks.
She had acquired a flock of fifty and she remembered that on
moonlight nights they would miraculously escape from their
house and promenade in single file round and round their
yard incessantly quacking salutations to the man in the
moon. A neighbor had violently protested and the ducks had
been sold.

If the Senator were awakened by Jemima she would be
sold, more likely beheaded, and Thalia would be brokenhearted. She was beginning to understand and like the child,

like her too much to have her hurt. She'd run down and lock the duck into the pen.

She flung a long chiffon scarf of pink and violet and pale yellow stripes across her shoulders and rapidly descended one flight. Stopped in the hall. Voices? In the Senator's study? She held her breath and listened. Not a sound. Must have been her overactive imagination again. Everyone would be in bed by this time.

She went on feeling as if she were running downstairs in a dream, floating down, the stillness of the house was so unnatural, so tomblike. That was an exhilarating thought. Duke was right, she was wasting her talents as a social secretary, she should be writing mystery stories full of chills and shivers.

The eerie feeling persisted when she reached the door of the conservatory. The fragrance of damp earth and flowers fitted into the sense of unreality. She rubbed her hand over her eyes. Was that a round spot of light moving across the floor, or was she seeing things? A sound!

The dream sense vanished. She was awake. Someone was moving. The same someone who had robbed the study? If so, she might catch him and clear Ben. She touched the light button.

For an instant she saw only the towering palms swaying, yellow acacia nodding as if roused from sleep, the marble bench by the blue pool with a slash of scarlet scarf someone had forgotten. Heard the startled peep of a parakeet. And then she saw a man with an electric torch gripped in one hand standing at the open door of the terrace as if turned to stone by the sudden light.

"*Count!*" she whispered incredulously.

For a stunned instant they stared at each other. Carrilski clicked off the light. The spell was broken. She was beside him as he backed to the terrace.

"Eet ees another amusing situation in which we find ourselves, ees eet not, Mees Jarvees?"

"If you call it amusing to sneak into a house in which you have been a guest, it is." Her voice was hardly more than a whisper.

"But you don't understand."

"I understand that you'd better go out the way you came in and make it snappy."

"Permit me to explain. At supper here I lost part of a cufflink." A diamond flashed in the gold button he drew from his pocket. "Eet ees an heirloom. I feared the servants would sweep eet away. I came to look for eet."

"I will tell the butler about it in the morning. Go! I'll follow to be sure the gate is locked behind you."

"You are very beautiful, Mees Jarvees. I like much blazing eyes and red scornful lips. I like eet so much I think I kees you."

He caught her in his arms. His lips missed her mouth and landed on her ear.

"Let me go. Quick, or I'll scream and rouse the household."

"You scream. I hold you like this and say—'I came by appointment.' Eet ees nicer than your word 'assignation,' ees eet not?"

With a wrench she freed herself and crossed the terrace to the steps. Better get him as far away from the conservatory as possible in case someone in the house had wakened. Should she tell him she knew he was faking an accent? Better not. It would put him on guard. He might disappear from the city before she found out what he was scheming.

"You couldn't go to town on that story, Count. I don't care for foreigners, I've seen too many. You *may* have come for that cuff-link. I'll give you the benefit of the doubt—if you go at once."

"I kees your hand. Next time I kees your lips. They were made for—"

"Going?"

"I go—Mees Jarvees."

She followed him down the steps. Along the garden path, Jemima quacked vociferously as they passed. At the gate he paused.

"Eet would be better eef you forget my veeseet, Mees Jarvees. Better for your brother, ees eet not?" He vanished into the dusk.

Faith closed the gate and locked it. Her heart choked her with its clamor. He knew. Knew that Ben had opened the Senator's safe! But Ben hadn't done it. He hadn't! *He hadn't!*

She swished her skirt at the quacking duck until it waddled into its pen. Barred the door. Raced along the path, up the steps across the terrace. Into the conservatory, the pink and violet and pale yellow scarf trailing behind her. Stopped beneath a swaying branch of acacia. Her heart turned a cartwheel. Near the fountain Duke Tremaine was holding a light to his cigarette.

"What's the big idea running round the garden at this time of night?" he demanded.

For one horrible second her mind spun like a rudderless skiff in a whirlpool. How long had he been here? How much had he seen?

"My w-word, how you frightened me. I thought ev-everyone was a-sleep. That's why when I heard that o-odious Jemina quack—I—I stole down to shut her in so she wouldn't waken the family. She was moonstruck. I had some ducks once who'd bay the moon every chance they could get."

"So you had some ducks once." His voice ran over her explanation with the crushing finality of an army tank. "That wasn't by any chance Marshall to whom you were saying a lingering good night, or was it? He stood back to the conservatory so his face couldn't be seen. Careful guy, isn't he?"

"And if it were Wayne? When it comes down to that, why shouldn't he be here as well as you, at this time of night?"

"If an explanation is in order, I've been having a conference with the Senator. He called me back as I was leaving. Besides, you see, I wasn't kissing you."

"Duke! You saw—"

"Plenty, but I closed my ears. After all, as you reminded Ben and me, you are free, white and twenty-three. Who was the man?"

"Try to find out. *He* kisses me in the conservatory. *You* kiss Kitty in the hall. Only difference is the choice of location. I don't consider it any of your business who it was."

"No? Well, it's the Senator's, and the Senator's business is mine when it comes to men dodging out the back gate at midnight. Going to tell me?"

"I am not."

"I think you will—later. Better go to bed or someone else may pop in and wonder what you and I are doing here. Go. Quick."

She went. Went without another word. In her room she slipped out of her frock, pulled on a yellow housecoat. She closed her eyes in a futile effort to shut out Duke's stony face. Only his eyes had been alive and they had burned into her heart like red-hot augers. Why should he get all excited because he believed she had been meeting a lover? He was practically engaged himself, wasn't he? Better for him to think she had met someone by appointment. He wouldn't suspect then that he was the one man in the world she wanted.

He had said she would tell him. She wouldn't until she found out what Wayne knew, or was pretending to know about Ben. "Better for your brother, ees eet not?" Carrilski

had warned. Lucky, in her surprise at seeing Duke, she
hadn't revealed who had kissed her. She was caught in a
bedeviled jungle of intrigue. Whichever way she turned a
sinister brood of consequences to Ben threatened her.

Duke Tremaine had followed her to the hall. Watched her
till she was out of sight. A lump of lead had moved in where
his heart had been. Who had kissed her? Marshall had
whispered something to her at the door of the conservatory
that had turned her face paper-white. She had made a date
to meet him at the Memorial tomorrow—it was today, now.
Had he returned at midnight to finish the story? Had he
kissed her to comfort her?

The memory of those few moments occupied his thoughts
as he drove to the Club; it was too late to return to Argyle
House. Perhaps it hadn't been Marshall. He had seen
only the man's back; his head was bent over her. Who had it
been? Who could it have been but the man who called her
"darling"? What did "darling" signify? Nothing. From over-
use the endearing term had lost all its tender meaning, it
was nothing but a conversation word now. She couldn't love
him—but, did she?

In his room he pulled from his pocket the slip of paper
Marshall had handed to the Count in the Teele drawing
room. He had had a queer hunch that the torn page had a
secret significance. If so, it had been a clever trick to deliver it openly. Later he had upset the goblet of water in
the hope that Carrilski might pull a handkerchief from the
pocket into which he had thrust the paper.

If the stunt had been planned on stage or screen it would
have worked; but in real life it stood about one chance in a
hundred of coming through. It had made the grade. The
handkerchief had been hastily produced, something white
came with it, had dropped to the floor. He had surreptitiously picked it up and—here it was.

He spread what looked to be a jagged half of the page
of a notebook on the desk. It had been torn through the
middle of Ben Jarvis' home address. Ben's address! The discovery sent little chills slithering down his spine. Marshall
had said that it was the address of a Personal Service Bureau. Why had he lied? Did those scrawled letters mean that
Ben or his wife were to be caught in a web of scandal or
conspiracy?

He frowned at the paper. Ben or his wife . . . It was
Irene who was mixed up in this, if one of them was. Only
tonight Nancy Carr had said that she had been almost hys-

terical in her demand for money for a trip to New York. She had wanted to leave Washington when the season was at its height and every day and night crowded with social events. Why?

She had gone. Who had financed her? Not Ben, he was short of cash at present. Had it been Marshall? Through his mind echoed Magnolia's voice:—

"I bet them two's just rolling in money. Zeke had to make change for a hundred-dollar bill. *A hundred dollars.*"

The cold hand of suspicion gripped his heart. Had Marshall or the Count given Irene that money for information received?

XV

IT seemed years, sleepless years, to Faith before the smiling dusky-skinned maid, in soft green uniform, appeared with the breakfast tray.

"My stars, you up an' dressed so soon, Miss Jarvis? You sure look awful nice in that white wool sweater and the red skirt an' the silver beads. Your eyes look kinder tired, though."

"Miss Kitty and I are taking a badminton lesson this morning, Zinnia. I slept with one eye on the clock. The instructor glares at us if we're a minute late. I hate to be glared at."

"I guess not many folks glares at you, Miss Jarvis." Zinnia set the tray sparkling with glass, glinting with silver, colorful with primrose-sprigged china, on a table by the window. "Leastwise not gentlemen. You sure got 'em comin' with their tongues hangin' out. I suppose sometime you'll be gettin' married, huh?"

"I hope so. I can't hand much to this day. It's gloomy and last night there was a moon. You needn't wait. I have everything I want. Toast and coffee and orange juice. Have you taken a tray to Miss Kitty?"

"Sure, an' the Senator's having his breakfast now on the terrace with Miss Thalia. If you've got everything you want I'll get on with my work. Miss Kitty may seem soft as melted butter but she don't miss a trick running this big house. Ma says if I make good here I'll be all set to get a

job in heaven dustin' off angels' harps. Don't sound ex-
citin' to me, no, mam."

The giggling maid whisked from the room. No wonder her
eyes looked "kinder tired" Faith thought. She hadn't been
able to get Duke's face or his voice out of her mind since she
had bolted up the stairs last night. He had been so sure he
knew who had kissed her. When she found out what Wayne
had to tell her should she tell him?

She wondered about it again in the afternoon as, hands
thrust into the pockets of her checked tweed topcoat, beige
sports hat with a green cockade pulled down on her dark
hair, she sat on a bench at one end of the reflecting pool
and looked up at "Lincoln Triumphant" in his shrine. The
poise, the strength, the benignancy of the heroic figure was
like the touch of a tender hand on her bruised heart.

She rose. Paced back and forth. She couldn't sit still. Why
didn't Wayne come? He must know that she would be mad
with anxiety to hear what he had to tell her. He must have
informed the Count or he wouldn't have threatened her with
that sinister warning about Ben. Why should he tell him?
Hadn't he intimated to her that he was suspicious of Carrilski?

She shivered. The sky was gray as pewter without its luster.
The atmosphere was dense with an out-of-season fog and
mist. It was her proud boast that her spirit never was affected
by the weather, but this day had her down. It seemed to have
crept inside her. She was chilled to the bone. Her teeth
showed a tendency to chatter. Stark branches of leafless trees
swayed like drifting ghosts. She watched a group of tourists
mount the three marble terraces and move slowly up the
thirteen steps of the Memorial. Men removed their hats. The
shrill voices of children ceased.

She had thought that this spot she loved would be the
place of all others in which she could straighten out her
tangled problems. "Tangled" wasn't the word. They were tied
in hard knots, and Duke's belief that she had kept a date
with a man in the conservatory was one of the toughest. That
belief would be funny if it weren't possible that it might breed
a lot of scary consequences. Suppose he told the Senator that
she was carrying on a clandestine love affair and the Senator
asked questions? He had said that it was the Senator's business. If only she could tell him what it was all about, go to
him as she had gone to him with her perplexities when she
was young. She couldn't. Not yet. Not until she knew what
Wayne had to tell her?

Was life like this for everyone who grew up? The day she had arrived at the Union Station she had wondered what lay ahead and had assured herself buoyantly that whatever it was she could take it. Little she had thought, then, that she would be caught in a dark, swift undercurrent of suspicion and intrigue, would find herself devastatingly in love with a man who loved someone else.

Suppose she were in love? Would she let the intolerable hurt of it beat her? Was love like this for everyone? Maybe something always jabbed at one's heart and squeezed it to pulp, stabbing, wringing, hurting, till it became numb. Perhaps hers would go dead wholly and never hurt any more while she lived.

"Walking in your sleep, Faith? I've spoken to you twice." Wayne Marshall's voice broke into her troubled self-questioning.

"Sleep! Do you think I could sleep after what you told me?"

"I didn't sleep either. I've done a lot of thinking since I left you last night."

"Hurry! Tell me what you meant by saying that Ben opened the Senator's safe."

"Here?" He shrugged and raised interrogative brows. Beneath the brim of his black Homburg his eyes were noticeably light. "A little public, isn't it, for the story of a crime?"

"Don't use that word in connection with my brother. I won't permit it. If you think I believe he did it, you're crazy."

"Then why are you here?"

He was right. Why was she here, if she didn't believe him? She watched a white-throated sparrow scratching back and forth for food like a chicken, before she answered:—

"I'm here because no one can accuse Ben of a thing like that and get away with it. Let's go down the steps where we won't be overheard."

As they followed the path beside the pool, which shone like a huge oblong platinum tray etched with the reflection of the Monument, rose and lavender and green spread tint above tint in the west till it fused with the cool clarity of a winter sky. Near the horizon glowed a superb star. The air was clearer.

"Fair tomorrow!" Faith thought, and wondered what tomorrow would bring.

"Cold?" Wayne Marshall asked and slipped his hand under her arm. She promptly shook it off.

"No. That shiver was nerves. Go on, tell me what you think you know. Let's get it over."

"Don't be in such a hurry. This is a ticklish situation and

we've got to move with caution. Understand, you're not to let your brother or Tremaine suspect that I know what happened. I'm not so sure Tremaine isn't mixed up in this, too. I'd give a fortune to fasten it on him."

"On Duke! You're crazy. Why would you give a fortune to fasten it on him? You gritted that between your teeth like a movie villain."

"Because I hate him. He has tried to get me in wrong with you. Snubbed me. Didn't invite me to the dance he's giving for you."

"Why should he? You're the only person who can get yourself in wrong with me. Get back to Ben and the Senator's safe, quick."

"Promise you won't repeat what I tell you, until, if ever, I say you may?"

"I promise. Don't keep me in suspense." She choked down a sob of excitement. Was she an accessory to the stealing of those specifications memoranda by making that promise? Why worry? Of course Ben hadn't stolen them. Why should he? He had access to them if he wanted to see them, hadn't he? As for Duke's having a part in it, Wayne must be losing his mind even to think of it.

"You saw the Senator's study after the safe was opened, but you don't know what went before." Marshall nervously pulled his hat lower over his eyes; his voice was tense. Faith's blood chilled. He wasn't making up this story, he believed it. But, why should he be tense over something Ben had done?

"Never mind what I saw or didn't see. Go on! Go *on!*"

"Remember that the Senator dragged me away from you at the Mayflower, said he wanted me to send a cable?" She nodded. "I sent it. Met two men I knew and stopped to have a couple of drinks. Then I returned to the Teele house, opened the door with my key and went to the Senator's study to —to look for some notes I thought I had left there, notes I would need in the morning, intending to go from there to my lodgings to dress. Your sister-in-law was to dine with me at the Russian place. The room was lighted, the long crimson curtains were drawn across the windows as usual. As I was looking for my notes I heard the doorknob move. There was something in the cautious way it turned that made me suspicious. I slipped behind a pair of curtains and held my breath. Then came the sound of drawers being pulled out. Papers rustled. A click. I cautiously peeked. A man was turning the knob of the wall safe. A man who knew the combination."

His excited whispers sent thousands of chilly caterpillars

crawling under Faith's skin. Duke had said that the safe had been opened by someone who knew the combination. Wayne was right about that. It had happened. She knew by the break in his voice, the light in his pale blue eyes that he had seen it. She put her hand to her throat in an ineffectual attempt to loosen its tightness.

"Well, my hero, if you were so sure the safe was being robbed why didn't you dash out and take a crack at the burglar?"

"Thought of it. Decided that a criminal would be armed. Why should I risk my life for the Senator's property? I stayed where I was."

"Second thoughts are often the best—and safest. Go *on! Go on!* Unless you want me to scream with impatience."

"I didn't dare watch what he did. After a minute that seemed a year I heard the door softly opened. I peered from behind the curtain. As the man stepped to the hall I saw his face and one hand. It was your brother. He wore gloves."

Faith's knees shook. She dropped to a bench before they could give way under her. Marshall seated himself beside her.

"Sorry, if I've upset you."

"Upset! You accuse my brother of stealing and say you're sorry I'm upset. Did you think I would be laughing my head off at your melodrama? If you believed that Ben had dishonestly opened that safe, why didn't you rush after him? Stop him? Why didn't you report at once to the Senator? He's your boss. Where is your loyalty to him?"

"I didn't report to the Senator because I didn't want him to know I had been in his room. You heard him roar at me the night of the supper when you and I came out of his study. He doesn't suspect that I knew, before the safe was opened, that he is putting through a deal for a demon bomber. It's no longer a secret. He broadcast the fact when he sent for the police. Evidently your brother was bribed beyond his strength to resist. Money is useful and he has an extravagant wife."

Memory stabbed. Irene had demanded five hundred dollars. Ben had replied: "Can't give it to you, money's tight." She had gone to New York. Where had the money come from to finance the trip?

"Leave my sister-in-law out of his. What's your price for covering up Ben?"

"I don't like that word 'price.' "

"Don't be upstage. Call it—'condition,' then; it is a prettier word. How can I save Ben?"

"Get the stolen memoranda for me. I've been told they are

complete enough to serve as specifications for an aircraft technician."

"Why do *you* want them?" Gone was the urge to escape with which every nerve in her body had been twanging. What lay behind his demand? Had someone a hold on him? Was he being forced to get possession of the memoranda?

"I may be dazed from shock but I can't see how that would help. You are bound by law, aren't you, to give information about a crime you have witnessed?"

"Listen. I told you at the Mayflower that I was sure someone whom the Senator trusted was double-crossing him. Now I know it is your brother. I knew he was hiding something when his wife and I, unexpectedly to him, walked into his den. His confusion tied up with what I had seen not so long before in the Senator's study. He's probably waiting his chance to turn the memoranda over. Find them. Give them to me. I'll return them to the Senator. I want him to do something for me. If I produce his stolen property he'll do it."

"And if I don't?"

"I'll let the story of the theft break. Then watch your brother's business, his career, go up in the smoke of scandal."

She sprang to her feet. She couldn't sit there another moment. "I believe you're crazy. I haven't the slightest idea where to find the stuff unless I ask Ben."

"Ben! Do you think he would give it to you? You're smart enough to find it yourself. Well, is it a bargain?"

"Give me twenty-four hours in which to think it over."

"Promise you won't hint to anyone that you know who opened the safe?" He was cold, cruel, taut.

"I promise. Wayne, what has changed you? You seem so callous, so heartless. You were never like this before."

"No? There's a little of the villain in each one of us. Takes circumstances to germinate it. I never had a chance before to bargain with such big stakes. I've told you I want something from Joe Teele; I've got to have it."

"Are you a *spy?*"

"Now *you're* crazy. If I got hold of those memoranda and turned them over to interested parties, the Senator's enemies, I wouldn't be doing anything more dishonest than some of the statesmen, so called, who are working their heads off to get certain bills rushed through without inspection or debate. They trade, don't they? I'm doing the same thing. I don't want to turn them over to them. I'm trading your brother's reputation for—for my own security."

"How do you know so much about what these 'interested parties' want? That doesn't look too good to me."

"How can I help hearing gossip? The cloakrooms buzz with it. Now, understand this, just in case you're tempted to break that promise: the walls even in lawyers' offices have ears. If a whisper got on the air that Ben Jarvis had the working specifications of that superbomber, his life wouldn't be worth a nickel, not a nickel. I'll repeat, there are people who want them,—not all Americans,—who don't care what they do to get them."

"Then be careful yourself, Wayne. If someone discovers that you know where they are, perhaps your life won't be worth a nickel. Thoughts get on the air as well as whispers."

Et would be better eef you forget my visit, Mees Jarvees. Better for your brother, ees eet not? The words bubbled up from Faith's unconscious. Carrilski knew.

"Have you told anyone else of this?" she demanded.

"No. Do you think I'm fool enough to share a valuable beat like that?" His voice was convincing, but his eyes shifted.

"Beat" was a reporter's name for a scoop, she knew that. She knew also that Wayne was lying; he had told the Count. If he would lie about that, wasn't there a chance that he hadn't told the truth about Ben and the safe? That thought helped.

"My roadster's in the parking place. Wait at the steps until I come, Faith."

"No. I'm going alone. I want to think."

"Just as you say. I'll see you this evening. Remember, if you're tempted to break your promise, that silence spells safety for your brother and talk may put him on the spot."

She watched him stride away. With him went her affection for him. It was as if something warm and living had gone out of her life, leaving a space which echoed queerly with a voice that was gone for her for all time. She had liked him. He had been her friend.

She'd walk until she met a taxi. If she didn't find the stolen memoranda of the specifications and deliver them to Wayne Ben's career would be ruined, he had warned. That was his ultimatum. Suppose she did find them, turn them over to him, could she trust him? She could not. He had said that he had told no one but herself that he had seen Ben at the safe. But, Carrilski knew. She hurried on half running, half walking.

"Hey! Watch the traffic light! Want to be arrested for jay-walking?"

A hand pulled her back from the street into which she had

stepped. Aware of the rush of blood to her cheeks she struggled to say gaily:

"Hey, yourself, Duke! What brought you here?"

"Must have been divine providence which sent me in the nick of time to save you from being trundled off in an ambulance in nice, messy pieces—or to the hoosegow. Saw you leave the memorial, and trailed you. You're pretty fast on your feet. Don't you ever watch traffic lights or do you believe you bear a charmed life?"

She drew an unsteady breath of relief. He had ignored that scene at midnight.

"I was thinking—"

"Of what Marshall said to you last night at the entrance to the conservatory that turned your face paper-white?" The note of badinage had left his voice. "I heard you make this date with him. Thought I'd look into it. What's it all about?"

"Shame on you, prying into the secrets of a maiden's heart. You interrupted Wayne in the study, so he begged me to meet him in the wide, wide spaces where he could tell me that he loved—"

"Don't say it. It isn't good enough. He wasn't telling you in the study or on that path by the pool that he loved you, he was telling you something about the safe-opening at the Senator's, wasn't he?"

"Duke! How do you know? He made me promise—"

"So he made you promise? Was that why he returned at midnight to the conservatory? Your face gives you away. Here's a taxi. Hop in. Sorry I can't go with you. I'll be seeing you at the White House Reception tonight. Meanwhile, make up your mind to tell me about it. Ben and I won't stand for your having clandestine midnight meetings with any man, no matter how old or how worldly-wise you are. If you don't tell me, I'll go to Marshall. I know a way to make him talk."

"No! No! Duke, please. Wait—" He motioned to the driver. The cab started.

XVI

DUKE TREMAINE watched the departing taxi till it was lost in a welter of home-going traffic. Faith's startled plea echoed in his mind. Why was she afraid to have him question Marshall?

He had conquered the urge to go with her, to hold her slim, warm body close till her tense nerves relaxed. With head against his shoulder she might have confided the cause of her heartache. But, he had an important appointment at the Club. Darn it, he always had some compelling business on hand when he wanted to be with her.

He had flung that cryptic boast about Marshall on a crazy impulse. He knew no way to make him talk. He suspected plenty but he *knew* nothing. Apparently the Senator liked him. He didn't. Hadn't since the first day they had met in the Senator's office. He couldn't tell why. Would the reply to his letter of inquiry explain his aversion? It was due any day, now. Perhaps he didn't need that letter, perhaps if he could fathom the reason for that torn address he would have the explanation in his hand. Better for Faith to think he took the romantic interlude in the conservatory seriously. Hang it all, he did take it seriously. Perhaps she did love Marshall.

The Senator had phoned that he would meet him at the Club. Otherwise he would have taken Faith home. What a crisscross of actions and reactions their lives were at present. There were some threads he couldn't seem to work into the pattern. The half of the Jarvis address was one of them. That conclusion brought his thoughts up bang against the reception at the White House. Senator Teele was to dine with the Presidential party and had suggested that he escort Kitty later. A little concentrated devotion on his part to her, he and she had agreed on the plan last evening, would lay the ghost of gossip about her and Ben Jarvis. Her presence at the dinner and dance he was giving at Argyle House tomorrow, for Faith, ought to give it a decent burial.

What could Marshall have told Faith this afternoon? His mind picked up that thread again. It was so unlike her to be frightened. She had been such a valiant child and girl. Joyous in play, fearless in adventure, prodigal in affection. What did the man know that would bring fear to her eyes?

Could Ben explain it? He had had no chance to talk with him except about business since the night the safe had been mysteriously opened. There were times when he suspected that his partner was dodging a talk-fest. He would look him up later and sound him out. He had been frequenting the Club more and more at this hour, had been giving a convincing imitation of a man who hated to go home. He would have to be handled with gloves, nice, soft, plushy gloves. He was confoundedly edgy these days, as if all that was needed to blow to smithereens his rigidly maintained self-control was a spark of rage.

"Has Mr. Jarvis come in?" he asked the green-uniformed, brass-buttoned doorman at the Club.

"Yes, Mr. Tremaine. About ten minutes ago, sir. Senator Teele has been asking for you."

Long . . . Luxurious . . . Subdued in light and color, the Club lounge vibrated with tradition. As he passed, members looked up. Some smiled and nodded. One glowered. Others waved a hand in greeting. Gray heads. Bald heads. Singly. In groups. Muted voices. Sound of deep breathing from an armchair. The fire murmured as if aware that a snap, a crackle, would be a social blunder. In a secluded corner Senator Teele sat smoking.

"Got you S.O.S. sir, and here I am. What's on your mind?" Tremaine inquired. He wouldn't speak of the torn address, he decided. No use stirring up the Senator about it until he had worked out the puzzle himself.

"Didn't know but what you'd like to report on what went on in the conservatory after you left my study last night?"

The blood flew to Tremaine's temples.

"That—that was a little matter which concerns me, alone, Senator."

"I'm not so sure. Anything which goes on in my house concerns me in these days of double-crossing and personal betrayal."

"If I thought it menaced you in any way, I would tell you sir."

"You're right. I know you would. Sometimes I think you and Ben are the only persons in this city I can trust."

"How about your confidential secretary? You trust him, don't you?"

"Sure, Duke, *sure*. He's efficient. Very efficient." The Senator's praise was hearty.

"Perhaps this isn't relevant to the 'little matter' in the conservatory last night,"—Tremaine knew by the twinkle in his eyes that he was sure it was,—"but my chief reason for asking you to meet me here was to advise you that if it will help to tell Miss Jarvis that your announcement that Kitty is your girl was a chivalrous gesture to shield her brother, to save the gossips from tearing her to shreds and incidentally getting at me, go ahead and tell her—but no one else. Understand?"

"I understand, Senator."

"And by the way, you might let it be known that you're through in South America for the present. Business completed. All washed up. I think you've been watched. It's being done, you know. Perhaps sometime my opponents on the Hill will quit playing politics by fighting my demand for an increased counterespionage appropriation, and agree one hundred per cent to a co-ordinated attack on the anti-American propaganda menace. That isn't the only activity that needs watching. There's a little game called 'combatant secret service,' sabotage to you, which has been developed to the nth degree.

"Having got that warning off my chest and having been firmly and politely assured that the slight disturbance in the conservatory last night is none of my business, I'll move on." He chuckled as his jibe brought the color to Tremaine's face. As he walked through the lounge members sprang from their chairs to greet him; some tried to detain him but he shook his head and went on.

Tremaine's eyes followed him unseeingly, his mind busy with the statement that there would be no more South American flights for the present. Suited him. He wouldn't have to leave Faith. So, he had been watched. Was that why Marshall had asked Faith if he really had been there? He had, but he had made an important stop *en route*, which fact was supposed to be off the record.

"Mr. Jarvis has just gone to the pool, Mr. Tremaine," an attendant replied to his query.

In the locker room he changed to trunks. He found Ben sitting at the edge of the pool, one knee clasped in his hands, one foot dabbling in the water.

"Well, see who's here!" Jarvis exclaimed.

"Why shouldn't I be here? You haven't taken on the exclusive right to this pool, have you?"

"Don't be a nut. What are you trying to do, start something? A letter marked Important came to the office after you left this P.M. Sent it up to your room here. Tried to get you by phone at the Club after I left the Senator's last night. Decided we'd been a little highhanded with the kid. Where were you?"

"Joe Teele kept me late in his study. Seen Faith today? She and Kitty were to take a badminton lesson at my gamehouse, Johnny told me."

He introduced her name in the hope that Ben would say something which would give him a chance to inquire as to her men friends, if he suspected she were in love with one of them.

"Great exercise. Wish I had time to perfect my game. Speaking of Kitty, thanks for the life-belt you flung me when that pest-child of the Senator's broke loose the other night with her skit, 'Romance as seen in the front hall.' I kissed Kitty. I love her—but that's all there is to it, ever can be.

"Forget it. Quick. I was crazy to admit it. I know there has been more or less whispering about us. I took her to the Inn one night for dinner, but that was enough to set tongues wagging. The place was full of people we knew. She wanted to give a luncheon there and the Senator asked me to introduce her to Zeke and Sophy. Lord, I'm so fed-up with *people* and *problems*. This place is apt to be deserted at this hour. I thought I might be able to think things through here." Elbows on his knees, he rested his head in his hands.

"Anything I can do or say to help, Ben? If there isn't—"

"Sit down again. If anyone on God's earth could help it would be you, but I've got to work things out myself. What I need most is that course being offered by one of the Universities. 'Social Adjustment within the Family.' I hope the lifeguard act hasn't put you in Dutch with anyone."

"I can take it. Ben, have you any idea what's troubling Faith?"

"The kid? No. Didn't know she was troubled. You don't suppose she's still sore at you and me for the stern-parent act we staged about Marshall at the Teele supper, do you? We did give her a raw deal. I was upset by Irene's determination to rush off to New York and said more than I meant. After all, she's right. She is free, white and twenty-three, old enough to decide what she wants. If she's gone overboard for that fourflusher, Marshall—the possibility makes me sick. Oh, come on! Let's swim! See if we can't get these plots and counterplots, these confounded problems, out of our minds."

They dove. Floated. Crawled. Raced hand over hand. Swam under water. Glowing from exercise, dripping with coolness, mentally refreshed, they pulled themselves out and shook the moisture from eyes and hair. Ben Jarvis drew a long breath.

"That's the stuff! Got my values straightened out. Guess I'd gone a little haywire. What makes you think the kid is troubled, Duke?"

Tremaine told him. Told him of Faith's whitening face as Marshall had talked with her at the door of the conservatory,—omitting the midnight kiss,—of what he had seen at the Lincoln Memorial.

"And what conclusion has your legal mind deduced?"

"This isn't the moment for the light touch, Ben. It's a serious situation. I believe Marshall knows who has the missing bomber memoranda. I asked Faith if he had spoken of the safe-opening. She answered breathlessly: 'He made me promise—' and shut up like a clam."

"Good God!"

Ben Jarvis cleared his throat so loudly that Tremaine wondered if he had imagined the startled exclamation.

"Duke, you're crazy. How could he know—unless . . . You don't suppose he's a plain-clothes man doubling as a secretary for the Senator, do you? That's an idea. I wouldn't put it past Joe Teele, with his 'right hands' and 'left hands.' "

There was a note of repressed excitement in his voice. His color had heightened. He nervously brushed back the lock of wet hair dangling over his forehead. A suspicion that was four-fifths conviction flashed through Tremaine's mind. Ben knew something about that rifled safe he wasn't telling.

"Quite an idea, Benjamin. Good enough to be buried in a capsule for the use of a future generation. Too bad that at the time you worked out that brilliant solution you didn't remember that whatever it may be that Marshall knows or *thinks* he knows, the result is the same. He's making Faith infernally unhappy about something. If you can't or won't do anything about it, I will. That's that. . . . Now that Irene is away, come stag to my party for Faith tomorrow, will you? Three of my young-married neighbors are giving dinners before the dance. Some of the best steppers in town will be there. Think it over. Let me know in the morning so I can phone Johnny about the table. Good night."

He dove, swam the length of the pool. As he entered the locker room, quite empty of members, Ben Jarvis was at his heels.

"What's the matter with you, Duke, breaking away like that? You're prickly as a hedgehog. Sure, I'll come to the party. Just so she has feet and can dance, my partner may be the pig-face lady. I got to be gay! I just *got* to be gay." He tapped out a rhythm to the accompaniment of snapping fingers and grinned.

"Sick of being low in my mind. Playing round with the younger set will put pep into these old veins. I'll talk with Faith. I'm sure you've got an attack of heebe-jeebes about her. I passed her this morning on the way to school with the pest-child. When she smiled at me I thought, 'Nancy Carr's right. The kid glows.' "

"Going to the White House reception tonight?"

"Sorry, can't make it. Planning to work late in my den. Great chance with Irene away and the house quiet. I've given the maids twenty-four hours off. Amos and I, with 'a hey-nonny, ho-nonny,' will keep bachelor hall. So long."

Tremaine thoughtfully regarded him as he disappeared into an alcove and drew the hangings. He hadn't appeared

so lighthearted in months. Was he emerging from the shadow of Irene's temperament? Temperament! "Cussedness" was
the word for it.

Ben wasn't telling all he knew. Neither was he. He hadn't
told him that Faith had had a date at midnight in the conservatory or that the Count had dropped half of the Jarvis' home address from his pocket. Were he and Ben working along parallel lines? Well, if they were, sometimes parallel
lines brought up at the same terminal.

In his room he slit open the letter marked Important. An
answer to his query at last. His brows knit. Two statements
stood out on the white page as if typed in red:—

No family, titled or otherwise, named Carrilski in the
country in which the Count claims to have estates.

And:—

Marshall hit the high spots socially abroad. Country
houses. Cards. High stakes. Only half-American. His father
married a foreign opera-singer.

XVII

IN the marble foyer of the White House the Marine Band
in scarlet jackets was playing "As the Caissons Go Rolling
Along" with flair and zip. Duke Tremaine and Wayne Marshall were waiting as Faith in a frock of filmy yellow, bro-
caded with silver plumes, and Kitty Teele in pale blue,
mounted the stairs to the Central Corridor.

"Just in time," Marshall approved. "The Crowned Heads
haven't gone in yet."

"I should hope not. This is my first White House Reception and I'm all tingle, tingle. See those gigantic branches
of pussy willow! Makes one realize that spring is tiptoe-
ing up from the South, doesn't it?"

She caught his surprised look at her. Was he wondering if
she had forgotten so quickly his revelation of a few hours
ago, his proposal to trade silence about Ben's theft in return for the bomber specifications? All the way home his
assertion that he had not told the Count had kept flashing
in her mind like a crossroads traffic warning. The Count

knew. If Wayne had lied about that, he would lie about Ben, wouldn't he? The conclusion had helped clear away the fog of terror and unbelief in which she had lived after hearing his story. Had all this color and brilliance done its part in restoring her mental balance? Conversely, had the mist and dullness of the afternoon contributed its depression to her horrified conviction by the pool that he was telling the truth?

"I can't make you out," Wayne Marshall complained. "This afternoon you were—"

"Low in my mind? That was this afternoon. That's what makes me so nice, isn't it? Never the same. Contrasts. Sunshine and shadow. Gaiety and gloom. Always surprising. Never, never dull—hear me say it—that's Faith Jarvis. Now I'm on the crest of the wave. This is a red-letter evening. I am much more thrilled than when I was presented to the King in Rome. My heart is pounding like a trip hammer. Can't you hear it?"

"Was that the *tum-tum* I heard?" Duke Tremaine asked. "I thought it was a drum in the marble foyer. Don't overwork that heart of yours. It's too precious."

"Tremaine had better attend to his own girl and leave mine alone," Marshall growled.

"I'm not your girl."

"Look here, you're not going to let what I told you—"

"But you tell me so many things, Wayne," she interrupted sweetly. "Isn't that music grand?"

She didn't sense his muttered reply. She was wondering what Duke had meant by, "It's too precious." Her heart certainly wasn't "precious" to him. Did he really believe that she had stolen down to the conservatory last night to meet Wayne? Apparently he intended to ignore the incident. So much the better. She had determined before she left home to slam the door of her mind hard tonight against her love and her fear for Ben. There was some simple explanation of his presence in the Senator's study, there *must* be.

As they entered the Red Room the pageant of splendor and color switched her train of thought. Palms and great stone tubs of incredibly luxuriant ferns . . . Mantels banked with red carnations . . . Glamorously beautiful women who trailed exquisite frocks, blazed with jewels, glittered with sequins, radiated gaiety and alluring scents. Other women, not glamorous, not beautiful, simply dressed, were like a minor strain running through a scintillating symphony.

Men in the blue full dress of the Army, men in foreign uniforms, men in white ties and tails, with broad ribbons across their breasts and medals on their lapels, distinguished-looking men in evening dress with neither ribbon nor medals, men in tail coats of ancient vintage which smelt faintly of mothballs, walked and talked to the women.

The sudden fanfare of a bugle . . . Voices were hushed. Guests turned expectant faces toward the corridor. The orchestra swung into "Hail to the Chief." The White House Aides, two abreast, in their full dress lavishly adorned with gold braid, preceded the President and his wife, the members of the Cabinet and their wives, in the stately march to the reception rooms.

From that moment, Faith's impressions were a colorful blur floating on a perfumed sea of music. When she was presented she was aware of a deep voice repeating her name, of a woman beside the President in a brilliant green frock which sparkled; of immense gold eagles aloft in the cornices of the Blue Room; of low silver bowls of pink roses among the lavish array of sandwiches, cakes, confections on the long, candle-lighted table in the magnificently paneled state dining room; of the portrait of Washington over the mantel.

"Had anything to eat?" Duke Tremaine's voice roused her from her absorption in a world which had no sense of reality.

"I couldn't eat now. I'm feasting on the color and beauty and music. In Europe I used to read about these White House affairs, but the reports made them seem, well, stodgy is the word. This is excitingly beautiful."

"I told you you'd been too long abroad. Where's Marshall?"

"A man with a ribbon across his shirt-front spoke to him. Wayne said something about getting coffee for me and vanished. Perhaps he's caught in that mob about the table. The guests have descended on it like a swarm of locusts."

"Locusts is right. Come on, if you won't eat we'll join Kitty in the East Room. Don't wait for Marshall, he shouldn't have left you alone here. There are two receptions. The Presidential party and Joe Teele."

"Is the Senator so popular?" Faith asked as they edged their way through the crowd.

"Yes. He's going to town on his, 'Set our own house in order, give the people a sense of economic security before we dip into foreign affairs' drive. That has started a big writing and telegraphing campaign. Thousands of messages arrive daily. He's recognized as Presidential timber, that's why, to an extent, he's stealing the show tonight. His friends and enemies are trying to hop on the band wagon."

"President! What a great responsibility."

"That word 'great' is a masterpiece of understatement, lady. 'Terrific' fills the bill. Whoever is elected will inherit every mistake, every liability, every heart-breaking problem of his predecessor. But no man ever was known to refuse the task."

"And the honor. Being First Lady must be a thrilling occupation."

"Think you'd like it?"

"I'd love it."

"We'll have to see what we can do about it. Would you mind being a Senator's lady first? You have what it takes."

She looked quickly away from his laughing eyes.

"If you think such humble citizens as you and I can get near her, let's join Kitty."

"You haven't answered my question, but we'll lay it on the table for the present. Come on. Nancy Carr is with the Teeles. She'd be a natural for first lady. Pity she isn't younger so that the Senator could marry her."

"Men so rarely marry the woman they should," she answered bitterly as she visualized Irene.

"Snap out of it, Faith. Ben will ride the gale. Don't worry."

She thought, as she had thought the afternoon of her arrival, that he always had had an uncanny knowledge of what she was thinking—and told him so.

"That's E.S.P. Extra-Sensory Perception, to you. I'm one of those sixth-sense guys." He turned her confidence off lightly. "Look at our Senator. He's positively sparkling. Having the time of his life. Listen, and learn how to be a politician."

Faith listened and learned, learned a little of what was expected of a man in public life socially. Heard Senator Teele respond cordially to a barrage of salutations. "Hi, Joe!" "Meet the wife, Joe!" "Joe, this pal of mine's come all the way across country to see what you look like." "We're ready to give you anything you want, out there, Joe. What'll you have?" "A case of your Grade-A grapefruit, Scott," the Senator evaded deftly and the crowd around him laughed.

Nancy Carr's white hair was coiffed in the latest mode, her face reflected the glow of her velvet frock, clear, pure color, the red of a Cardinal's robe. Her dark eyes were brilliant as stars as she said:

"They're giving Joe an ovation. I wonder how many of these people will stick a knife into his bill tomorrow. Where's Ben, Duke?"

"I saw him at the Club, before dinner. Working at home tonight, he has an important case on tomorrow. He had given the servants twenty-four hours off. Said he and Amos would go very bachelor-hallish."

"He wasn't at home when I telephoned him. I want him to join us at supper at the Russian place. I've engaged a table. Kitty and the Senator are coming and of course you and Faith, Duke. I'm always hollow as a puff-ball mushroom after one of these affairs. I'll go ahead. Try to get hold of Ben, will you?"

"When did you phone, Nancy Carr?"

"Just before I came here. Don't look so apprehensive, Faith. He probably found he couldn't work at home and is burning the midnight watts at his office."

Faith didn't hear the last of the sentence. She was hearing Wayne Marshall's voice: "If a whisper got on the air that Ben Jarvis had the specifications of that demon bomber his life wouldn't be worth a nickel." Ben had told Duke that he would work at home, and he had not answered the telephone. Had a whisper got on the air? She must get to him. The threat of danger to her brother acted on her like a stimulant. She felt as if her mind had been sharpened to razor keenness.

"That supper party is nothing less than inspiration, Nancy Carr," she approved. "I adore that Russian place with the Cossack waiters speeding back and forth with *shashlik* flaming on the huge iron skewers. I'll get my wrap. If you see Wayne, tell him where I've gone, will you, Duke?"

"In case you see him, Duke, he is *not* included in the invitation," Madam Carr instructed sweetly. "That man is a flat note in my song of life."

Faith deliberately lost her in the crowd milling in front of the cloakroom. In her impatience it seemed hours before she slipped on her short white fox jacket. She left the house in the midst of a group of departing guests for fear Wayne or Duke would see her and stop her. From the East room drifted the music of "Anchors Aweigh!" The Marine Band was swinging it for dancing. The green and gold sunset had belied its promise. Snow was falling. The air was white with floating feathers.

She waited for a taxi to roll up. Gave her brother's address. As the cab started she thought she saw Duke step to the front of the waiting guests. Did he so possess her mind that she saw him everywhere? He couldn't have retrieved his coat so quickly. The sound of snow-shovels on sidewalks, the clang of iron, the scrape of wood accompanied her thoughts.

Where was Wayne? She hadn't seen him since he had left her in the dining room. How long could she keep him waiting for an answer to his proposal to trade his silence for the stolen memoranda? Of course she wouldn't turn them over to him were she to find them. Equally of course she wouldn't find them, but she must let him think she would try while she played for time to discover the truth. If she didn't discover it—Well, let him break the story. Who would take his word against Ben Jarvis' denial?

But, the Count knew. Where was he tonight? What had been his real errand in the conservatory? That broken cufflink had been a blind. The cab skidded to a stop. She had reached Ben's house and she had not decided what to say to him. She must have a squirrel-cage mind. It whirled round and round, never by any chance going forward to a solution of her problem.

She paid the driver and ran along the path which led to the door. Lucky the snow was light! She could feel the dampness through her yellow sandals. There was no response when she rang the bell. The windows were dark. No glow in the hall. Where was Amos? Had Ben decided to work in his office instead of at home? How silently the snow came down! She shivered. Drew herself up tensely. Shivering wouldn't get her anywhere. She would try the terrace door. One of the long windows of the living room might be unlatched.

She caught up her filmy yellow skirt and hurried to the back of the house, slipping on the snow, swallowing her heart at every crack of a twig. Idiot! What had she to fear? Nothing but the bogies of imagination. She tiptoed up the steps. Someone had mounted them before her. The glass door was swinging. What did it mean? Should she go in? . . . Why be a quitter?

She crossed the terrace and cautiously turned the knob of one of the French windows. It opened easily, too easily. She entered the dim room. Far ahead a shadow moved. Four shadows. Her heart stopped. She crept on. The shadows came nearer. She swallowed a hysterical ripple of laughter. She had been terrified by her own reflection in the mirrored screen!

She snapped on lights and the living room sprang into clear colors and glinting surfaces. Nothing had been disturbed. How still it was. It might be the palace of the Sleeping Beauty under a magic spell.

She touched a bell to summon Amos. Somewhere in the house a faint buzz sounded. No slow footsteps responded to the summons. She fought the fear which seized her like a black demon. Then in her mind sounded Duke Tremaine's voice:

" 'That youngster has the heart of a winner. She never asks herself 'Can I?' She says to herself 'I'm going to win.' "

Fortified by the memory, but with a horde of apprehensions clutching at her imagination, she stopped in the hall and cautiously unlatched the front door. (She might want to run.) The door of Ben's den was ajar. She touched it with reluctant fingers. It swung open as if slowly pulled from within. From the threshold she could see the whitened trees in the garden swaying like pale wraiths. The silence was weird. Uncanny. She shut her teeth hard into her lips. Snow crunching. On the front walk. On the steps! Who was it?

She groped for the electric light button. Pressed it. Lamps glowed. The room was in order. No cigarette ashes in the trays. Ben hadn't been here. Yes, he had: the top drawer of the desk was pulled out. Her racing thoughts jangled to a halt. Something sprawled by the hearth. Sprawled horribly . . . Nightmare? She closed her eyes. Opened them. She was awake. It was a man.

XVIII

IN topcoat, opera hat in hand, Duke Tremaine restlessly waited in the corridor. There had been a strain in Faith's voice when she accepted Nancy Carr's supper invitation which had set his suspicion-nerve atingle: a touch of blitheness which hadn't rung true as he remembered the whiteness of her face when she had heard that Ben had not answered the telephone. Was the man who had kissed her last night in the conservatory a part of the puzzle? Puzzle! Girls had been kissed before, hadn't they? Why be so sure that Faith hadn't welcomed that embrace? Hang it! That was what was getting him cockeyed. Perhaps she had.

"Where's Faith?" he asked as Madam Carr, swathed from neck to ankles in Russian sable, joined him.

"I thought she would be waiting with you. She left me to get her coat and I stopped to refuse an invitation to lunch after the Monday Musical. Had to explain that I was entertaining guests myself before the woman would take No for an answer. Perhaps she's on the portico looking for us."

"More likely she shot for Ben's." He reminded her of Faith's sudden pallor. "She's worried about him. If it's Marshall's Machiavellian touch, I'll break his neck."

"You'll have to catch him first. As I crossed the Corridor he strode past in that theatrical Inverness he affects which makes me think of the wings of a bat or his Satanic Majesty in person. Women fall for it. The fancy wrapper still sells the goods as it did in War time. Two men who looked like embassy attachés stopped him, he didn't appear too pleased to see them. Perhaps Faith resented my exclusion of her boy friend from the supper and slipped off with him."

"Then I'll slip after them. Kitty is busy with the glad-hand stuff among her brother's constituents, she and the Senator will come along together. I'll find Faith and bring her to supper, it may be nearer breakfast but we'll show up. Excuse me if I don't wait to escort you to your car? Every minute counts."

As he reached the portico he saw Faith step into a taxi. He raced and dodged after it. Lost it. Picked up a cab on the highway and gave Ben's address.

Trees sparkled as if sprinkled with star dust. Snow lay like fluffy blankets of down on lawns and roofs. He sat on the edge of the seat and scowled at the white ribbon of road striped with tire tracks winding ahead. Tried to relax. Lighted a cigarette. Why had Faith rushed away from the White House? He recalled every word of hers in the short time they had been together in the late afternoon. What had Marshall said to terrify her? Had he sent someone to the conservatory last night with a message? Would a messenger kiss her? Why had he left the reception without waiting for her? Who was the man who was pretendng to be a Count, to be the owner of ancestral acres which didn't exist? Was Wayne Marshall loyal to his father's country or to the country of his mother?

"Here you are, sir."

The driver's voice startled him from his absorbed attempt to solve the problem. He paid the man, started for the house. Stopped.

"Wait for me." If Faith were here they would go on to supper at once.

"Very good, sir."

The lighted windows patterned the snowy lawn with squares of gold leaf. High-heeled footprints dented the path. Faith had come here. She had found Ben, if not, why the illumination? He had pictured her in the grip of a foreign spy. Funny, what love did to a man's common sense. Made him get screwy ideas. Why should a spy want her?

When he had told her over the phone the night of her arrival at Ben's that she could marry him, he had meant it as he never had meant anything before in his life. She had laughed. Why not? She hadn't seen him for years. They had been together so few times since. Sometimes she was so coolly friendly that he wondered if she really liked him. Would she laugh tomorrow night at Argyle House when he showed her the contents of the silver box he had for her? There was the little matter of the kiss in the conservatory to be explained. She was too fastidious to permit that unless she cared deeply for a man.

He flung away the memory with his cigarette and ran up the steps. The front door was open. Apprehension tingled along his nerves. Something queer about it. A stifled shriek. In Ben's den?

"Faith! Amos! *Amos!*" he shouted as he charged through the hall.

No response. Silence. He could feel the hard thump of his heart as he reached the open door. He saw her braced against the desk. Staring. Eyes wide. Horrified.

"Faith! Faith!"

"Duke! It's you! It's *you!*"

She was in his arms. "Look! By the hearth!" She shuddered. "I saw it—only a minute ago—is it—Ben?"

He crushed her face aganst his breast and looked over her head.

"No. No, dearest. It's Amos."

"*Amos.* I thought—" She drew herself erect. "Quick! We must help him."

Together they bent above the butler. Tremaine rolled him over.

"He isn't dead. Stunned. Hit his head when he fell. Brandy. Hurry!" She ran from the room. He lifted one of the man's hands. Something was clenched in it. Something white. Gently he pried it free. He glanced at the open drawer of the desk before he thrust the torn paper into his pocket. Faith hurried in with decanter and glass.

"Here it is. Is the skin broken on his head?"

"No. A big bunch, that's all. He's coming out of it."
He held the glass to the man's lips. "Swallow this, Amos.
Make you feel fine."

Fright flashed in the butler's eyes like lightning through a
dense cloud.

"Thank you, Mistuh Duke, I don' need nothin' to drink."
He sat up. Dropped his grizzled head into his black hands.
"Seems if everything was a whirlin'."

"Who hit you, Amos?"

"If yo' all jest give me a hand, I'll git to my feet." Erect
he swayed and clutched the desk. "You don' have to hold
me, Mistuh Duke, I'se fine, now. Sorry, Miss Faith. You
look's white's if I'd scared you' mos' to death."

"I was frightened, Amos. I rang the bell. No one answered. I ran round to the terrace. Saw footprints on the
steps. Found a window unlatched. Came in that way and
then—then saw you."

"Them footprints were me, Miss Faith. I answered the
phone. 'Twas Mistuh Ben telling me he wouldn't be home
till late—then I went out on the terrace an' down the steps
to see if they needed sweepin' off—Mus' a left the winda
unlatched w'en I come in—an'—"

"Who hit you, Amos? Who opened the desk drawer?"
Duke interrupted the wandering, hesitant explanation. Making due allowance for the daze resulting from the nasty
crack on the man's head he was convinced he was lying.
Why?

"I didn't see the drawer wus open. No one hits me as
I knows of, Mistuh Duke. Hones' to Gawd, it was a
dizzy spell. I'se been havin' 'em quite frequently lately.
Mistuh Ben's said as how I oughter see a doctor, yassuh."
He glanced furtively at the hearthrug, at the floor near the
desk.

"What are you looking for?"

"Nothin' 'portant. Someone come to de do' just aftah
I answered de phone an' lef' a note for Mistuh Ben. I come
in here to put it on de desk an' I swear to goodness dat's
de las' I knowed till I looked up an' sees yo' an' Missy
Faith abendin' over me. If yo' don' need me, Mistuh Duke,
I'll go up an' git into mah bed. Mah haid sure am agoin'
roun' an' roun'."

"I'll go with you." Duke steadied the man by an arm
across his shoulders.

"Try for Ben at his office, Faith. Tell him we'll stop and
take him along to Nancy Carr's supper. Amos will be okay

as soon as he gets into bed. I'll phone the doctor to drop in and look him over. Come on, boy, Easy does it."

Faith watched them pass into the hall, heard them stumbling up the stairs. Duke must be half lifting, half dragging Amos. She sank into a chair before the telephone. Now that the excitement was over she felt limp as a—as a limpet. She didn't know what a limpet was but it sounded the way she felt.

She dialed. Heard the bell in Ben's office. No answer. Tried again. The insistent ringing had a lonesome sound. Was the room empty? Ben had phoned Amos that he would work in his office? Where was he? She cradled the instrument as Tremaine entered.

"Ben doesn't answer."

"That's nothing to be frightened about. Maybe he couldn't concentrate, maybe he felt fagged and decided to take in a show. I've done that loads of times and have returned to work feeling wacky and gay and confident that I could twist the world round my finger. I could let loose a swarm of maybes without a sting among 'em. Have you kept on that fox jacket all the time you've been in the house? You'll freeze when you go out."

"How about your topcoat? Things have happened too fast since we came into this room to consider clothes."

"Right, but now that there's a lull in the excitement we'll think of them. Your sandals are soaked. Run up and borrow a pair of Irene's. Then we'll beat it."

"If we go, Amos will be alone in the house."

"He's all right. Doesn't want a doctor. Said he'd had 'spells' like this before. Scram. I promised Nancy Carr that come hell or high water I'd bring you to supper."

He waited until she had reached the upper hall before he looked into the open drawer of the desk. The few papers had been rumpled. He examined the scrap he had found in the clenched black hand. It was a torn page from a note-book, mate to the piece Carrilski had pulled from his pocket while at supper in the conservatory, the piece he, himself, had surreptitiously picked up. It completed the Jarvis house address. Marshall had given Carrilski one half and here was the other. Was this the "note" for Ben which had been given Amos at the door? Was his story of his "spells" on the level or had he been knocked down by someone he knew, the same someone who was faking a title and claiming to be hereditary owner of mythical estates? Footsteps in the hall. He thrust the paper into his pocket.

"What the dickens are you doing here, Duke? Thought you were at the White House."

Ben's voice. Ben on the threshold. A mighty tide of relief swept through him. He hadn't realized until this minute that he had feared for his best friend's safety.

"Well, see who's here!" He cleared his voice of gruffness and tried again for the light touch. "If it isn't Benjamin large as life and twice as handsome. Faith and I've done everything but set the G-men on your trail. Nancy Carr wants you to join her at supper at the Russian place. For Pete's sake, when you tell me you're going to work at home why don't you work at home?"

"Sez you. Couldn't settle down. Dropped in at a show. So what?"

Ben's jibe set the world right-side-up again. If Marshall really had anything on him serious enough to terrify Faith he couldn't grin like that, could he?

The sound of running feet on the stairs. The silken swish of a skirt. Faith tucking her hand under her brother's arm.

"Ben! Ben, where were you? We've been trying to reach you. Amos had one of his 'spells'."

"Amos! Spells! What are you talking about, kid? Does she mean he's drunk, Duke? Can't be. The boy never touches liquor."

Tremaine told him what she meant.

"Spells! Doctor! Heart's a little tricky, but I hadn't heard of these spells. Never told him to see a doctor. I'll go up and take a look at him."

In an unbelievably short time they heard Ben running down the stairs.

"He's gone!" he reported breathlessly.

XIX

FROM the garage Duke Tremaine crunched across crisp snow to the Georgian Colonial house with its spreading wings which had been the home of his family for generations, in which George Washington had been a guest. Gorgeous night for Faith's party. Moonlight picked out the bricks in the red walls, gilded the white blinds and doors, threw shadows of towering frosted trees on the slate roof.

Frozen branches rang a soft chime of welcome. Every window was a blaze of light. There were cars at the side door. That meant that the Club chef had arrived and was on the job. Filipino José, who usually did the cooking, was good, but he was needed in the dining room.

Johnny, the houseboy, flung open the front door. His grin revealed teeth as white as his immaculate jacket. He snapped his middle finger and thumb incessantly.

"Heard you drive in, boss. It sure is a swell night for our party." The boy took his coat and hat.

"Couldn't be better. Everything under control, Johnny?"

"Everything goin' fine, boss. Chef, he come. Flowers, she come wif a man to fix 'em, an' music, he phoned he'd be long time you said; Sophy, she sent maid to help wif ladies' wraps."

"Did you find the seating-chart and placecards I left in my workroom?"

"Sure, boss. They all fixed fine an' dandy. Soup an' fish, all ready in your bedroom."

"Where'd you get that soup and fish stuff, Johnny?"

"You laugh easy tonight, boss. I guess you happy. We learn soup an' fish at night school. Teacher say, José and me comin' along fine in Eenglis'."

"I'll say you are. I'll be down in time to put the flowers at each place."

He took the stairs in triplets. Faith was coming! The thought had run through his mind like a joyous refrain during a day which had been packed with conferences, between which he and Ben had squeezed in efforts to track Amos. The butler's disappearance following so close to the "spell" didn't look too good. Ben had gone white when he had looked at the open desk drawer but had made no comment. Did he suspect Amos of treachery? He hadn't told him about the torn address. Was it connected with the yarn with which Marshall had terrified Faith? Who was the man who had kissed her in the Teele conservatory? He would get at the truth of that before she left the house tonight.

Why think of it now? She was safe. She was coming. He had phoned her before he left the office. Had told her he had a silver box for her, a very special silver box. He was on the top of the world. Whistling exuberantly, he entered his book-walled workroom. The tune broke on a high note.

"Greetings, Duke," Irene Jarvis welcomed jauntily.

Her hair gleamed like red gold against the back of the tan leather chair in which she was slumped with her knees nonchalantly crossed. Her black frock accentuated the

dead whiteness of her face. Her mocking eyes shone like
emeralds, her vivid lips were a scarlet slit. A short beaver
coat was thrown over a chair. A hat topped it. Looked
as if she'd settled down for the evening.

"Thought you were doing the Big City, Irene. What's the
idea? Did Johnny let you in?"

"Don't bite, Duke. Neither Filipino boy knows I'm here.
I parked my roadster with the cars at the back of the house
and under cover of chatter in the kitchen slipped in the side
door and upstairs. I ought to be able to slip into Argyle
House. I did it times enough when I was young."

"You're not young now. Why did you come?"

She sprang to her feet.

"Because I need your help. I knew this was the night of
Faith's party, knew I'd find you here."

"You came to *me* for help?"

"Don't be nasty, Duke. To whom else could I go? You're
the oldest friend I have. You've *got* to help me." The last
words were a whisper. Her face had been white before. Now
it was ghastly.

"Help you? How? What have you done? Come clean,
Irene."

"Close the door."

Was this a blackmailing scheme? If he closed that door
would she scream and bring the servants on the run? He remembered Nancy Carr's warning: "Look out for Irene. She'll
stop at nothing to break you with the girl you love." Was
she planning to stage a scene before Faith's party or was she
after money? It sounded like the wildest melodrama, but
after finding Amos knocked out last evening could he
doubt that the city was reeking with it?

"You'll say what you have to say with the door wide
open. Sit down. We won't be overheard. The Filipino boys
are busy."

Seated on the edge of the deep chair she clenched her
hands in her lap. She tried twice to speak, the words died
on her lips.

"Go on. Give!" he prodded. "I have guests coming." He
thought the contraction of her white throat would choke
her.

"Duke! Duke! You've got to help me."

"That has been said before. Why?"

"I'm—I'm married."

Good lord, had her tempests of anger finally resulted in
insanity? He had heard that it sometimes happened.

"That's a news-flash! You're telling me. Wasn't I best

man at your wedding?" How could he speak so flippantly when he felt a chilly premonition of disaster?

"Don't laugh, Duke. I mean—I mean I was married abroad. I thought the man died. He didn't. What shall I do?"

If this were true she wasn't Ben's wife. Ben would be free. *Free!* His exuberance took a nose-dive. It wasn't so simple as that. There would be shame and scandal and searing front-page publicity.

"How long have you known that the man is alive?"

"Don't be such an iceberg! Can't you see I'm mad with anxiety? If the truth comes out my life, my social career, will be ruined."

"How about Ben's life? His career?"

"You would think of him. I believe you're glad, *glad* this has happened to free him. I presume you are thanking your lucky stars you didn't marry me."

"I never considered marrying you. Keep your voice down, unless you want this stuff broadcast by the servants." He glanced at his wrist watch. "I'll give you ten minutes, not a second more. I will help you if possible, because you're my best friend's wife. I shall think you are his wife until I've dug up proof that you're not. Quick. What happened?"

White-knuckled hands clenched on her lap, in a low, unsteady voice she told of a secret marriage in Paris five years before to a man she had known but a month, Eric Stratton. She had been madly in love with him. There had been a short honeymoon in Switzerland, after which they had gone to London where he was liaison man for an important industrial concern; that was why he had been in Paris. They had lived in separate apartments because the firm wouldn't employ a married man in his position. He had promised that as soon as he moved up to the stay-at-home job he was working toward, they would announce the marriage.

"Not like you to be taken in by such a phony yarn, Irene."

"I told you, Duke, I was mad about him. He was sent to Africa. Three months later I received a letter from there on the firm paper announcing his sudden death. Enclosed was a news clipping confirming it."

"Didn't you follow it up to make sure it was true?"

"I didn't dare tell anyone about it. I was glad I was free. The secrecy had killed my infatuation for him,—that was what it was,—had humiliated me beyond words. I, whose family for a hundred years and more had been at the top socially, had been living a double life like a cheap woman."

"How did you hear he was alive?"

"The—the Count. He was a witness at the ceremony in

Paris. Eric had run across him that day. He had known him in Africa."

Carrilski! Had he told Marshall? Had Marshall in his turn told Faith? Was this what was worrying her? Not the safe-breaking at the Senator's? He said as calmly as he could with that possibility whirling in his mind:—

"If you were so sure your husband was dead, why did you deliberately upset that kettle when the Count appeared on your terrace? Why be frightened?"

"You saw that? You would. Sees all, knows all Tremaine. For an instant I was terrified for fear the man would exclaim, 'Mrs. Stratton!' I upset the kettle to give us both time to think. I had not told Ben of the secret marriage. I didn't want him to know. It was past, done with. He loved me; and believe it or not, I wanted to keep that love, it was the finest thing that had come into my life."

"Has Carrilski been blackmailing you?"

"No. He—he—well, he just promised not to say anything about it."

"What price did you pay for that promise?"

"N-nothing. No price. I've been almost crazy with uncertainty. I asked Ben for five hundred dollars, felt I must get away; he said he hadn't it. I tried Nancy Carr. She refused unless I explained why I wanted to go. I went. Pawned the pearls in New York that she gave to me for a wedding present. I couldn't stay in the house with Ben, knowing I was not his wife, could I? I had to get away to think things over."

She had paid something for Carrilski's silence. He knew by her hesitation. What?

"I don't know how you could have lived with him for a minute after you heard this. Have you thought that the man you married in Paris may have died as you were first informed? That this *Count* Carrilski may have cooked up the yarn for the sole purpose of getting a hold on you?"

She was on her feet.

"Duke! Duke! Could it be possible?" The light went out of her face. "No. He has told the truth. I know it. He had a letter of introduction to me from a man I had met at one of the embassies abroad, but he was stunned with surprise when Marshall brought him to the house and he saw me. He has shown me letters Eric had written him, after the date of the announcement I received of his death. In one he wrote that he had decided to stay in Africa, that he was breaking all ties with England, that I—*I* had died. I knew his writing to the last loop of a *g*. It was from Eric Stratton without a doubt."

A clock chimed. Tremaine pulled a notebook from his pocket.

"Quick. Give me Stratton's full name and the address of his firm when you married him. Have you the letter telling of his death?" She nodded and drew an envelope from her bag.

"Give it to me. Go back to New York. No, you musn't do that tonight. Home won't do either. Go directly to the Inn from here. I'll phone Sophy. Stay there *incommunicado* till you hear from me. I will talk with my London correspondent tonight after the party. He'll ferret out the truth. I'll get in touch with you as soon as he reports. It ought not to take long; there must be records. Go. Quick. Before you are seen here. Step on it. If Carrilski tries to get in touch with you—phone me and—"

"Hey, Duke!" It was Ben; Ben, sending his voice ahead as he charged up the stairs. "Here I am all dressed up and somewhere to go. I've quit worrying, I'm on the crest of —*Irene!*"

Dark color surged to his hair, drained away leaving him white. The incredulity of his eyes as he looked at his wife flamed to fury as he turned to Duke Tremaine.

"So this is where she's been, you—you doublecrosser! New York! Like fun she's been there! So this is what your fighting like cats and dogs has meant, a cover up for a love affair! You—"

"Hold everything! You're crazy, Ben."

"Crazy! *Crazy!* Sure I'm crazy, crazy enough to give you the licking of your life." He flung off his coat, "Come on, my *friend.*"

"Telephone for you, Mr. Jarvis." It was Johnny's soft voice, Johnny on the threshold snapping his fingers nervously. "Take it here? Man said tell you it was Amos. He mus' talk to you, quick, *very* quick."

"Amos!" The name penetrated Ben Jarvis' fury. He seized the phone. Tremaine caught up Irene's hat and coat and drew her forcibly to the hall. Before he closed the door he heard Ben's voice:—

"What happened, Amos?"

"Duke! Duke, what shall I do?" Irene whispered. "I'm sorry. I was a coward. I—I didn't know what to say. I hid behind you. I—I love him, really I love him. Would it help to tell him now?"

There was a tone in her voice he never had heard before.

Had the shock of Carrilski's news penetrated even her self-ishness?

"No. Why torture him till we're sure? I can take it. He'd just about reached the limit of endurance when he barged in on us. It needed only a spark to set him ablaze. Get out of the house as secretly as you came in. Stay at the Inn until you hear from me. Get going. Make it snappy."

He waited till he heard the side door close. Listened. Ben was still on the telephone. He would run down and take a look at the table. By the time he returned to dress Ben would have cooled off, would have realized that his suspicion had been wildly improbable. Irene married! Stratton and she must have have been two of a kind. Nothing would cut a diamond but another diamond. He must have been as hard as she. What price had she paid for Carrilski's silence? The answer to that question might be the clue to the safe-robbing and Amos' assailant.

In the dining room the flames of wax tapers, in the cut-crystal chandelier dripping with prisms and dangles, were reflected a dozen times in the gold-framed mirrored plaque which held a mass of yellow freesias and the feathery softness of buddleia; picked out the delicate pattern of the lace cloth and daintily touched the purple bloom of the great bunches of Hamburg grapes in graceful gold comports, flickered on the gilt braid of the uniform in the portrait of a long-gone Tremaine above the mantel.

"Here the flowers for the ladies an' gents, boss." Johnny's voice broke his tense absorption. "You look worry? Anything you don' like 'bout table, boss?"

"Stop snapping your fingers, Johnny, or you'll have me cockeyed. Everything's fine!" He laid a spray of pale green and white orchids that smelled like honeysuckle and gardenias at the plate on the right of his at one end of the table. "Place the other flowers. You know how. Orchids for the ladies. Carnations for the men. . . . Hear a car, Johnny?"

"Sure, one just goin' out. Come from back door. I go see who come an' gone?"

"Never mind. Attend to the flowers. I'm going to the kitchen to speak to the chef, then I'll dress."

Later as he mounted the stairs amazement at Ben's outrageous suspicion flamed into rage. How dared he accuse him of carrying on an affair with Irene? Irene, of all the women in the world! He'd tell him a thing or two. Reason laid a restraining touch on his blazing anger. He and Ben never had really quarreled during years and years of friendship. The furious outburst had been the explosion which was bound to result from repressed, hurt unbelief and rigidly controlled anger as the nature of the girl he had loved and married became apparent.

Married! If Carrilski's story were true he wasn't married to her. If only he could be told that now. No. The Count's statement must be verified first. Lucky there was no child. Ben had been so eager for a son.

He felt as if he were marching up to a firing line as he crossed the corridor. He braced himself and turned the handle of the door. Opened it. The room was empty. Ben had gone.

"That's a break," he said aloud. "Now for Sophy."

He gave the black woman directions over the telephone. "Glory, Mistuh Duke! You sen' dat Irene chile here? W'at I do—"

"Do as I told you." He smacked down the receiver in the middle of another "Glory." Thank the Lord, Ben had had the sense to beat it before Faith's party.

Faith's party . . . This was the night he had planned to explain to her about Kitty Teele, to tell her he loved her, to ask her to marry him. After that it would have been a simple matter to find out what Marshall had told her by the pool. Had it been the story of Irene's secret marriage? Where did the man in the conservatory fit into the scenario?

He couldn't tell her tonight. Not with his mind full of Irene's deceit and Ben's furious anger. It would be like dragging his love through shambles. What price had Irene paid for Carrilski's silence? He might have believed her denial if the "N-nothing" had not been breathless. She *had* paid. *What?*

Dressed, except for his tail coat, he opened a heart-shaped silver box. A large emerald-cut diamond in its white velvet nest shot out sparks of iridescence. When he gave that ring to Faith he didn't intend to be hurried, and tonight as soon as the guests left he would burn up the road to his office and put in a call for London. With the difference in time between the two cities he would be able to contact his man. Business, Ben's this time, *vs.* love again—and business won out.

"Come in," he locked the box in a drawer as the door opened. "What is it, Johnny?"

The houseboy's mouth stretched in an excited grin.

"The peoples are coming."

"All right. Did—you—did you see anything of Mr. Jarvis?"

Under cover of settling his white tie he watched the boy's

face in the mirror. How much had he heard of that blow-up in the workroom?

"Gosh, I near forgot. Mr. Jarvis he come down while you talkin' to chef, he say he mus' leave for office p.d.q. I don' know that Eenglish word. Not in schoolbook. He say tell you he ver' sorry to miss party, but he mus' go to office. He say 'office' hard second time. Then he say, '*Sure* you tell him this, *too*: "I'm sorry. I did go crazy." ' Did he go crazy, boss?" The boy's eyes were black pools of fright. His fingers snapped like castanets.

The world came right-side-up for Duke Tremaine. Ben was "sorry."

"Johnny," he said. "We all go crazy from pain some time or other. . . . I hear another car. The party's on!"

XX

DUKE TREMAINE joined in the laughter and badinage, played to the hilt his role of host at the dinnertable. In the ballroom of the game-house—done in Chinese lacquer, gilt, black and red,—he danced and cut-in to the music of winds and strings and horns swinging the latest song-hits; declared to his partners that he was completely sold on short curls and the long-sleeved dinner frocks they were wearing, all to the accompaniment of an aching memory of Ben's unjust accusation and a smarting anger at Irene for her deception.

Ben had sent word by Johnny, that he was sorry, that he had gone "crazy," had told him to relay the information that he was going to his office, the second time "hard"—which, translated from the houseboy's lingo, meant that the word had been emphasized. Had it been a tip for him to follow as soon as he was free? He had planned to speed to his office and phone his London correspondent the moment the last guest departed. That would fit in with Ben's hint, if it had been a hint. Something evil was in the wind. Were Marshall and Carrilski involved? What price had Irene paid for the "Count's" silence about her marriage to the man Stratton? Did she know that he was faking the title and estates? Nancy Carr's words suddenly echoed through his mind. "To get himself and his friend the Count into the Army and Navy set, especially the aeronautic branch." Was that the answer?

Had he forced her to secure information for him? Information as to Senator Teele's air-research activities? Irene and her marriage in Paris . . . Amos' disappearance and his sudden return from the port of missing men . . . The torn address . . . The memoranda of specifications stolen from the safe . . . Were they tied together? Did Carrilski hold the end of the thread which would unravel them? Had it been he in the conservatory the night of the supper, looking for the paper he had pulled from his pocket? Had he kissed Faith?

"Thinking up an argument to hurl at a jury, Duke? If you're not careful you'll step on my pet sandals. It would be a crime, they're such snappy numbers. Silver braid all twinkle, twinkle with rhinestones. Watch your step or you'll lose the reputation of being the best dancer in the District of Columbia and points west and south."

It was Faith's voice with laughter and a hint of unsteadiness. She was in his arms and his mind had been seething with thoughts of Ben and Irene and a probable web of intrigue. Which fact only went to prove the wisdom of his decision that this was not the time to ask the girl he loved to marry him.

"Boy, what a reputation to live up to! We were moving in such perfect rhythm that for a minute I forgot where I was. Born to dance together, weren't we?"

"We—Where's Ben? When you phoned this afternoon you said he was coming stag. Each time the door opened I thought it must be he. Why isn't he here? I haven't had a chance to ask before."

"Steady. You're breathless. He's okay. Arrived just before dinner looking like a million and announced that he was all set for a good time, that he'd slapped down ol' black debil Worry for the night, when along comes"—he had almost said "Irene"—"Amos, and his high spirits collapsed like a pricked balloon."

"Amos! In person? Did he explain why he staged the disappearing-act last night?"

"That 'along comes' was a figure of speech. He didn't come, he phoned. I don't know what he said. I had to dress. Ben did a fadeout. Left a message that he had gone to his office."

"To his office! Something about that sets merry-pranks jitterbugging down my spine. Are you sure it was Amos calling?"

"I heard him say, 'What happened, Amos?' "

He answered her whisper as if he hadn't asked himself the same question a dozen times, hadn't thought of the torn address, hadn't visualized the sprawled figure on the hearth in Ben's den, hadn't been tense with impatience for this party to be over, finished, that he might follow Ben. Faith's party, on which he had lavished so much tender thought, which he had hoped might end with his ring on her finger . . .

"Must have been Amos." He was reassuring himself as well as her. "Ben couldn't be fooled. He learned every tone of that black man's voice during the days he was on trial for murder. Murder! How did we get switched to that gruesome subject? 'Pause for station announcement.' Now, let's talk about your party. Like it?"

"Love it. The dinner was delicious. This music is enchanting. Dated as it is, there never will be anything more perfect to dance to than 'Night and Day.' Sorry Kitty isn't here. When I told her you had phoned that Ben was coming she was seized with a violent headache. Her absence must have scooped the icing from your cake."

His arm around her tightened.

"I still have the cake. Never was crazy about icing. Why don't all girls with dark hair and eyes and perfect skin, like yours wear a frock of silver tissue which looks as if it had been spun of frost?"

"Maybe it's because they haven't a mother who, having cut off their allowance, sends them clothes from gay Paree to dope an uneasy conscience. Does that answer your question?"

"It does. I love your voice with a laugh in it. How did you get here? I thought you and Ben would come together. Didn't drive yourself, did you?"

"No. I arrived in Senatorial state in the large car. Storker, the chauffeur, is to wait and take me back."

He resisted the temptation to tell her he would dismiss the man and drive her home. It wouldn't do. He must reach his office as soon as possible. He couldn't rid his mind of the uneasy hunch that complications were lurking just around the corner that would tax his intelligence and initiative to the limit. What price had Irene paid? That darn question again. Faith freed herself from his arms.

"Didn't you hear that last long-drawn note of 'Good night, ladies,' Duke? Time you were in the hall speeding the parting guests. Thanks for these exquisite orchids, for—for everything. It has been a perfect party."

"Faith!" He caught her hands hard and as quickly released

them. He cleared his husky voice. "Plenty more parties where this came from. A whole lot more. Don't forget that, my dear. Good night."

The vision of her lovely upturned face was between him and his guests as they took their leave. His thoughts dwelt on her sweetness and gay charm as he changed to business clothes. He started for the door, returned and took from the pocket of his evening coat the torn paper he had pried out of Amos' clenched hand. The half he had picked up in the conservatory was in his office safe. This should be with it.

As he drove carefully but with mounting speed toward the city, Faith's low-pitched voice with the lilt in it—like splinters of sunshine—went with him to the accompaniment of the musical *klish-klish* of frosted twigs and the grating of tires on rough roads. She must have reached home by this time.

Headlights flashed dazzlingly on trees which were shedding their white coating,—the temperature was rising, there would be no snow in the morning,—gilded brick walls of historic houses; illumined the turgid current of a stream; etched the arch of a bridge in gold against the purple canopy of sky; glazed the black ribbon of the city highway.

As he locked the roadster in front of the office building he looked up. No light in Ben's windows. Had he gone home? He must have been here recently, as the outer door of the building was unlocked. Ben might have left a note on his desk. He'd look for it later. His first job was to get in touch with the London correspondent. That was Ben's business if ever anything was. Irene had brokenly protested tonight that she loved him. If she did, she had a queer way of showing it. If the man she had married in Paris were alive, good old Ben would be free. Would he? Irene could secretly procure a divorce from Stratton in Reno or some other accommodating place and go through another ceremony with him, couldn't she?

She rated all the scandal and suffering and headlining that would be handed her when the story broke. She had deceived Ben. Trouble was, old Ben would have to take the rap with her. Well, at least he would be free of a woman who had hurt him, humiliated him, disillusioned him. He wouldn't have to remarry her. In short, he would have another chance at happiness, he could marry Kitty Teele.

He reached that satisfying conclusion and the third floor at the same time, breathless from his sprint up the stairs. He disciplined a kid urge to shake a threatening fist at the name Carrilski on the door before he reached Ben's. No light showed through the ground glass there. He must have gone.

He put in the call for London. From the names and addresses Irene had given him made careful notes of what he wanted to say. Was she Mrs. Eric Stratton or Mrs. Ben Jarvis? Suppose his correspondent couldn't find out? He must. If he failed Duke would go to London himself, to Africa if necessary, until he dug up the truth. He wouldn't leave the sword of Damocles dangling over Ben's head even if Ben was unaware that it was there.

He passed through the outer office into his partner's and flooded the room with light. In perfect order. A note lay in the middle of the green blotter on the desk like a white boat in the midst of a calm malachite sea.

Duke [he read]:
If you were wise to what I didn't say in the message I sent by Johnny, you'll follow me here. Amos hasn't showed up. Something queer in the wind. It's 11:30. I'm going home. Come along. I must tell you I'm sorry I blew up.
Of *course* I don't believe it.

                                                                    B.

Thank God that was cleared-up! The note had been written three hours ago. He'd have to wait till daylight to see Ben. He snapped out the light. Was that a sound in the dark room behind him? He lingered on the threshold. Must have been something in the street. He shut the door.

How time dragged. Probably the man he was trying to contact wasn't in his office. He compared the wall clock with his wrist watch. Alike to the minute. He paced the floor. Queer how unfamiliar the place seemed at this time of night. Darned lonesome. His desk chair creaked as if someone were rising from it.

This was his chance to compare the torn slips of paper. He opened the safe. Laid the piece he had found in the conservatory beside the one Amos had clutched. They fitted, letter to black letter. Why had Marshall given Carrilski an address he already knew? He frowned at the papers on the green blotter.

A ring! At last! He seized the phone. A tense moment of question and answer before he heard his correspondent's voice coming from across the sea.

He gave instructions. Spelled out names. Heard Big Ben sonorously tell the hour and for a magic instant was transported to London, sat again in the musty Law Courts and heard the boom of the great clock outside. He impatiently shook off memory.

"Don't leave a stone unturned to find the record of Eric Stratton's death and be quick about it. Spare no expense. Cable both my office and Argyle House an hour before you phone. The message will be relayed to me and I won't miss the call. Send documented proof by air. Duplicate by ship, understand?"

"Yes."

"Speed, man, *speed!* Good-by."

"Good-by." The voice which had been so clear had a faraway sound. It lingered in the still room like a ghostly presence.

He shook off the spell and looked at the papers fitted together so neatly on his desk. What did they mean? Whatever they signified, the safe was the place for them.

As he shrugged into his coat he had the feeling that there was something more he should do, as if some thought were trying to take form. He had spoken lightly to Faith of a sixth sense. Sometimes he thought he had it. A psychology expert would doubtless explain his present uneasiness as vibrations pouring into his intelligence, as some mind trying to reach his. It wasn't Ben. He was at home. Must be a case of jitters, resulting from his hectic anxiety for Ben's safety and his disappointment that his ring wasn't on Faith's finger.

As he closed his door Carrilski stepped from his office, looked cautiously up and down the hall, stood motionless for an instant as he saw him. He squared his shoulders and smiled.

"Oh, Meester Tremaine, you work late, too? I came here only a moment ago to prepare mail for the early morning post. My friends in the city are so hospitable that I have to work een the early morning," he explained with easy urbanity.

Duke's eyes met his, smiling but secretive. If the Count had arrived only a moment ago, why did he act as if he were vibrating with impatience to make his getaway? The statement about his work and his appearance didn't hang together.

If getting off mail made him look like something the cat brought in, heaven help him if he ever went on a bat! His face was white, his deep-set eyes looked as if they had been rubbed in with a dirty finger, his open topcoat revealed a crumpled shirt-front, there was an angry bruise on one hand.

"You are looking at my hand, yes? That—what you call the 'cord' broke and let the window down on eet."

"Too bad, Count. I'll bet it aches like the dickens. Good night. I'm in a hurry."

"You feenish your work as I begeen mine. Good night—eet ees good morning, ees eet not?" He entered his office. A key clicked.

Tremaine regarded the closed door with speculative eyes. What was Carrilski's business that he had to work at this time of night, or rather morning? Perhaps he was wondering at this moment what business took a man named Tremaine to his office at this unholy hour. . . . Too late to go to Ben's. He'd go to the Club and turn in.

Curious that Carrilski should have been at the office building, he thought again, as he snapped on the light in his room. Why was he there? What price had Irene paid for his silence? The question would continue to bob up like a jack-in-the-box till he found out. He would take that up next. The six days he had been back in Washington had been devoted to picking up the affairs of impatient clients. Only six days! Incredible. So much had happened in that time that it seemed six years since he and Faith had dined at the Inn.

Was the Count preparing mail at this minute or had the explanation been a blind? Perhaps he had been in a fight and had gone to his office to repair damages. Fight! *Fight!* What had he been doing in that office next to Ben's looking as if he'd been in a knock-down and drag-out? Perhaps Ben hadn't gone home! Perhaps Carrilski had hinted at Irene's secret and Ben had pitched into him.

He broke his own speed record reaching the telephone. Called the Jarvis house. "The party doesn't answer," singsonged a colorless voice. "Keep ringing, operator! Keep ringing," he commanded fiercely. After a few minutes he dropped the phone. Ben wasn't there. Where was he? What had Carrilski been doing in that building? Ice formed round his heart. Had Amos' call been a fake? Had the Count lured Ben there? Had Ben's mind been trying to get an S O S to his?

XXI

ONLY one thing to do. Back-track to the office building and
start his hunt from there. Why was he so sure the Count
knew where Ben was? A vision of the man's battered appearance as he had faced him in the corridor flashed an
answer.

The memory sent him running down the clubhouse stairs.
He tiptoed past the dozing hall-man. Better not be seen.
Carrilski might be interested in his movements, might want
him out of the way as well as Ben. Ben out of the way!
His blood chilled. Why dwell on that hideous possibility?
Every shred of thought was needed constructively. He
would walk. There was a chance he might meet someone
who had seen Ben.

A white milk-wagon passed. The *clap-clap* of the horses'
hoofs made a staccato accompaniment to the ring of his
quick footsteps which echoed through the early-morning
quiet of the dozing city. A man with hat pulled low over
his eyes wove his unsteady way past. A shabby boy offered
a newspaper. No one else on the broad street. Dawn dipped
its paint brush in bright pink and slashed it across the eastern
horizon. The moon regarded the effect with jovial eyes as
it slanted toward the west, sending rays of light through the
fleecy clouds surrounding it.

He must find Ben before his trail was lost in the crowds
and rush of the day. First, he'd rout out Binks, the janitor
of the building, and ask him what time he let the Count in
and in some way get into his office. His office! Had Ben been
behind that door while he had stood talking—Ben, perhaps
helpless?

He tried the door of the building. In his apprehensive impatience, shook it. Locked . . . The janitor answered his
ring. He blinked sleepy owl-like eyes.

"You, Mr. Tremaine? Anything wrong? You look kinder
white. No? Maybe it's the dim light. Don't see you round
much this time of night or rather mornin'."

"See enough of it in the daytime, Binks. I cut out night
work if I can."

"Not much like that Carrilski fella. He's here long before

daylight every morning. Says he works better when ever'-thing's quiet, leastwise that's what I think he said. Can't understand his foreign jabber."

"Well, you may bet your life I'm not here to put in night work, I'm after papers." He thrust his hand into his trousers' pocket. "Boy, wouldn't you know it! I've left my keys. Loan me your passkey, will you, Binks? I'll return it as I go out."

"Sure, Mr. Tremaine. It would be kinder queer if the owner of the building couldn't get into his own office." He detached a key from a bunch. "Here you are, sir."

"Thanks. I won't be long."

So, the Count could work better when everything was quiet, he thought, as he forced himself to mount the stairs slowly and listened to the janitor's retreating footsteps on the flagged floor. As the sound died away he ran up the next two flights. Looked up and down the corridor before he approached Carrilski's office. No light . . . Preparing his mail hadn't taken long.

He knocked before he gently inserted the passkey. His heart appeared to have split, and gone on location in each ear, where a half pounded heavily. Suppose the man hadn't gone? Suppose he had figured on his return? He hadn't liked his smile. Never mind who else was there, would he find Ben?

He entered cautiously. Snapped on the light. The room was in order. Not much furniture. A flat desk with a tele-phone. Two chairs. Scrapbasket overturned, but that might not mean anything. A closet. He tried the door. Locked. Was Ben in there?

"Ben! Ben!" he whispered close to the keyhole.

His tightening throat threatened to choke him. The room behind him was so quiet he could hear his heart thump. Would the passkey do the trick here? What would he find when he opened the door?

Nothing. He strangled an urge to shout from relief. A big closet with a washbasin in one corner, a typewriter on a table, and a stool. . . . Darned queer place for a—wires! Wires connected to a typewriter! It wasn't a typewriter! It was a *teletype*.

So that was what the bogus Count worked on nights! Sending messages. Where? There was printing on the sheet of yellow paper in the roller. If he could see that . . .

Footsteps in the corridor! The Count returning? He softly closed the closet door. What next? He mustn't be caught here. He pressed the light button. The room went dark as Ere-bus. Listened. Could he make the balcony? He tiptoed across the floor, pulled up the sash of the window. Heavy as lead. His head was partially through the opening when it fell with a crash which set a million stars making whoopee behind his eyes.

Boy! Carrilski hadn't been lying when he had said that a window had come down on his hand. No wonder it was bruised.

He struggled to force up the heavy frame. He must raise it. Suppose Carrilski were to enter and find him half in and half out of his office window? The situation would take some explaining. Was the confounded thing made of iron? At last! His shoulders were free!

He lowered the window noiselessly. Pressed a hand to his throbbing head. Lucky he hadn't paid for his investigation with a fractured skull. The balcony was out as a hideaway. He listened. No sound in the corridor. He'd let the teletype investigation go over for the present. Ben wasn't here and he was after Ben. He softly opened the door to the corridor.

Now what? he asked himself, as safely in his office, he held his hand to his throbbing head. Steps! He flung open the door to the outer office.

"Ben!" he exclaimed incredulously. "*Ben!* I've gone nuts trying to find you."

"Why? What's up, Duke? You sound as if—Has anything happened to the kid? You've had her on your mind."

"*No. No.* She's safe in bed by this time. She left Argyle House long before I could make my getaway. Johnny gave me your message. I figured you wanted me. Found the note you left about fifteen minutes ago. Phoned your house from the Club. When you didn't answer, got a bad attack of jitters and hot-footed it back here."

"Well, brainless, what d'you mean by getting jittery about me?"

When he had finished telling Ben what he meant, he added:

"For the last hour my nerves have been acting-up like a lot of electrical conductors. I presume it's nerves. Never knew before I had 'em. Got a queer hunch that there's something wrong, terribly wrong and that I ought to be doing something about it. That's what brought me back here on the run. When I reached my room I couldn't get that battered Carrilski out of my mind. He said he'd come here to attend to business, but I had a hunch that you might have caught him in your office hunting for something and—"

"Hunting for something!" Ben Jarvis' voice trailed after him as he sprinted through the outer office to his own. A lamp glowed into pale green light. His feet made no sound on the thick rug as he crossed to the desk and unlocked a drawer. He drew a deep breath of relief.

"It's okay! He didn't get 'em."

"What d'ye mean, didn't get 'em?"

Ben Jarvis held up a long blue envelope and dropped it back. He turned a key and pocketed it.

"We can talk better in your office."

Perched on a corner of his desk Tremaine folded his arms across his chest.

"Stop walking the floor, Benjamin. You're white as a sheet. Give! What *didn't* Carrilski get?"

"The specifications for the bomber. I have the complete memoranda of them in that blue envelope I showed you."

"Then it was you, *you* who took them from the Senator's safe?"

"It was. He planned it."

"The Senator! Planned it with you! There wasn't by any chance a red herring round? Don't stare as if you thought I'd gone screwy. Let's have the story. Quick!"

"Joe Teele never has really trusted Marshall, whose mother returned to her native country after her husband's death. He believed that his distant cousin asked for the secretary-job with him that he might pick up some of our aviation research to use in an anti-American deal."

"Hasn't trusted him! Why didn't he tell me? He's put on a grand show. I thought the dapper Wayne was his white-haired boy. Sorry. Didn't mean to interrupt. Go on. I feel as if I'd go cockeyed if I didn't get a move on, go somewhere. If the Lord knows where, he isn't telling."

"You're on edge, the whole country's on edge with the United States facing more great problems than ever before in her history. A spy psychosis is in the air. The Senator's nutty on the subject; that's why he ordered me to remove the memoranda of the bomber specifications from his safe, mess up the room to suggest burglary, take them home and as soon as advisable transfer them here. We had it planned, but no time set for pulling it off. At the Mayflower reception he told me to go to it at once. He was cool, but I sensed that something had happened to get him worried."

"I'm beginning to see light. One of the Senator's red her-rings. Go on."

"I don't get that red herring stuff. I didn't like the job. Didn't believe in it. But he insisted. He was sure that Marshall would show his hand if he thought the information had been snitched by an agent of a foreign country. He figured that if he got him, he'd get others. Declared that if his confidential secretary proved to be on the level he'd make him a present of two grand. A conscience payment for suspecting him."

"Did the Senator also plan that Marshall was to see you take the memoranda of the specifications?"

"Of course not. What d'you mean?"

"That he saw you at the safe, has told Faith you're the thief."

"You're crazy. Why should Teele double-cross me?"

"Keep your shirt on, Benjamin. Perhaps he hasn't. I don't *know* that Marshall saw you, I suspect it. Perhaps he is the Senator's extra hand, he says I'm his right, you're his left. He didn't tell me you were to snitch those 'complete memoranda.' I believed they'd been stolen. He may be playing a third-handed game. You're not listening to my words of wisdom."

"I'm thinking while you're wise-cracking. Perhaps Marshall did see me at the safe; he might have stepped behind those red curtains when I opened the door. They are always drawn across the windows when the room is lighted. Never thought to look. Haven't been doing much burglarizing lately. My technique's rusty. I remember now that as I was locking the papers into the drawer in my desk at home Irene came into the den with that stuffed-shirt in tow. I jumped as if a jumbo torpedo had been dropped behind me. There was something about his slick, smiling assurance, that made me wonder if he would recall my start when the news of the theft broke. At that minute I hated the Senator and all his works. After they'd gone I calmed down. How could he know? I asked myself. Now, I'm beginning to believe he did."

"Joe Teele must have gone potty to suggest keeping material of such importance at your house or here in a desk. Suppose there had been a fire?"

"The papers I took are his memoranda in compact form for easy reference at hearings. There are blueprints in a bank vault. I don't know where. Neither do I know where the super-demon bomber was worked out. Only Joe Teele knows. He won't allow the name of the technician to be revealed for fear he would be seized and forced to give up his designs. That shows the hectic state of our Senator's imagination."

"Where does Amos fit into the scenario?"

"He was to let it be known in certain quarters that he had information to sell for a price. The Senator figured that because the Negro had been tried for the murder of his wife there were plenty of people who would take it for granted he would be dishonest and would listen to his whisper of 'information for sale.'"

"Another red herring. Joe Teele is wasting his time and talent in the Senate. He should be in Hollywood writing continuities. Who took a crack at Amos in your den? Who broke open the desk drawer?"

"Don't know. Don't know where he went last night. He phoned me at your house to say he would meet me at my office, that he had something important to tell me, quick. I stepped on the gas getting here—stopping only long enough for a flat and to pick up a ticket for speeding. He wasn't here. I beat it home. Someone had gone through my den, that's why I had been lured to the office I presume. Amos wasn't there. The other servants were off duty. There was no one to ask about him. I waited and waited thinking he might phone. Decided to return here on the chance that he'd doubled back."

"Certain he's on the level?"

"As certain as I am that you are." A crimson tide mounted to Ben Jarvis' light hair. "Sorry, Duke. You were right. I—I went crazy."

"Forget it. Sometime I'll explain Irene's presence in my house. She—she had something on her mind, she didn't want to worry you about."

"*Money?*"

"In—in a way. Let it go now, Ben. Trust me, won't you? We ought to get busy. Carrilski had been mauled. I know it. By whom? Boy! Perhaps it was Amos! That black man could put up a terrific fight. Where would he put him? The balcony? That's an idea! the window crashed down on my head and I saw only billions of stars. Let's go! I have a key. We'll—"

"Listen, Duke! Someone's coming."

Dragging footsteps in the corridor echoed through the empty building. A fumble at the knob . . . The door opened slowly. A bedraggled man swayed on the threshold, his breath came as if pumped up by an engine.

"I—I—saw de light, Mistuh Ben." Jarvis caught Amos as he lunged forward and drew him to a chair. "Shut de do'. Th'all may trail me."

Tremaine filled a glass at the water-cooler. Was this what E.S.P. had been trying to get through to him?

"Drink, Amos. Don't talk for a minute."

"Thanks, Mistuh Duke. I come upstairs so quick, set my heart gallopin'." His harsh breathing was the only sound in the room. Gradually it quieted. "All right now, Mistuh Ben."

"Take it easy, Amos. Answer my questions but don't rush.

What did you do after I told you to let Mr. Marshall know you had information to sell? I want Mr. Tremaine to hear."

"One night when he brought the Madam home from dancin', I said low as I handed him his hat, jus' as you tol' me, 'Is you int'rested in army plane 'provements, suh?' He looked at me quick, 'You're the man who was tried for murd'rin' his wife aren't yo'?'—I'll never live that down, Mistuh Ben—and then he said, 'The whole world's int'rested in army planes, Amos,' an' took his hat an' left."

"Go on. Be quick."

"Each time he come to the house after that he say very low w'en I open de do', 'Any new dope on army planes, Amos?' The day Madam lef' fer New York he came to say good-by an' he ask that again. 'You might fin' a plan of somethin' new in this house, suh,' I tole him.

"He looked sharp tow'd de livin' room to see if yo'all was lookin', then pulled a piece of paper out of a book, wrote somethin' on it, tore it across. 'See this?' he say. 'Keep one piece. W'en a man comes with the other half show him w'ere to fin' that thing yo're talkin' 'bout. Yo'll get money on the spot. Keep this paper in yo' pocket. You may need it in a hurry. If you double-cross me, yo'll go out lak a candle, won't even leave a grease-spot, get me?' "

That explained the torn address. One piece had been given to Amos, the other to Carrilski. Why to him? Tremaine wondered before he asked:—

"What next?"

"Nothin' happened till the night Mistuh Ben phoned he'd work late at the office. I went to de terrace to see if steps needed sweepin', it was snowin', an' w'en I come in I went to Mistuh Ben's den. It wuz all dark 'cept fer a spot of light on de desk. A man wid a black band wid holes in it across his eyes wuz leanin' over it. He wuz pokin' in the drawer. He heard me.

" 'Don' snap on that light, nigger,' he said rough an' low. 'Come across wid that plan.'

" 'W'ere de paper dat matches this?' I say. An' pulled the torn piece Mistuh Marshall give me from my pocket.

" 'Never min' that,' he say. 'Give me—'

" 'Not till I sees the other half,' I say, an' hol' my piece tight in my han', an' all the time the spot of light dancin' on de rug. I heard someone movin' outside. That's all I know till I look up an' sees Miss Faith an' Mistuh Duke bendin' over me."

"Did you recognize the man?"

"No, Mistuh Ben. He had on a big coat an' wid that black

ban' across his face I wouldn't know my own brudder. He mus' have snatched the torn paper out of my han'. I never could fin' it since."

"Where did you go that night?"

"I slipped out de back way hopin' to get to your office, Mistuh Ben. Someone hustle me into auto. I was locked in a room. Las' night th'all ask me where yo'd be at that hour. I tol' 'em they might try Argyle House, jus' to put 'em off yo' track. Then they held me before de telephone an' said tell you to come to yo' office quick, or they'd shoot me. I wus awful surprised when yo' answered. I said what th'all wanted. You tol' me, Mistuh Ben, to do what they say."

"Okay, Amos. How many men were there?"

"Two's all I see."

Two! Tremaine remembered that Nancy Carr had said that two men had detained Marshall in the Corridor of the White House, that he had not appeared overjoyed to see them. Had they been giving him instructions? That same night the masked man had appeared in Ben's den.

"P'raps hour ago man who kep' me wen' out fer a drink an' locked the door. I waited. Broke a window. Jumped. Crouched an' listened. Ran. Picked up a taxi an' went to our house. An' then—"

A telephone rang. Rang again and again with the ear-splitting persistence of a fire siren. Ben Jarvis looked at Tremaine.

"That's in my office. Who'd know I'm here at this time of night?"

Amos pulled himself to his feet. His black face turned yellow as he followed the two men.

"Perhaps it's Mistuh Storker, Senator Teele's chauffeur, Mistuh Ben. I forgot to tell yo' he called our house. Said he mus' talk to yo' an' I tol' him yo' might be here."

"Storker! The Senator's chauffeur! What did he want?" Tremaine's face was chalky.

"He talks so fas' I couldn't understan'. I think he meant he los' Miss Faith somewhere, Mistuh Duke."

XXII

FAITH snuggled into a corner of the limousine as it rolled away from Argyle House. She tried to crowd from her mind the memory of Duke's eyes as he had said good night. It stubbornly resisted ejection. What was it all about? Why did he look at her as if he loved her when he was practically engaged to Kitty Teele? His line, of course. Hadn't Irene warned her?

Why spend a moment thinking of him when her brother was in trouble? Trouble! Now that the evening's gaiety was over memory engulfed her like a tidal wave. If Wayne's story were true "trouble" was too tame a word. Was the story true? He had assured her he had told no one, but Carrilski knew. Had it really been Amos whose phone call had sent Ben rushing back to his office? How had the butler known he would be at Argyle House? She had a feeling that Duke doubted that Amos had been the man at the other end of the wire. Perhaps that was why he had been so pre-occupied while he danced with her. His conscious mind hadn't been in the ballroom, it had been thought-miles away.

She remembered his laughing "Born to dance together, weren't we?" and she remembered the impulsive answer "We were!" which she had caught back with terrified haste, and her substitute question, "Where's Ben?" He had answered "Steady. You're breathless." Lucky he hadn't suspected that he, not Ben, had been the cause of that breathlessness. He was dominating her thoughts again and it was *Ben*, Ben of whom she should be thinking—and what a chance for constructive thinking, alone in the great car! She seemed alone, the motionless figure of fur-coated Storker on the other side of the glass might have been a robot, so little she sensed him as a person.

All about lay a shimmering world, changing from white, to silver, to purple, as fluffs of cloud floated across the face of the slanting moon and cast grotesque shadows. The soft air which drifted in through the half-open window suggested a quick thaw, smelled of spring. Mile after mile the tire-rutted road swept, dipped and climbed ahead. Snow crunched under wheels. Ghostly trees rattled like skeletons. Two dots of green light shone in the road. Immovable. Fascinated.

A black shape scuttled into the shrubs. Thank goodness! The creature had saved itself at the last minute. Had instinct broken the spell of terror which had held it as the car approached? Was there always a chance of escape if one could find the way. A gate in every wall? If Ben were in trouble could she help him find a way out? Not unless she could know the truth about his connection with those missing memoranda. Wayne had said that he was the only person who knew who had taken them, that he would keep silent if she would get them for him.

He must have a low estimate of her intelligence if he thought she believed that, if she didn't know that a man who would try to put through such a deal had no honor in him. Honor? What was honor? If it came down to cases how would she stand the test? Would she tell Senator Teele who had opened his safe before Wayne had the chance?

She settled deeper into the soft corner and closed her eyes. She could think better if she shut out the dazzling beauty of the night. And she must think, must figure out a way to help Ben. Where had she better start? At the moment when Wayne had first whispered: "It was your brother."

She shut her teeth into her lips to steady them, and sent her thoughts hurrying on to that stunned instant in the conservatory when the Count had faced her. Improbable as it was, she might have believed he was there in search of a missing cuff-link if he had not threatened, "Eet would be better for your brother, ees eet not?" Wayne's explanation at the pool had followed. It *couldn't* have been Ben at the Senator's safe. She wouldn't believe it.

"Steady."

Duke's voice. Duke's reminder. It rang through her mind as clearly as if he were beside her. She unclenched her hands. He was right. Jitters wouldn't help her think things through. What next? Find Ben, of course. Wayne had demanded a promise that she would not tell her brother what he had told her. How sacred was a promise? All her life she had been guided by a code of which keeping a promise was a part. Ben had a right to know of what he was accused. How could he know unless she broke that promise and told him?

Should she tell Duke instead? No. No one but Ben. She would find him wherever he was and tell him what she had heard. If he had the stolen memoranda—oh, but he hadn't.

She knew it. He was caught in a trap. Perhaps an international one. He must be warned. Duke had told her that he was to meet Amos at his office. She would go there.

She sat forward on the seat. Ahead she could see the shining gold cap on the white shaft of the Monument. The boom of a clock drifted in through the window. She must plan quickly if she intended to find Ben. She picked up the speaking tube, saw the chauffeur bend his head toward his end of it.

"Storker, I—my brother left word at Argyle House that I was to stop at his office on the way home. You know where it is. You've taken the Senator there many times, haven't you? You may leave me there."

"At this time of night, Miss?" the voice was gruff with surprise.

"What difference does the time make if Mr. Jarvis is waiting for me? Drive there, Storker."

"Very good, Miss."

His round, red face registered disapproval when he opened the car door in front of the office building. For some inexplicable reason Faith's spirits had mounted since she had made her decision.

"Don't frown, Storker. Look up. There's a light in my brother's office. It's the third window from the north corner on the third floor. Right?"

"Right, Miss Jarvis. Just the same I don't like leaving you here. I'll wait."

"Indeed you won't. I've kept you out late enough. Mr. Ben will bring me home. I may return to his house, his wife is away. Good night."

She stood in the dark doorway and watched the red light dim in the distance. When it blinked out something caught at her throat. Was she crazy to stop here? Being alone on the street at night never had been her strong suit, and the prospect of prowling round an empty building did things to her breath. Why worry? Ben was in his office. She had seen the light. Could she get in? Were office building doors unlocked for tenants or would one have to ring for the janitor? She turned the handle, the heavy door swung open. Why not? Hadn't Ben come here?

Buoyed by that certainty, she went upstairs so quickly that she was breathless when she reached his door, which was ajar. She pushed it open. He was bending over the desk. She had been right to come. "Obey that impulse," she thought, and laughed.

"See who's here, Ben. I've come—" the word rattled in

her throat. The man who wheeled to stare at her wasn't
Ben, it was Wayne. Wayne Marshall! He put his hand behind him. A drawer softly closed. A key turned.

He crushed papers into the pocket of his dinner jacket.
Hatless, topcoatless, he stared at her incredulously.

"What are you doing here, Faith?"

The harsh question drove back the fright which had
gripped her at the discovery of his identity. She walked toward him, one part of her brain registering the certainty
that he had been lying when he had said he saw Ben at the
Senator's safe, the other that she must be very careful what
she said.

"And just what are *you* doing here, Wayne?" she inquired
sweetly. "I came to hunt for those memoranda you are so
sure Ben has. Have you beaten me to it? Are those they,
stuffed into your pocket?"

His face turned crimson, then white. His mouth pinched
into an ugly line. His eyes narrowed. Could this be the
man who had been her friend, who had asked her to marry
him? The person staring at her was a stranger. She was alone
with him in an empty building in an empty office—Was it
empty? Where was Ben? Duke had said he was coming here.
From the curb she had seen the light. She glanced at the
clock. Had he come and gone?

"You see, I didn't trust you, Faith." He kept his voice
light with evident effort. "You're so emotional. Even to save
your brother—"

"Where is my brother? What have you done with him?"

"Who, Ben? My dear girl, be reasonable. What could
I do with a man his size?" She caught his furtive look at
the closet door. "I haven't seen him. When I thought it over,
I decided you were right, I should have told the Senator. I
did. He sent me here to try to find the specifications memoranda."

"That's a lie! He didn't send you. You've hidden Ben
somewhere."

"Where? Read that note on the desk. He wrote Tremaine
that he was going home."

She glanced over the slip of white paper on the blotter.

"Doesn't that convince you?"

"No. You've done something to him. Put him out of the
way somewhere."

"You're crazy. I'm here on an errand for my boss. You
still don't believe me? Only one place he could be hidden.
Look in the closet."

The electric light came on as he flung open the door.

Only a washbasin in one corner and overcoats and a lot of scarfs and an old hat hanging on hooks, and a three-legged stool and a pile of books on the floor.

"You see, Faith? No one there. You're jittery. I don't wonder. I shouldn't have told you that I saw Ben at the safe. I'm going to get what I want from the Senator myself. Joe's a good egg." He pulled a silk scarf from a hook. "Left my topcoat in my car. I'll borrow this, Ben won't mind. Come on, I'll take you home. Let's go. It would be a front-page scandal if the janitor came in and found us here together at this hour."

"I'll risk the scandal, Wayne. I don't believe one word of what you've said. You're the one who's jittery. Your hands are shaking. Give me those papers in your pocket. I shan't go until I get them. Neither will you."

"No? All right, I know when I'm licked. You'll have to do a tall lot of explaining when the Senator finds you have these specifications. Take them and we'll go."

He held out a folded paper. As she moved nearer he flung the scarf across her mouth, tied it tightly at the back of her head. She choked. He pulled off her white fox jacket.

"You were right when you said you wouldn't go, Faith. I'm sorry to do this but—I must. *You* stay. *I* go."

He held her like a vise in one arm while he reached for other scarfs. With teeth and one hand he knotted two together. She kicked him viciously. He put a foot on hers and held it down. She freed a hand, grabbed at his black tie in the hope of choking him, but it merely became unbowed. She clawed at his cheek and left the marks of four pointed nails. He tied her arms down. Set her on the stool in the closet and lashed her ankles to that. Threw in her jacket. He stood on the threshold. His face was livid. His eyes were desperate.

"Sorry about the rough stuff, Faith. But, it had to be done. You're going to hate me for this but some day remember that I loved you, hoped to marry you, and try to think a little kindly of me. I had to choose between you and—the Senator. I'll leave the key in the lock. You'll be let out in the morning. Good—good-by."

She hadn't imagined it, his voice had broken on that "good-by." He couldn't lock her in. He wouldn't dare. Her eyes blazed in protest. The only part of her she could move . . . If she could speak, tell him what she thought of him, it would help some. She couldn't. She was trussed as tight as a turkey ready for the oven. She hadn't done such a bad job herself. He looked as if he had been flung into a spinning plane-propeller. That helped.

In a fury of rage at her stupidity in being caught like this, at him, she gathered all her strength and shoved herself and the stool forward. She was so near that her skirt almost touched him. He slammed the door. The key grated in the lock.

She strained against the scarf on her mouth, at those bound round arms and ankles. No use. They wouldn't give. A voice! Explosive! As if someone were surprised. Who was it? Who had come? Had it been Ben? Growls of rage. She must scream. Her voice gurgled in her throat. Wayne was expert at trussing his victims. Perhaps it was part of a secret agent's training. Wayne a secret agent? Even now she couldn't believe it. Who else would steal papers from a man's desk? Had he really been after the stolen memoranda for the Senator, or had he been caught in that tricky current of "temptation" of which Nancy Carr had spoken, and wanted them to sell?

She strained and twisted. She couldn't move the scarfs. If she relaxed would they loosen? Lucky the closet was large. Dark and spooky though. The light had gone out when the door closed. Who had surprised Wayne in the office? Had it been Ben? Had there been a fight? Was Ben on the other side of the closet door, injured, perhaps dying? She strangled rising panic.

"That's enough of that sort of thinking, my girl." She felt like Alice in Wonderland talking to herself as she dropped down the well. "Ben is safe. He wouldn't let himself be beaten up. Wayne asked me to remember that he loved me! Loved me! That's a joke. Oh, forget Wayne and his treachery. Thank your lucky star you never loved him. Think of the pleasant things you've seen and enjoyed since you left Rome."

That was an idea. She recalled the books she had read and liked; pretended that the darkness was a silver screen on which were projected plays and movies she had seen; knelt in Church and offered a little prayer for Ben's safety— was he on the other side of the door unconscious, hurt?

With all her mental strength she forced back the terrifying thought, hummed bits of music, classical and swing; shut her eyes tight and fitted together the names and faces of individuals she had met since she came to Washington. Her mother had taught her that, had insisted that to be a social success—social success was her fetish—one must remember the persons one met, their faces, names and interest, that the way to fix them indelibly in her memory was to name and visualize them before she went to sleep at night. It had become a game with her. She had played it so long that now it was second nature.

The telephone. Ringing. Ringing. Ringing. Who would call Ben at this time of night or morning? It had stopped. Perhaps the person who wanted him would come here for him, would free her. Would they find him? If he were safe and unharmed when she was free she never would worry again in all her life. Free! Perhaps Wayne would send someone to let her out. Wayne! Why think of him! If only by some telegraphic transmission her thoughts could reach Duke. Would a mental S O S contact him? He said he had the sixth sense.

"Duke! Duke! Help! Come!" she repeated over and over. Just thinking about him gave her courage.

She was tired, desperately tired. She had not closed her eyes the night of the White House reception, had danced her sandals thin at Argyle House. She was bound so tight that her hands and feet were numb. If only she were near a wall against which she could lean. She wasn't. She'd better stop being sorry for herself and think of something else.

She lined up senators and representatives she had met and racked her brain to remember the bills each one was sponsoring; lucky she was a newspaper addict!

That had taken time. It must be getting toward morning. A sound! A door opening! Someone in the office. Wayne again? Had he come back to let her out? Silly. He wouldn't come back. He would be miles away with those specifications. Was it Ben? Had her thought-call reached Duke?

She must make a sound. She strained at the scarf which bound her mouth. Frantically tried to move her arms, her feet. If only she could kick the door. She was so near her skirt brushed it. No use. She twisted her head in an effort to free her mouth. Stopped struggling. A bang. The door! Whoever it was had gone.

XXIII

"THE kid! Lost!" Ben Jarvis stood as if turned to stone. The room had become subtly and intangibly charged with tragedy. Tremaine grabbed the telephone.

"Jarvis' office. Tremaine speaking. Who's calling?"

"Storker! Storker, Senator Teele's chauffeur. It's about Miss Faith, sir. I left her at the office building."

"*What* office building?"

"*Yours,* sir."

"Did she go in?"

"I don't know, sir. I told her she hadn't oughter do it. But she said as how she was to meet her brother there. She told me not to wait."

"How long ago was that?"

"Don't know the exact time but we came straight from Argyle House, sir, and then I left her. I got worried. Phoned Mr. Jarvis' office. The operator rang and rang. No answer. I waited in the hall a long time for the Senator to come in; I live in the house, sir. I told him. He swore something terrible, you know how the Senator is when he's excited, sir, and he said try Madam Carr at the Mayflower, Miss Faith might have gone there. I did. She hadn't seen her. Then we rang Mr. Jarvis' house. The butler answered. He told me to call the office again. I'm weak as a rag, now that I've reached you, sir. The Senator'll be there in a few minutes. He took a taxi. Said to tell you he was coming." Tremaine banged down the phone. Tried to speak.

"You needn't tell me, Duke. I heard. What's our first move?"

"Carrilski! She came here for you, Ben. May have caught him at your desk. Break in his office door. No, no. I have a key! She's there. His hand was bruised—my God! If—"

"Found her, boys?" Senator Teele bolted into the room. His face was as colorless as a ruddy face can be, his voice was hoarse.

"No."

Rapidly Tremaine told of his meeting with the Count in the hall. Of the man's battered appearance. He stopped. Stared.

"What's that glittering on the rug?" He swooped up a rhinestone. "Silver braid all twinkle, twinkle with rhinestones." Faith had said that about her sandals. Faith had been here. When? Where was she now? His eyes flashed around the room. A scrap of silver gauze glinted in the crack of the closet door.

He lived through an eternity of agony till he turned the key and flung it open. Faith was there. Faith with mouth and arms and ankles bound. Her eyes were closed. Her cheek rested against a bare shoulder. Was she dead? Smothered? Would this picture of her flash on eternally within his mind?

"Dearest! *Dearest!* I love you! LOVE YOU! *Love* you!" Was he saying that? He, who had waited for the perfect moment in which to tell her he loved her? He lifted the stool from the closet and shouted to the three men who stood motionless, staring.

"Quick! Open the window, Amos! Water, Senator! Ben for God's sake wake up! Free her arms. I've got the damn thing off her mouth."

A rush of clear cold air. The girl's long lashes stirred. Lifted. She looked up into the haggard face above her. Smiled.

"That message was a long time getting through, Duke."

"What message?"

In answer she drew a deep breath and flexed her stiff arms. As the scarf fell from her ankles she stood up. Tried to stamp her feet. Tremaine caught her as she swayed and held the glass to her lips. She drank thirstily.

"Thanks. Sorry I passed out but that closet is not airconditioned, perhaps I only went to sleep. I'm all right, Duke. My feet and hands are coming to life. Oooch, how they prickle!" Color flooded her white face. Her startled eyes flashed from one man to another.

"My mind's prickling to life, too. Running on all cylinders. Where's Wayne?"

"Wayne Marshall? Take it easy, dearest. You mean Carrilski, don't you?"

"I mean Wayne. Don't talk as if I were a baby, Duke. Go after him! He has Ben's papers from that desk."

"No, he hasn't, kid. They're safe in the drawer. Calm down."

"Calm down! What d'you mean, calm down? I'm telling you that Wayne Marshall was taking something from that desk drawer when I came in. I thought he was you. He saw me and turned a key. I ordered him to give up your papers and then he—said the Senator had sent him for them and he—he—" She choked on the word.

"Did he—" Tremaine's voice bogged in his throat. Fear whipped up his imagination. He tried again. "Did he—did he *hurt* you?"

Color burned in her cheeks like red spotlights, her eyes flamed.

"*Hurt* me! Not unless losing faith in a friend hurts, unless making me so mad at my own stupidity that all I could see were red neon spots on poison-green, was hurting me. The tussle had its moments, though. Tying me up was nothing to what I did to him. I tried to choke him and clawed his cheek—with these." She held out pointed, faintly tinted nails.

"What time was it, Miss Jarvis?"

She glanced at the clock.

"A little over an hour ago. Only an hour! It seemed years shut up in that closet. An hour! He could go a long way in that time. Why are we standing here, talking, everlastingly talking, when Wayne is making his getaway with the memoranda of the bomber specifications he said Ben stole from your safe, Senator?"

Why, *why* had she repeated that? Before she had had a chance to break her promise to Wayne and beg Ben to tell her the truth about the safe-opening, she had betrayed her brother. Break her promise to Wayne . . . That was a joke! He had freed her from that promise when he had robbed Ben's desk.

"Wayne told me he saw Ben steal papers from your safe, Senator. That he had known for some time you were putting through a deal for a demon bomber."

"Ben steal! I suspected Marshall had been torturing you with some such yarn. The heel!"

"Just a minute, Duke. You're sure it was my 'confidential secretary' who took those papers from here, Miss Jarvis?"

"Sure? What else was he doing? He wasn't here to play marbles. Would he have tied me up if he hadn't stolen something? He—he looked so—so evil."

"Show her the papers, Ben. Quick. Better sit down, Faith. You're shaking."

"Sit down! You've forgotten, Duke, that I've been sitting down hard for an æon or two."

The laughter in her voice and eyes contracted his throat. She was a grand sport. Such a lovely sport, standing there with ugly red bruises on her arms, in her torn silver gauze, smiling with unsteady lips. If he had driven her home instead of attending to that rotten business of Irene's, she would have been spared all this—but, it had been Ben's business too.

"Here it is, kid."

Ben's voice snapped his mind to attention. He was holding up a long blue envelope, drawing a paper from it.

"Safe as—" He stared in utter disbelief at the blank sheets in his hand. His face was colorless as one by one he let them drift to the floor.

"Ben! Ben! I *told* you he had them," Faith cried. "Go after him! Why don't you go after him, quick!"

"Just a minute, Ben." The Senator opened the door in response to a rapid tattoo. Madam Carr brushed past him into the office. She was hatless, her sable coat hung open over a heliotrope gown. Her eyes glistened like black diamonds behind a mist of tears.

"Faith! My dear, my *dear,* you're safe, thank God!" She sank into the chair Ben Jarvis pushed forward. "If any harm had come to you out of this—" Faith gently patted her shoulder.

"No harm has come to me, Nancy Carr. I had an idea and did something about it, but it didn't go over so big. Now who's here?"

Senator Teele flung open the door. His mouth set in a hard line, his eyes narrowed as two stony-faced men pushed Carrilski forward between them. He had changed to gray business-clothes. His bruised hand was covered by a glove. His monocle swung by its ribbon. He glanced quickly at Madam Carr, speculatively at Ben Jarvis. Was he planning to trade with Irene's grandmother and husband his knowledge of her marriage to Stratton for freedom? Tremaine's heart stopped. On second thoughts, why should he have to trade? He hadn't stolen the papers, it was not he who had locked Faith into the closet.

"We found this guy pussyfooting round your house, Senator, and grabbed him. Your chauffeur said you were here, so we brought him along," explained the man at the Count's right. His mouth, already lifted at one corner by a purple scar, tipped up in a grotesque grin. "Mr. Tremaine's orders, sir. He has had us shadowing your place since Sunday, said he thought you needed a guard."

The Count shook off the heavy hand on his shoulder.

"Eef I may be permitted to speak, Meester Senator. I was not pussyfooting, ees eet not ever done in thees country for a man to walk the streets for air after he work late? Meester

Tremaine has made a meestake having me brought here. But, I forgeeve. I weel make a trade, not with heem, but with you, sir. I weel—"

"I insist that he make it with me, Senator. I had him watched. Let me handle this. Keep out of it, will you?" Tremaine pleaded hoarsely. Good lord, did those men glowering at him think he was mixed up in this dirty deal? He must shut Carrilski's mouth till he had the facts from London as to Irene's marriage.

"I'll handle this myself. He was snooping round *my* house, wasn't he?"

"Senator, let me—"

"What's the matter with you, Duke? Think I'm incompetent to attend to my own business? Apparently you do, setting a guard round my house. Why should anyone want to sneak in?"

"It was done once, wasn't it? My mistake. I didn't know then what really happened. Perhaps this—er—Count is another red herring—"

"Meester Senator," Carrilski interrupted, hastily. "Do not be so angry with your right-hand man—you call heem that, I understand—he is only chivalrously trying to shield"—Tremaine's fists clenched. Would the cad dare mention Irene's Paris marriage?—"the charming young lady whom I keesed in the conservatory, ees he not, Mees Jarvees?"

"Now that the horrible truth is out, why were you prowling there with a spotlight, Count?" Faith inquired. "He said 'kissed,' not killed, boys, so you needn't look so murderous. I have been kissed before, but never quite so clumsily." Her disdainful shrug brought a chuckle from the Senator and a dismayed "Hmp!" from Madam Carr. The Count clicked his heels and bowed with theatrical humility.

"My apologees, for clumsiness, Mees Jarvees. The next time—"

"You are in the conservatory, you won't leave till you've told why you are there. Why were you?"

"Eeet was—now eet may be told. A torn piece of paper wheech I pulled from my pocket when Meester Tremaine overturned the glass of water. He has both pieces now, yes?"

"I have. Why did Marshall give it to you?"

The Count glanced at one guard, then at the other and shrugged.

"It looks as eef I cannot get away, so, I make what you call my confession, my come-clean, ees eet not? That paper was my passport—ees that what eet ees called—to obtain certain papers about a magnificent bomber at the home of Meester Jarvees. I lost eet, and my accomplice played what you call a lone hand."

"If you lost that chance what were you doing round my house at this hour? Come across with the whole story and come quick." Senator Teele's command was a roar.

"And when you make your 'confession,' Count, why not drop that accent?" Faith suggested crisply. "I've known you were an American since the duck chase. Emigrés from border countries do not speak of a 'three-ring circus.'"

"Thanks for the permission, Miss Jarvis. I didn't know I shed my accent that day. You and the duck were so funny," memory shook his voice with laughter, "that I forgot my role and felt free for the first time since I reached the city."

"Free to send teletype messages to New York newspapers? I presume that machine explains your early-morning work in the 'headquarters' where you have been handling 'important family affairs,' investing a fortune. He's not a secret agent, Senator. He's the 'pipeline' you were wondering about," Duke Tremaine declared.

"A reporter! I don't believe it. It's a trick. He's been hand-in-glove with Marshall." For the first time since he had known Joe Teele, Tremaine saw him genuinely surprised. "Where is my confidential secretary now? You and he have been meeting and scheming at Zeke and Sophy's, haven't you? Speak up!"

"We have been meeting there. He has done the scheming; and take it from me, he was good after he learned the ropes. You'll find him in his room, under guard, Senator. He was skulking out of this office as I was entering mine. He explained his battered condition as the result of a fight with a panhandler. Like a fool I believed him. I had been instructed, never mind by whom, to appear to be in sympathy with his subversive activities. He accused me of double-crossing him by losing the slip of paper, said he had been forced to carry on himself, had knocked out the Jarvis butler while searching for the bomber memoranda. Then he lit into me. I dragged him into my office. I was preparing to get him out when you saw me in the corridor, Tremaine."

"You looked as if you'd been battling a heavyweight champion."

"He scratched me up some, but nothing to what had been handed to him previously. Miss Jarvis, had I known then as I can see now what he had done to you in this office, I would have beaten him to pulp." He coughed as if to loosen his tight throat. "I had seen you and admired you on the ship—but I had never before met your sister-in-law. She has been most kind to an absolute *stranger*."

Tremaine drew a deep breath of relief. The man was telling him that he would keep the secret of Irene's marriage to Stratton.

"Here are the specifications memoranda. I found them on Marshall. Lucky I was on the spot to get them before he had a chance to turn them over, Senator Teele." Carrilski drew crumpled papers from his pocket. "I was trying to reach you, thought you wouldn't mind being routed out of bed to get them—when I was arrested by these two guys, for pussyfooting. Later, I'll tell you where they were to have been sold, though I suspect Tremaine knows even more than I about that."

The Senator looked at the papers, then at the man who had offered them. His face burned a choleric red.

"Look here! Who set you—"

"Snooping is the word, Senator," Madam Carr interrupted airily. "I set him snooping. Now, don't lose your temper. He has been working for me. He's only one of the 150,000 reporters in the country, but he has put across a good bit of favorable publicity under my instructions, for you, Joe Teele."

XXIV

KITTY TEELE, in a morning frock of sheer white wool, tucked a sandaled foot under her, little-girl fashion, in the deep chair and clasped her hands behind her head. Her eyes were the dark purple-blue of larkspur as they rested on Faith Jarvis in a dusty-pink frock writing at the desk.

"The snow has gone. Melted as if by magic. We'll have spring with us by the end of the week. You haven't told me about the dinner and dance at Argyle House last night. Was it exciting?"

Last night! It seemed years since last night! *Ben hadn't stolen the specifications*. That thought had been running through Faith's mind like the theme of a symphony since she had left his office at dawn. Exciting! She'd say the evening had been exciting. She gently rubbed her left arm. It still ached from the pressure of that scarf. The Senator had pledged them all to secrecy, so she couldn't tell Kitty that the

Count was not a Count but a newspaperman in Madam Carr's service. She didn't know what had occurred after she left. Ben had hurried her home before the other men had started to find Wayne.

"Well? Was it exciting? Perhaps I shouldn't ask. Perhaps something so wonderful happened that my question has sent you into a dream trance."

"Dream trance." Nightmare, she'd call it. If she didn't answer quickly Kitty might suspect she was hiding something.

"Nothing especially wonderful happened. It was grand fun. Perfect host. Delicious eats. Rare orchids. The girls wore their swankiest numbers. The men had been picked for brains as well as flawless dancing, not a moron among them. Enchanting music. Between dances a violinist specialized in gypsy airs and a glamorous young chanteuse, who had the decency not to make a play for the men guests, put on her act. All in a gorgeous setting of gilt and red and black lacquer, red curtains with gold stripes, under a golf-leaf ceiling. How's that for description?"

"Thrilling. It sounds like something straight out of *A Thousand and One Nights*. Was the—the host particularly attentive to any one girl?"

"He wouldn't be. He's really engaged to you, isn't he?" She'd said it. She felt as if she'd pulled out the long, sharp splinter which had been hurting unbearably.

"No! He's neither really, nor tentatively, engaged to me. He sprang to my rescue—my mistake, to Ben's—when Thalia turned tattletale. The Senator and I selfishly grabbed at his help. It won't be needed any longer. Joe and I talked it over at breakfast. I'm going abroad for a year. It has been one of the dreams of my life. I'm to take Thalia, and put her in a school in Switzerland."

Duke wasn't engaged! The words rang like a pæan. *That doesn't mean that he'll love you,* a sober inner voice reminded. Suppose he didn't? Then it was just one of those things about which you could do nothing but keep your chin up and smile, smile, smile and—in time, *perhaps* love someone else.

"I said that I was going abroad for a year. Come out of your dream, Faith. I believe something did happen last night you're not telling."

"I heard you. It's a grand arrangement, but what's to become of me?"

"I've been trying to hold your attention long enough to tell you. The Senator wants you to go with us."

"*No.* No *thanks.* I don't want to go back. I like this country. I feel something in the air here so different from what I have known during the last eight years. Courage, buoyancy, the if-you-don't-like-your-life-as-it-is-do-something-about-it spirit. I'll stay here. I'll find another job. I'll be a career woman. How soon are you going?"

"The first of the month. Thalia hasn't been told, yet. I'm asking you to break the news to her. I confess I haven't the courage. She'll hate it."

"If she goes, she'll make your life a nightmare."

"Joe wants her to get away. She's so crazy about sports that she lets her studies slide. Her misuse of words troubles him. He thinks she's being spoiled here, that she will grow up too fast. He has been a grand brother. I'm only too happy to help him. You said 'nightmare.' Life can't be much more of a nightmare than it has been here for the last few months." Her usually smooth, unhurried voice was shaken.

"I didn't mean that wail, forget it. I hear Thalia charging upstairs. What's her grievance now, I wonder? 'Disgusting' is her latest word. I'll vanish and leave you to battle with her."

"Just a minute, Kitty. Ben wants me to dine with him tonight. All right with you?"

"Of course. Here she comes. Keep your powder dry. Don't shoot till you see the whites of her eyes." With a tremulous smile and a wave of her hand she entered her bedroom.

Faith regarded the closed door through a haze of tears. Gallant Kitty. Had that broken "for the last few months" meant that she loved Ben? What a labyrinth of crisscrossing life-lines her own special world had proved to be!

"Come!" she answered a peremptory knock. Thalia burst in, nibbling a huge apple. Her brown frock had a white collar and cuffs. The Boston Bull was at her heels. Thalia here, and she hadn't thought what to say to her . . .

"Where's Jemima?" She played for time.

"Gone!"

"Gone! Stolen?"

"Nope. Given away. She never was Jemima, and I expecting every day she'd lay an egg and have a lot of little yellow ducklings. Sam laughed his head off when I asked him yesterday how soon they'd come and he said:——

" 'Lawsy, Miss Thalia, that pusson ain't no duck. She's a drake.' Isn't that perfectly disgusting?"

"But, it's your pet, don't you love it just the same?"

"Nope. It deceived me and I don't love anyone I can't trust. That's why I like you, Miss Faith. You're on the level."

"I'm glad you think so, Thalia. Sit down. I want to talk to you."

The girl dropped into the deep chair and draped her long legs over an arm. The Boston squatted beside her. With suspicious eyes she regarded Faith above the red-cheeked apple.

"You and who else? I'll bet that big stiff, Kitty, wants to put over something and got you to do it, didn't dare tackle me herself. Disgusting!"

Faith walked to the window, thinking what she would say. A patch of white on a distant slope which the sun had not reached gave her a cue.

"The instructor at the skating rink told me that you were his ace pupil. He predicts you'll be another Sonja Henie."

Thalia stopped nibbling. Gold motes danced in her brown eyes.

"Honest? You're not kidding?"

"I'm not kidding."

"Whoopee! Hear that, Stubs?" Her exuberance dimmed. "Why the dish of applesauce? What do you want? What does she want?"

"Your aunt? Nothing from you. What have you to give her except impertinence and heartache? What can a poor sport like you give anyone?"

That brought Thalia to her feet. Her cheeks were crimson, her eyes blazed.

"A poor sport! That's what you think! Haven't you just said I was tops on skates? I'm the best swimmer at the pool. I'm captain of the basketball team. I can tap-dance the shoes off the other girls. Didn't the chatter column say I could ride like a centipede—"

"Centaur, Thalia."

"Phooey! What difference does it make if the word isn't right? You get what I mean. I'm on the tennis team. Perhaps I'm not so hot in lessons, but what difference does that make? Duke knows I'm a good sport, so does Pop. What do I care what you think? I know I'm good."

"I still say you're not, Thalia. A good sport plays the game fairly, squarely. You don't."

"I don't! Lot you know about it. How could I be plus in sports if I wasn't on the level?"

"Plus in sports, but zero-minus when it comes to people."

"So what? The—the other girls like me." Her voice had lost its belligerent assurance.

"Do they? I wonder? I wonder if you can be nice to them when you are so disagreeable to your Aunt Kitty?"

"Hey! So that's the nigger in the woodpile. Well, she'd no business to come here. I didn't want her."

"But your father did. He's been a pretty fine father to you, Thalia, and you've been cheating with him. *Wait* a minute. He asked your Aunt Kitty to come here, first because he thought she would be a companion for you. Second, because he needed a woman to preside over this house. He's got to have someone. Of course if you prefer a stepmother, that charming Mrs. Carton, for instance . . . She'd accept the job before you could say Jack Robinson. She thinks you need a firm hand. I can see 'Mamma spank' in her eye whenever she looks at you."

"Gee, not that blond honey? That pussycat? She paws me and darling-childs me. Pop wouldn't marry that total loss. He knows I'd hate her."

"Men as a rule don't select a wife to please a daughter, Thalia. The Senator has been troubled about the way you let yourself go, a bad temper gets to be a mental twist in time. He has heard of a fine school in Switzerland—I've seen it— you'd love it. He wants to send you there but he is undecided."

"I'll bet I'd be crazy about it. Sounds grand. I'm sick of the school here. Why's he undecided?"

"Well, you see, your Aunt Kitty is going abroad. He would send you over with her, but he knows you would be disagreeable and make her unhappy, so it looks as if you'd have to wait another year."

The girl's face was crimson. Her eyes glittered with tears. "I want to go this year. Pop needn't be sure I'd be disagreeable. I can be nice, if I want to be. Duke likes me. I never believed Aunt Kitty was his girl. I have a hunch he's planning to wait for me to grow up so we can be married."

"If that's your idea, you'd better watch your step. Duke Tremaine is on his way to the top politically. He won't marry a girl who can't be agreeable, who leaves splinters in the heart of everyone she talks to."

"Maybe I can be agreeable at that. Crazy about him yourself, I'll bet. You'll get him only over my dead body."

"You see, Thalia? Now you're sticking splinters into me."

"I'm sorry, honest." Her eyes flooded with tears. "I guess I'm a pretty hopeless case. I guess perhaps I'll go into a convent and take the veil."

"You'd better learn to live in the world first, my girl. Answer the phone, will you?"

Thalia grabbed the telephone.

"Hi. Who's talking?" She turned.

"It's Duke!" As Faith took her place she whispered: "Tease Pop, to let me go—*please*. I'll be nice to Aunt Kitty—I promise. And—and I'll tell Duke you're crazy about him."

"Thalia!"

The slam of the door was the only answer to Faith's frantic protest.

"What's the matter?" The question came over the wire as plainly as if the voice were in the room.

"Nothing, Duke. I've been having a battle royal with Thalia, that's all. She got in the last shot. Plop in the bull's eye." She had tried to speak lightly but her voice broke on the last word as on the screen of her mind flashed his haggard, deeply lined face as she had seen it bending over her in Ben's office.

"Forget her. Ben wants Nancy Carr and me to dine with him tonight, says you'll be there. Right?"

"Right. Duke—did—did you find Wayne this morning?"

"We did. Are you crying? Don't tell me you're still in love with that double-crosser after what he did to you last night!"

"I'm not crying. I never was in love with him and my affection for him is as dead as a ten-year-old slogan, but I'm terribly sorry for him. Why did he steal the specifications memoranda?"

"When we found him the Senator gave him the works and he came across with the truth. Got mixed up with the wrong people across the water. Gambling debts apparently, a net of international intrigue actually. Didn't intend to be crooked when he wrote for the job with the Senator, really came because he was in love with you. But, he had got himself into a mess abroad and as soon as he reached this country the thumbscrews began to tighten. He couldn't stand the pressure. He became the tool of foreign agents a week after his arrival in Washington. Getting him was like pulling up a deep-sea net full of flapping fish. We knew they were at work. I've had a line on the leader, but couldn't land him. Now we've caught a whole school of undercover agents. Marshall's going back to Europe. His first try at the big bad spy stuff was a colorless flop. The rest is history. Feel better now?"

"Lots. Thanks. Were you surprised when you discovered that the Count was a newspaperman?"

"I had been sure for some time that he wasn't a Count, but you could have knocked me over with a feather when he announced that it was he who kissed you. We'll take that up later. Wear the pink frock and the diamond butterflies tonight, will you? Oh, by the way, I have a present for you, a silver box. Hope you'll like it. Good-by."

She sat looking at the telephone after she had cradled it. Poor Wayne. He had said, "There's a little of the villain in each one of us." In spite of his treachery to his country and his employer, his brutality to her, she couldn't think of him as a villain. Duke had suspected that Carrilski was not a Count; did he know that Irene had met him secretly?

"Has Thalia gone?" The soft question came through a crack at the bedroom door.

"Some time ago. Coast's clear."

"What did she say?" Kitty Teele perched on the arm of a chair.

"She wants to go to school, but—here she comes. Don't go. You've got to face her sometime. Come in, Thalia."

The girl entered hesitantly. Her face flushed a deep red as she held out a bunch of snowdrops.

"First of the season. I—I—brought them for you—Aunt Kitty."

Surprise dyed Kitty Teele's face a soft pink.

"Thank you." The sweetness of her voice tightened Faith's throat. "They'll be perfect with my blue crepe. Faith and I are making a round of official teas this afternoon. What time do you skate? We'll drop in to watch you. Your instructor says you're good."

XXV

DUKE TREMAINE stood back to the fire in the mirrored living room, watching Faith at the coffee table. For an instant he saw her with detachment, a lovely girl in a violet and pink frock. Her lashes looked exceptionally long against her faintly flushed cheeks, the diamond butterfly in the short upswept curls of her dark hair quivered, her rosy-nailed fingers were unsteady.

That realization brought him back to the present. Why the unsteadiness? If it had been his hand now, shaking because of the confirmation of Carrilski's statement about Stratton that had been phoned to him before he left his office, there would be some sense in it. His London correspondent had reported that there had been no trouble tracing Eric Stratton. He had not died in Africa on the date announced. He had passed away only six months ago in England and had left a widow. This time there could be no doubt.

Six months ago! The man was alive at the time Irene had gone through that ceremony in Washington. She had been Stratton's wife then, never had been legally Ben's. He had tried to reach her at the Inn. Sophy had reported that she had been out all day in her roadster. Had she been trying to escape her thoughts? He must get in touch with her.

His troubled eyes rested on his friend, who was slouched in a deep chair smoking, with head tipped back, eyes on the rising smoke. Nancy Carr, whose crepe gown was the color of violet hyacinths, was nibbling the end of a pencil as she frowned over a crossword puzzle.

"What's another word for 'confusion,' Ben? A word of five letters?"

"Chaos."

"Right. It fits."

"It fits my state of mind like a glove." Ben Jarvis rose and straightened his shoulders as if throwing off a weight of troubled thought. "This old globe spun to a fare-thee-well when I discovered at dawn that Count Carrilski was a one-time foreign correspondent."

"And special writer and roving journalist for the string of papers I once owned. A reporter with a sense of moral responsibility and decency of outlook," Madam Carr explained.

"The day you came to my office I would have sworn you thought he was here to ferret out our air-research secrets, Nancy Carr."

"That was to find out what you thought, Duke. What's another word for 'sufficient,' a word of six letters?"

He dropped his hand on the puzzle.

"Never mind that now. Step on the witness stand. Look at me."

"And what do I see?" Her eyes sparkled with mischief. "An exceptionally tall man with an I-can-take-it-on-the-chin set to his shoulders. Compelling gray eyes, dark hair a trifle silver-foxish at the temples, a firm mouth which at times can look appealingly boyish, in short, the type of man men trust and women love. That's not original, I read it somewhere. How's that for characterization, Duke?"

"A masterpiece, but that won't let you off. Come clean. Why did you have that foreign-correspondent come to Washington as a Count? Did you fake that letter of introduction to Irene?" A chill trickled through his veins. Did she know of Irene's marriage in Paris?

"He came as a Count because this city, a certain stratum

of it, fairly eats up titled little boys. In a time when our world is changing and human life and liberty and the pursuit of happiness are threatened on every side, with alien termites trying to nibble at the foundations of our government, old methods of exterminating them are no longer adequate. I wanted a man to work for me whom I could direct, could trust. I've been experimenting with the result that a load of evidence to investigate is to be dropped on your shoulders, Duke."

"They're broad. I can take it. Most of the time your guess is as good as the facts other people present, Nancy Carr."

"I don't guess, Duke. I reason on a basis of straws blowing. When Joe Teele told me that Wayne Marshall was coming to this country to be his secretary—I had a hunch that perhaps he was being sent here. I got in touch with my pet foreign correspondent, whom I never had met, and directed him to look up Marshall. If he discovered that he was in a set which would bear watching, to follow him to this country. I sent him the letter of introduction to Irene. Until he presented it, I honestly didn't know that he was my man."

"Then his name isn't Carrilski?"

"What's in a name, my dear Faith? Something tells me that's been said before. Well, we've pulled through this mix-up, as I firmly believe we will pull through them all. Put your fingers in your ears, boys and girls, I am about to quote. Rousseau said: "There never was a time when civilization was in need of spiritual awakening that it did not arrive.' We're in need of it right now, and it will come, just watch it. What did you say the six-letter word for sufficient was, Duke?"

"I didn't say. Stop nibbling that pencil as if it were a lollypop. You're still on the witness stand. Is your reporter friend responsible for the build-up for Joe Teele in the papers?"

"Yes. Extraordinarily well done, weren't they? He's a writer of punch and discernment. Joe Teele's friends have been talking loud and long about the insidious forces working against him, taking it out in talking. With nobody doing anything, I took a hand. I'm quite proud of the result. I would have given a small fortune to have had a moving picture operator on hand in Ben's office when I announced that the fake Count was my contribution to the cause of democracy." Madam Carr's infectious laugh bubbled. "You looked like mechanical toys run down. Rigid. Dropped jaws. Staring eyes. You were so fun—"

"I've come back. I couldn't bear it another minute. I had to tell Ben." Irene in the doorway spoke with dispassionate precision.

Ben Jarvis sprang to his feet. Duke Tremaine took an impetuous step forward. Madam Carr's laugh stiffened into a fatuous grin as she stared at her granddaughter. Faith regarded her sister-in-law incredulously. It really was Irene, Irene in a black frock with a green turban which intensified the sheen of her red-gold hair. Had she come from New York? Her face was devoid of color, the knuckles of the hand with which she gripped the back of a chair showed shiny white.

"Have you told them, Duke?"

"No, Irene. The report came a couple of hours ago. I tried to reach you. Sophy said you had been out all day."

"I've driven miles trying to think things out. Was—was Carrilski's story true? He promised to keep my secret if I would agree not to let anyone know he was a newspaperman masquerading as a Count."

So that had been the price she had paid for the man's silence. He had misjudged them both, Duke Tremaine admitted to himself before he answered her question.

"His story was true. Stratton died in England six months ago."

"Is he really dead?"

"Yes. There can be no mistake."

"Say, what is all this?" Ben Jarvis emerged from the daze into which Irene's sudden appearance had thrown him. He impatiently brushed back his hair. His eyes flashed from his wife to his friend. Cords knotted on his forehead. His face was gray. Deep lines rayed from his eyes, slashed between his nose and the corners of his mouth, it was as if a make-up expert had suddenly transformed him into an old man.

"Who's this Stratton you're talking about, Irene?" his voice rasped. "What did you come back to tell me?"

He took a step forward. She moved toward him. The others were blurred into the background like the feed-parts in a play, only he and she had been stung into quivering life.

"That I was married to Eric Stratton in Paris five years ago. I honestly believed the man had died in Africa before I returned to this country, but," she shuddered, "you heard Duke say it. He died only six months ago. So, I'm not your wife, Ben. Never have been."

No one moved. It was as if a magician had turned them all to stone. Madam Carr was staring at her granddaughter with eyes shining like black coals in her chalky face. Duke had backed against the mantel. His eyes, which were on Ben, were dark with pain. Irene flexed stiff lips.

"I'm not your wife, Ben," she repeated. "You're free." She said it quietly, with no hint of self-dramatization.

"Free! *Free!*"

The word was an incredulous whisper. Light leaped into Ben Jarvis' eyes, color surged to his hair. Years dropped away. He was young. Militant. A soul escaped from bondage. As suddenly as it had flamed the light went out. Youth died.

"Is this true, Duke? Did she go to Argyle House to tell you this?"

"Yes, Ben."

"Cut this fool talk about not being my wife, Irene." His voice was hoarse. "You can't blot out our years together. Go up and pack a bag, *Mrs. Jarvis*. Be quick."

"Where are we going, Ben?"

"First to the clergyman who married us before. He won't need a new license. The old one will serve. He christened you, didn't he? He will understand. We'll leave the city for a while. Hurry."

Irene looked back at him from the threshold, tried to speak, stumbled as if suddenly blinded. Madam Carr put an arm about her waist.

"Come, my dear," she said. "I'll help you." They left the room together.

"Ben," Faith pleaded brokenly. "Why do you do it? She has spoiled your life. Half the time she hasn't behaved like a decent human being. You could be so happy with—"

"Soft-pedal, kid. You're speaking of my *wife*."

Faith's face burned. How had she dared crash in on his life with advice? Words had escaped which she had held back for months. No matter how she tried to scramble them up, no matter how deep in her mind she tried to bury them, always they would drift like uneasy wraiths between her and her brother. As if he divined her thoughts Ben tenderly patted her shoulder.

"It's all right, kid, it's *all* right. Don't worry, we'll ride the gale. Would there ever be any happiness for me if Irene wasn't legally my wife? Ask Duke. He knows. I've been a good deal of a fool, have allowed myself to dream of impossibilities, have let her get away with her temper. I could have stopped the outbursts, but I was so in love with her at first that I wouldn't see where we were drifting. You know she can be tender and companionable and lots of fun. I'll take a week off, Duke. Will you two come along as witnesses

to—to this marriage? Can't have a stranger in on this. Now
I'll get in touch with the clergyman—"

Tremaine's hand gripped his shoulder.

"I've seen him, Ben. As soon as I got the report from
London I did a little spadework. He is alone in the study
at the church waiting for you"

XXVI

"THOSE whom God hath joined together let no man put
asunder. I pronounce you man and wife."

It seemed to Duke Tremaine that the black-robed clergyman spoke the words with even more than his usual solemnity.
As he looked at the white-faced man and woman standing
hand in hand in the still, book-lined study, he had a sudden
flash-back of that first ceremony, the flower-decked church,
the green-robed bridesmaids, the veiled bride. How had Irene
dared. How had she . . .

Faith laid her hand on his arm. He could feel its unsteadiness. He caught her fingers hard in his and held them.
In her pink frock with the diamond butterfly trembling in her
dark hair she was like a splash of brightness in the somber
setting.

The clergyman drew Irene aside. Her mouth was set hard,
her eyes were downcast as she listened to his low voice. Ben
held Faith's fox coat for her, put his arm about her shoulders.

"Nancy Carr has gone to her apartment. She's pretty well
broken up over this. Stay at the house nights and keep an
eye on the servants till we get back, will you, kid?"

She nodded. She couldn't force her voice through her tight
throat. He pressed his lips to her cheek.

"Everything's going to be all right. Don't worry. Come,
Irene."

As Faith stepped into Tremaine's roadster she asked:

"Will you take me to the Senator's, Duke? I must collect
some clothes if I'm to stay at Ben's. I can't fare forth to
my job tomorrow in this frock."

"Sure. After you get the bag packed we'll go somewhere
and dance and forget this last hour. Let's pick up Nancy
Carr. She loves the night spots and she needs cheering."

A portion of golden moon was hanging above the Monument. Somewhere by the river a venturesome frog croaked and softly from the shrubs along the border of the tidal basin drifted the sweet startled note of a bird. High over the river roared a motor, its silver wings playing hide and seek with the stars.

"What a week!" Faith exclaimed. "When I think of the agony of mind I went through after I had been told that Ben had stolen the memoranda—which he had been ordered to steal—I could cheerfully wring our Senator's neck. Of course I shouldn't have believed Wayne for a minute, but he was so convincing."

"Joe Teele had me fooled, by the fake safe burglary, but he got the surprise of his life. He hadn't counted on Ben's being seen in action. Suppose we add that to the list of events to be forgotten, shall we?"

"Yes; I'd like also to forget my outburst to Ben about Irene. I'm terribly ashamed of it. I had a brainstorm for a minute when I thought of lovely Kitty Teele and what she would mean to him. Of course he is right about this remarriage. How could an honorable man do anything else?"

"If it will ease your conscience I'll admit that for a short time after Irene told me of that Paris ceremony I went haywire with relief. Then I realized that she was Ben's wife as surely as if that marriage to Stratton never had taken place."

"Will she ever conquer her temper? Ever make him really happy?"

"She's had a tough lesson. She has brains. Plenty of them. Ben's learned something, too. Let's believe that the going will be smoother. You've thought about them enough. From now on concentrate on me. Hard, understand?" To his intense relief she laughed.

"Fair enough, old-timer. I'll shut my eyes and concentrate, *hard.*"

He could feel her relax, heard her little quick sigh, half sob, could see her hair stir in the soft breeze. Thin, tenuous clouds floated across the face of the moon and vanished.

"Can't you smell spring in the air?" She drew a deep breath. "More April weather ahead." He didn't answer, his eyes were on the road. "Can't you? Not that I care especially; just to make conversation so that I—I won't think of Ben."

"I heard you the first time. I was figuring my chance at a vacation when Ben gets back. Never have seen California, have you? Wouldn't it be fun to fly there? Here we are."

"The Senator's in his study, Mistuh Tremaine," Sam announced before the door was fully opened. "He's been phonin' every place he 'spected you might be. He's awful anxious to

see you, suh. He was afraid he couldn't wait. He's speakin'
at a dinner in half an hour, an' his speech is goin' on the air.
He'll be talkin' to de whole country," he added proudly.

"I'll find him, Sam." Duke caught Faith's hand. "Lady, in
spite of the millions of words which have been written to the
contrary, love has to take a back seat in my life when duty
calls." His voice was low and not very steady. "All of which
translated means that I've got to see the Senator before we
can dance."

Faith's world was suddenly shot through and through with
warmth and radiance. She avoided his eyes for fear he would
see the light his words had brought to hers.

"While you are talking with him, I'll pack. Is Miss Kitty
at home, Sam?"

"No, Miss Jarvis. She an' Miss Thalia, they've gone to the
school play. They went out arm in arm. They wus laughin'
fit to kill, they wus."

"Of course. I forgot the school play." She started up the
stairs.

"After I've seen the Senator, I'll phone Nancy Carr that
we'll call for her, then I'll come up and help you pack. I
haven't told you yet why you're to concentrate on me," Tremaine reminded.

He watched her until she was out of sight. Apparently
she hadn't heard his frenzied outburst of love this morning
when he had found her trussed up in that closet in Ben's
office. Would he ever reach the place where he would be sure
of uninterrupted time to tell her he adored her? On that
question he opened the study door.

"What's that scowl for, Duke?" The Senator stopped his
restless pacing to bring a hand down hard on the younger
man's shoulder. "You'll hit the ceiling when you hear my
news. It works, boy! It *works!* And it's ours!"

The two men stood smiling broadly, shaking hands ex-
citedly in the middle of the room. Joe Teele sank into a
capacious leather chair and wiped his damp face with a huge
white handkerchief. Tremaine perched on the corner of the
desk.

"You put on a great act, Senator, with your red herring,
when you started secret agents chasing after the specifications
of a demon bomber, while the even more important invention
you were after was being quietly and unobservedly tested in
an obscure workshop."

"I had to put on an act and put it on quick. At the Mayflower reception I saw the Count's eyes narrow when, like a

fool, I asked you about the South American business. I had a hunch he suspected you hadn't been there, that you had been on a secret flight for me; of course, then, I didn't know we were being fooled to the hilt about him. It was time for a red herring so I gave Ben the high sign to rifle the safe to attract attention from you."

"It worked. The last time I saw the technician he was sure he had succeeded but he told me not to get your hopes up till he had made more tests. When did you hear the grand news?"

"Code message came through about half an hour ago. Been trying to reach you. When the contract with the inventor is signed, I'll tip that fake Count off to the news first. He's earned the beat for his paper. Nancy Carr had us all fooled. What a woman! Where's Ben? It's only fair now to tell him."

"Ben? Ben? Well, you see, Irene came home from New York unexpectedly and they suddenly decided to take a vacation."

The Senator's eyes bored into his. Tremaine's heart jumped, turned round and settled down again. Did Joe Teele know about that Paris marriage? He couldn't.

"Hmm! Sort of a reclamation project, reclamation of matrimony, isn't it? I hope it works. They haven't been hitting it off any too well. Kitty's going abroad," he added irrelevantly.

"I'm glad. I'm darned glad."

"You sound so. I wanted Miss Jarvis to go with them—"

"Faith! She can't. I won't—"

"I can see that my suggestion doesn't really hit you between the eyes, Duke. Relax. She refused." He chuckled. "I'm a little troubled for fear she'll be out of a job. Hard work getting positions now, you know."

"Make your mind easy about that, Senator. I'll find one for her. Ben asked her to stay at the house nights while he and Irene are away. She's upstairs now packing a bag."

"And undoubtedly needs your help. I won't keep you but a minute. You and I have carried this experiment through alone. We've got a plane that can't be grounded by an electric ray and it belongs to the U.S. in spite of grade-A espionage. Lord, when I heard of that devilish invention to bring them crashing down—" He cleared his roughened voice.

"If it hadn't been for you, we wouldn't have had it. You've made six trips to that workshop. You've given up business, pleasure and the companionship of the girl you love without a yip of complaint."

"Complaint! Why should I complain? It was my share of the job. I was proud you trusted me, Senator, happy that I could help."

"Without your help and loyalty in other matters I couldn't have carried on this winter. The evidence you've piled up will win that counterespionage appropriation."

"You could carry on anything, anywhere, alone, Senator. That's what I think of you. I honor you with all my heart and soul."

"There, there, boy. You—you—" Joe Teele blinked furiously and grinned. "Don't get nervous. I'm not about to burst into tears. Next, we'll set the economic house of the U.S.A. in order. It's got to be done. I'll hammer for that from now on and when I hammer I *hammer*. Run along. You're hearing nothing at present but a voice upstairs. What is it, Sam?"

"Taxi's at de do', suh. If yo' don' get goin' yo'll miss dat broa'cast. Radio, it don' wait fer no man, no *suh*."

"In the class with Time and Tide, eh?" Tremaine followed Senator Teele into the hall.

"It's my first time on the air," he confided nervously. "It's a sobering thought to realize that thousands may be listening to me, Duke."

"Thousands! Thousands are mere chicken-feed to the radio boys. They count in millions; so make it good, Senator."

Tremaine and Sam waited at the door until he waved from the taxi.

"He's a great man, he is, Mistuh Duke. Miss Kitty tol' me I might listen to him speak on her radio. Yo' come too?" the butler suggested.

"No. I'm going to telephone."

With her bag packed, Faith smiled radiantly at the pink-frocked girl in the wall mirror. She appeared so lighthearted! Why not? It really looked as if Ben's life problems would straighten out. Duke wasn't engaged to Kitty Teele, and—

Tremaine was laughing as he entered the room.

"Nancy Carr was pleased as punch to go out with us," he announced. "Said she's been feeling as lonely as a solitary pup in a dog-shop window."

"Than which there is no more forlorn sight. Sounds like her, doesn't it? Did you find the Senator?"

"Yes. He had a short report to make on a case we have been working on together."

"Was it a good report?"

"Couldn't be better. He's troubled because you are losing a

job. I assured him he need not worry about that." He sat on the arm of a chair. "Come here." He caught her hands and drew her close. "That day I met you at the station seems a long way off, doesn't it?"

She nodded without meeting his eyes.

"I realized when you smiled that you were the girl I'd been waiting for, that memory of you had kept me company across the years. That's why I didn't go off the deep end with one of those glamour girls, as you called them. Love me?" His voice was quiet, infinitely tender.

"But—Kitty—"

"That situation in the study, when Thalia dropped her bomb, was what we call in politics a minor crisis. I had to help Ben and the Senator. Believe me?"

Was she really hearing this? Believe him? Of course she believed him. The relief, the heavenly relief to know that he loved her. His hands tightened on hers.

"Look at me! Why don't you answer? Either you believe me or you don't. Yes or no?"

"Yes."

He caught her close in one arm.

"You lovely trouble-shooter. Didn't you know that I adored you? You're so cold, so sophisticated sometimes. Driving me mad by letting a man call you 'darling,' meeting another at midnight in the conservatory."

"I didn't meet him. I was as surprised to find the Count there as he was to see me. And when he kissed me—"

"That's another item for the forgotten list. Going to be a good girl and love me a lot?" he asked with his cheek against her hair.

"Not too good. As one pal to another, you wouldn't want me to be, would you?"

"I want you *any* way, my dearest." He steadied his husky voice. "Remember I told you I had a present for you? Here it is." From his pocket he drew the heart-shaped silver box. "With all my love."

"*Duke*, what a beauty!"

"Open it."

"O-o-oh," she breathed ecstatically.

"Hold out your left hand." He slipped the emerald-cut diamond on her third finger. "Perfect fit, isn't it? Plenty of room for a wedding ring there too. Like it?"

"Like it? I love it. It's perfect."

"I don't wish to appear mercenary, Miss Jarvis, but would you pay me a kiss on account?"

She was in his arms, her lips responding to his, her long lashes only partially screening her radiant eyes, ardent in her surrender.

"You *dear!* You *dear*," he said under his breath. "Lady, that was a perfect kiss." He drew her closer until she lifted her face again and tempted in a flare of reckless happiness:—

"As you reminded me about the dance, there are a lot, a whole lot more where that came from." There was mischief in her eyes, laughter and a hint of passion in her voice as she added, *"Darling."*

He kissed her the second time without tenderness as if his lips had been touched with flame. The sound of distant cheers, a man's voice responding, brought them back to the present.

"It's the Senator! On the air! Speaking at the dinner! Quick!"

Tremaine caught her hand. As they reached the hall a resonant, determined voice rose from the radio on the floor below:—

"I honestly believe that as a means of settling international difficulties war is on the way out and that it becomes more and more the duty of the United States to preserve peace, to insure the right of every man to life, liberty and the pursuit of happiness on this Western Hemisphere. But, we must set our own house in order. We must . . ."

Side by side on the top stair, his arm about her, her head against his shoulder, they listened to the tumult of applause.